Ripped Genes

by

Lawrence E. Rothstein

Tri-Star Investigations, Book Two

Ripped Genes

Cover Art by *Lea Schizas*

The Wild Rose Press, Inc.
PO Box 708
Adams Basin, NY 14410-0708
Visit us at www.thewildrosepress.com

Publishing History
First Edition, 2025
Trade Paperback ISBN 978-1-5092-5940-3
Digital ISBN 978-1-5092-5941-0

Tri-Star Investigations, Book Two
Published in the United States of America

Dedication

I would like to thank my wife, Jan, my son, Jeffrey, and my daughter, Alexandra, and my good friend and author, C.N. Hetzner for their constant support for my writing. Special thanks to my Willett Free Library writing group for their comments, criticism, and inspiration. Thanks to Alexandra for handling my website and social media presence for my novels. Thanks also to my superb editor, Lea Schizas, of The Wild Rose Press for guiding me through the publication process.

Chapter One

Alan Scanlon, M.D., Ph.D., entered his laboratory, passing through the third retinal scan protected security door into his private office. The first door had required a magnetic badge and a numeric code and the second had required a thumbprint.

The Rare Disease Genomics Laboratory he presided over at the Shabel Institute looked more like an impossibly clean and bright factory. It was filled, not with test tubes, microscopes, and lab benches, but with huge stainless-steel machines and computer screens. There was enough whirr, hum, and pocketa-pocketa to stimulate the daydreams of a hundred Walter Mittys.

At the door of his office, a white-coated, hair-netted, and gloved lab assistant handed Scanlon a printout from the tandem mass spectrometer. He ran the paper ribbon slowly through his fingers, scanning the peaks and valleys. Although this data was stored on a server and backed up on a DVD locked in a safe, Scanlon found the feel and look of the hard copy reassuring. Slowly, a half-smile took shape on a narrow, pinched face that was not accustomed to full smiles.

"I think we have it this time," he said, mostly to himself.

Carrying the waxy strip of paper, he walked into his adjoining office. He placed the spec readings on his desk, took one more pleasurably confirming look at them, and picked up the phone. He punched a speed dial number. After one ring, the well-modulated, slightly accented voice of a real, living receptionist intoned, "Bryan, Swayze, and Colter. To whom do you wish to speak?"

"Please connect me with Jack Colter. Tell him it's Alan Scanlon," said Scanlon, pushing his wire-rim glasses back to the bridge of his nose and proprietarily surveying his scientific domain through the glass wall of the office. The voice of Colter's hyperefficient administrative secretary, Tracey Gould, interrupted Scanlon's reverie. "Hello, Dr. Scanlon. Mr. Colter will be with you momentarily. Will you wait or shall I have him call you back? It won't be more than five minutes."

"I'll wait. No canned music, please," said Scanlon with a touch of impatience.

"Of course, Dr. Scanlon," said Gould primly.

Scanlon pressed the speaker button on the phone so he could log on to his computer. In less than two minutes, Jack Colter's voice boomed in the Research Director's ear. "A-a-lan." He drew out the first syllable. "How are you doing? Any news?" Colter asked expectantly.

"The news is excellent. I might even say 'Eureka'. We have substantiated and isolated the abnormality in the FERA gene on chromosome nine and the production of feraxin with excessive CAG repeats."

"Whatever that means!" blurted Colter with a chuckle.

The scientist pursed his lips and raised an eyebrow. "It means we have a clear genetic marker indicating the future onset of feraxia. I will send you some graphics and the necessary description of the gene with the marker tags, the isolation method, and the test. Let's do the patents now."

"Your name only on the patent applications?"

"As we discussed."

"No protests from your lab associates or the benefactors?"

"They don't know about it yet. And they won't for some time. The associates will get some authorship credit when we publish and possibly an additional monetary "bonus" for Elaine, who has worked closely with me on this. The benefactors…."

"Are you and Elaine still an item?" interrupted Colter.

"No. That maudlin ending was six weeks ago. She'll get over it."

"Yeah, but will you? She is *soooome* piece," crooned Colter, adding an appreciative whistle as he conjured up an image of Elaine Sessions long, silky legs spread invitingly. "Hey! D'ya think she'd go with me if I asked her now?" asked Colter, almost panting.

"Not once she gets wind of the patents you're doing for me," stated Scanlon matter-of-factly. "And as part of the incentive to keep quiet, I am going to send her on a long-deserved vacation to some island paradise where she will be unreachable. But as I was saying before you so rudely, or was that lewdly, interrupted."

"Both!"

"The feraxia support group was more than a little naive. They made no contractual arrangement concerning patenting when they contributed money, biosamples, and family histories to the institute. It was no strings attached. They expected, of course, to receive some medical and family planning benefits from the research and they will. As for the institute, the benefactors have little or no interest in scientific issues or day-to-day operations. In fact, they would prefer that the institute do nothing to create a public buzz. Thanks to your skill at covering up ownership paper trails, no one knows that you, I, and your secretary, Ms. Gould, are voting board members. Can she be trusted?"

"Of course. Tracey is extremely loyal and is well compensated. As a legal secretary, she understands and respects confidentiality better than most lawyers. I am also putting her nephew and niece through expensive prep schools. She dotes on them. She's mine. That's why I often use her as board secretary when I want to maintain control of a board of directors," said Colter with more than a hint of braggadocio.

"We'll need to discuss the details. I'll come to your office," interrupted Scanlon.

Chapter Two

Cheryl Dain parked her car in the lot behind her office building. The building was in downtown Marshfield, a nine square block central business district—old, slightly seedy, bordering on quaint. The town was only fifty miles west of Chicago, just off I-90, but had so far retained its countrified atmosphere. The law firm, Dain, Ross, and Klyberg, occupied a huge, three-story, remodeled Queen Anne house built in the late 1800s. The house was something of a Victorian *folie,* as there had been many additions early and late.

Cheryl snuck in through the back door that led through a kitchen directly to her office. She wanted to delay as long as possible breaking the glow that the glorious day had kindled. Her ground floor office was flooded with sun from the large French patio doors, now covered only with a diaphanous curtain material. *Too fine a day to be working. But the bike path will have to wait for the weekend–if then.*

Just as she sat at her desk, the office intercom buzzed. The lawyer picked up the receiver and said, "Good morning, Rosalie. How did you know I was in?"

"Oh, Ms. Dain, you always try to avoid me on beautiful days like this. But you're never late. Your ten-thirty is here."

Cheryl chuckled, hung up the telephone, and ran her hand through her close-cropped, dark brown hair.

Her appointment had arrived fifteen minutes early.

Dain decided to go out to the waiting room to usher the client in. Clients, particularly women, found this welcoming and reassuring, dispelling the aggressive, shark on the prowl stereotypes that made some clients leery to consult a lawyer. Of course, some clients were looking for a bulldog or "Jaws". If so, they had come to the wrong place. What they would find in Cheryl Dain was a Fred Astaire of the law–elegant, smooth, making the difficult look easy. With no compromise of her integrity, she outclassed her opponents with superior intelligence, hard work, and instinctive creativity in the use of the law for her clients.

"Ms. Merino, I'm Cheryl Dain. It's very nice to meet you. I'm glad you're early. I like that kind of energy and conscientiousness in my clients and colleagues. I am compulsive about time and details myself. Will you come with me?" said Cheryl with a warm smile. Golda Merino looked up and couldn't help returning the smile, if nervously, as she rose to shake the attorney's outstretched hand.

The client was a pleasant-looking woman of about forty-five. She wore little makeup but had clear, glowing skin with a smattering of freckles around her nose. Her forehead showed some worry lines that might well have been of recent origin. More marked were the generous smile lines at the corners of her mouth. She had large, luminous, frank, gray eyes and long dark hair streaked with silver. She wore a somewhat dated and slightly rumpled dark business suit paired incongruously with open-toed, flat-heeled sandals. She was tall, almost a head taller than the five foot four Dain, not overweight, but slightly soft looking.

The lawyer ushered the woman into her office and indicated a brown leather chair facing her desk. Merino sat, wriggled to a comfortable position, rearranged her skirt, and folded her hands on a battered-looking leather portfolio she had placed in her lap.

Dain had already perused the brief intake file prepared by a paralegal when Merino had made her appointment and done some preliminary research. Dain sat behind the desk in her leather swivel chair and leaned back. "Our paralegal, Denise, has already explained to you the kind of retainer agreement we would have you sign should you decide to engage our firm. There is no fee for this first appointment to decide if you wish us to, and we are able to, handle the case. After that, we generally charge three hundred dollars per hour plus expenses for our work. However, we give you an estimate of the total cost and will not charge more than a hundred twenty percent of that estimate, plus our costs no matter how many hours we end up devoting to the matter." Merino nodded her understanding.

The lawyer cocked her head a bit to the right and fixed on the older woman's eyes for a full two beats. Golda Merino didn't flinch. She returned Cheryl's gaze with a wide-eyed, open expression on her face.

"Now, what can I help you with, Ms. Merino?" Dain asked with an interested, but serious look.

"Please, call me Golda."

"Okay. And I'm Cheryl. Please, go on, Golda."

"Well, as I told your paralegal, Denise," began the client hesitantly.

"Golda, I know you outlined your problem to our paralegal already," cut in Cheryl, "but I want to hear your narrative in detail. Our paralegal takes some of your information for three purposes: to help decide if our firm is the appropriate one for the matter and which of our lawyers might best handle your case; to get the names of participants in the matter to check for conflicts of interest with our past and present clients; and to give us enough advance information to make this first appointment as productive as possible." Cheryl paused and smiled encouragingly. "So please start from the beginning. I am very interested, not only in the facts you can recount but also in your feelings about the matter."

The woman took a deep breath, bent her head down, and closed her eyes for an instant. When she looked up again, she began, "Our daughter, Terri, was born three years ago with feraxia. It is an extremely rare, hereditary, developmental disease that can lead to severe mental disability and early death."

"I am so sorry to hear that."

Golda sighed. "Well, we were somewhat lucky. There just happened to be a pediatric resident at the hospital where she was delivered who had had a cousin with the disease. He recognized what looked like a yellowish patch of skin under the armpit that sometimes appears and is associated with the disease."

Golda hesitated. Cheryl could see that the distraught woman had committed this recitation to memory. Probably the only way she could do it without breaking down. The attorney nodded and her brow crinkled. Best not to interrupt the narrative and keep it going with open questions.

Taking a deep breath, Golda continued, "There is no cure as of yet. Diet management can lessen the damage the disease does. We must restrict Terri's intake of certain proteins found in milk and, unfortunately, also in soy substitutes. We go to a drug compounding pharmacy to prepare the formula for her. Her development is nowhere near normal, but at least she is not wasting away like so many other victims of this disease."

Golda stopped and could not completely stifle a sob. Cheryl's tightly compressed lips and furrowed brow conveyed the sympathy she felt for this distraught mother. Thinking of Terri and other less fortunate infants, the attorney had to blink to hold back a tear herself.

"Terri is very lucky to have you and such a strong family caring for her. Do you have other children?"

"Yes. Two boys, Roger and Michael. They're fourteen and sixteen. Terri was an unexpected late bonus." A very small smile flickered on Golda's lips.

"Are the boys healthy? Any sign of feraxia?"

"They don't have the disease, thank God, but they could be carriers. My husband and I must be carriers for Terri to have it while we don't." Golda Merino sighed and her eyes glistened with tears.

"Can you go on, Golda, or would you like to take a moment? Some coffee or tea?" Cheryl said softly.

"N-no thanks. I'd like to go on."

The attorney nodded.

"As soon as we learned of Terri's condition, we began to research the disease on the Internet and discovered a support group in the Midwest region. The support group mostly provided people to talk to who shared the problem and was good for advice on how to handle certain aspects of the care. Many of the support group members' children had already died of feraxia, often because of the lack of early detection. The group was a godsend. It kept us sane."

Cheryl shook her head and exhaled between clenched teeth. Golda's head lowered for a moment, but she quickly returned to her recital as if too long a pause would make her forget it.

"It was my husband Sam who said to me: 'If this is a genetically transmitted disease, maybe someone could develop a genetic test for early detection or even for pre-natal carrier detection?' I thought immediately that this is what the support group should be working toward. You know, we could contribute and raise money and provide biological samples and family histories for medical research and find an institute or hospital that would work on a test and possibly a cure for feraxia. So I decided to take on this project with the help of Sam and several support group members."

"You are an amazing woman, Golda. But I gather you have already carried out many of your plans and are working with the Shabel Institute in Skokie. What can I help you with?"

"Well, that's just it, Cheryl. We were working with that lab headed by a Dr. Scanlon. We raised money and donated samples and histories so the lab could research feraxia. We hoped the research would lead to a test for early detection and possibly even a cure."

"And has the research progressed?"

The client looked down with half-closed eyes. "In a way it has, but that's where we ran into a major problem."

When Golda hesitated, Cheryl prompted her. "What was the problem?" asked Cheryl, leaning forward and raising an eyebrow.

Golda let out a long sigh. "We just learned that three months ago Dr. Scanlon patented a method for isolating and tagging the feraxia gene and a test for identifying it."

"That sounds like good news."

The woman moved forward in her chair and looked at Cheryl wide-eyed. "We thought so at first, although we only learned of it when one of Dr. Scanlon's associates contacted us. She, a Dr. Elaine Sessions, was very upset because the whole patent business seemed to be a secret and underhanded ploy."

Cheryl made a mental note to follow up with Sessions and determine her involvement in the research and the patenting. But she didn't want to interrupt the rhythm of Golda's rote presentation. This would clue the attorney in on Golda's performance as a witness and the depth of her commitment to moving forward on her claim.

"What did you do?"

"Well, as president of the support group, I tried to contact Dr. Scanlon immediately. It was difficult. He seemed to be avoiding my calls and emails. After ten days of fruitless efforts, I finally went to his lab in Skokie. His secretary tried to put me off saying he wouldn't be in until a very important meeting later in the afternoon. Then he would have no time to talk to me. She said to make an appointment for next week."

"And did you?"

"No! I said I would wait if I had to camp outside his office for a month."

"What happened then?"

"After two hours, I asked the secretary where the

nearest restroom was. She directed me around the corner of the hallway. But just as I was about to enter the women's room, I had a flash that it was not a good idea to abandon my post. I quickly returned to the waiting area and, sure enough, there was Dr. Scanlon sneaking out of his office."

"Did you confront him?"

Golda's eyes narrowed and her eyebrows arched. She let out her breath. "I sure did. I asked about the discovery and the patenting. I said that I didn't even think a gene could be patented. But he said that they had added a tag to the gene and the tagged gene, the procedures for isolating it, and the test were covered in the patent. He tried to reassure me that this was standard procedure so the institute would get credit for the research and protect their ability to make further progress. He said that he had instructed a colleague to notify the support group immediately, but there must have been some glitch. He said they could begin testing newborns very soon."

Cheryl could see the anger behind Golda's controlled recitation. "Did you believe him?"

"Not by this point. He seemed very uneasy and kept looking for a way to escape me. I told him that I would contact the support group members and other researchers who had been in touch with our group to let them know of the discovery. I would also ask the other members to start notifying local hospitals that there was a test available. I said that I expected he would make the research results and the test widely available as soon as possible. After all, there were lives to be saved." Golda seemed to be out of breath for a moment.

Cheryl nodded, pursed her lips, and asked, "How

did he respond to that?"

After three deep breaths, Golda continued, "He said not to go off half-cocked. That I should notify the support group members, but that he would take care of disseminating the information to researchers and hospitals. He was very fidgety, shifting his eyes all about and tapping his foot. He said he had to go to his meeting, although it was only noon, and abruptly departed down the hall. I thought of running after him but decided rather to get to work on my end."

"What did you do then?"

Golda smiled slightly. "Everything I told him I would do. I telephoned and emailed our support group. Asked them to spread the word. I notified all the researchers on my contact list. Within ten days, I was getting calls and messages saying that those who tried to contact Scanlon and the Shabel Institute were first getting the runaround and finally being told they would have no right to use the feraxia gene for research or to administer the test without paying an exorbitant licensing fee. Several hospitals did sign on to give the test to parents and newborns but weren't sure how long they could continue paying the fee. None of the researchers are presently willing to license the gene."

"A sad but, I have heard, not atypical story with rare diseases," said Cheryl, frowning and shaking her head. The attorney was always wary of the overblown expectations of clients. "What do you expect to come out of my involvement in this matter?"

Golda leaned forward in her seat and steepled her hands under her nose. "Our support group contributed money, tissue samples, and family histories to Scanlon and his laboratory. We did so while letting him know that we wanted to stimulate as broad an interest as possible in finding a test and cure for feraxia. We expected him to make his work widely available to others pursuing the same goals. Doesn't his taking the contributions create any legal obligation on his part?"

Cheryl did not answer immediately. She could not reassure Golda.

Realizing no answer was immediately forthcoming, Golda continued, "Now the best we can hope for is that through legal action or the threat of it, we can shake loose Scanlon's grip on the discoveries. That's what we hope you will be able to do."

Cheryl took a deep breath and stared down at her desk for a moment. "Golda, as I said, this is not an atypical situation. But I must tell you that courts have generally held that individuals have no ownership rights in tissue samples once removed from their bodies or in family medical histories when given to others. Did your group make any formal agreements with Dr. Scanlon or the Shabel Institute regarding the use of the contributions or the money?"

"No, but he seemed to be agreeable with our wishes," said Golda, her voice cracking.

"Did he make any specific promises, oral or written, concerning the use of his research or discoveries?"

"Well, he did say, as did the Shabel Institute literature, that his lab and the institute were non-profit organizations whose purpose was to further medical research and to make available medical discoveries to patients."

"That's something. I would have to look over all of the literature and your correspondence with Scanlon and the institute. It is possible we may have a claim of fraud or unjust enrichment which might be leveraged against them."

The attorney paused with a faraway gaze over the client's shoulder. "Now you've given me something to work on, but before you leave, you must give Denise the names of everyone you can think of from your support group, Terri's doctors, people at the institute, and even your contact list. It is necessary to determine if we have a conflict of interest with anyone who might be involved in the case. If you would like to engage our firm, specifically me, you can sign the retainer agreement with Denise or you can go home and think about it for a few days. Discuss it with your husband and support group."

The woman looked slightly bewildered, not sure if she was being dismissed.

Cheryl got up, walked around her desk, and took Golda's right hand in both of hers. She looked into the woman's eyes, smiled reassuringly, and said, "It was so good to meet you. I'd also like to meet Terri and your husband. I hope we will be able to work together to untie this knotty problem."

Golda Merino smiled back at Cheryl, rose from the chair, and nodded before turning toward the door. She opened the office door and, before exiting, turned back to Cheryl and nodded again. Cheryl felt that this was a nod of approval and that Terri's mother would be a client.

Chapter Three

Dr. Alan Scanlon sat in his office at the Rare Disease Genomics Lab of the Shabel Institute glumly staring at the papers he had just been served with. According to Jack Colter, his lawyer and fellow institute incorporator, the institute, too, had been served as a defendant in the case. The feraxia support group and its members were suing for fraud and unjust enrichment (*Whatever that meant?*) based on their contributions to his research and his patenting and restricting the use of the discovery of the feraxia gene and the test for it.

Scanlon was outraged and worried. *Didn't those ingrates understand that, without him, there would have been no isolated gene or test for feraxia?* Although he expected to win the lawsuit, he was apprehensive about the effects of the case on the funding for the institute.

The office intercom buzzed. The receptionist's hesitant voice informed him there was a man on the phone who insisted on speaking with him but would not give his name or business. He just said to tell the doctor that his major benefactor wanted to talk to him.

Scanlon's head sank to his chest and he closed his eyes. "Okay. Tell him I am on another line and will be with him in a moment. Give me thirty seconds before you put him through."

"Yes, sir, but he doesn't sound like he will wait

patiently."

"Just do it," snapped Scanlon, and switched off the intercom.

What could this be about? The patent under his name? The lawsuit? Missed payments?

Scanlon shuffled some papers on his desk to collect himself. The phone rang. He picked it up and said, "Hello, Victor. How are you?"

"No good since I heard about that fucking lawsuit," said the gruff voice on the other end of the line.

"How did you hear about it so fast? We just found out today when we were served."

A hoarse grunt was the response. "We have very good connections down at the courthouse. Who d'ya think you're playing with here?"

Scanlon could only utter, "Uh" before his benefactor continued. The doctor's knuckles turned white as he gripped the receiver harder. He bit his lip.

"We don't like this suit, we don't like what you did to bring it on, and we don't like how this jeopardizes our sweet deal."

"I can understand that but—"

"There ain't no buts. End the suit now. Settle before discovery gets going and financial information's requested. Give 'em what they want."

"But we'll win the case. The law is clearly on our side."

"Don't think ya heard me. There will be no case. We don't give a shit about who wins. We need to keep our business with the institute out of court. You have three days. After that, we know how to end the matter conclusively. You get me."

"Yes," rasped Scanlon. There was a click at the

other end of the line. The scientist held the receiver near his ear for several seconds. He could feel a cold sweat on his forehead. His hands were shaking. Finally, Scanlon let the receiver drop on his desk.

The lab director knew he couldn't give up everything. The patent and licensing of the feraxia gene and test were too much of a boon establishing both his scientific and tough business reputation in an extremely lucrative industry. However, he thought that he and Colter could work out a satisfactory settlement of the suit. He convinced himself that the benefactor's threat was for the Merinos and the support group and that it would help ensure a favorable settlement.

Chapter Four

KELAN SU

I slammed shut and locked my locker after my morning *Qui Gong* workout. The meditation, strenuous physical activity, and a hot shower made my mind and body tingle. I was ready for action, although there was none on the agenda this dreary Saturday morning. At least I would have a nice lunch and a long *tête-à-tête* with Cheryl, my former roommate and big sister at U of C. She was coming in from her law office in Marshfield for the day. We had arranged to meet at Café Rom.

I slipped into my jeans and T-shirt. Sitting on a bench, I put on and tied my running shoes. Everything in black today, unoriginal as usual. When you are a six-foot Chinese-American woman, you don't need anything to make you more conspicuous.

As I reached the door of the *kwoon*, my *Shifu* waved goodbye, with a slight bow. I lowered my head in respect. He had conducted a superb master class on the connection between spiritual balance and the most effective defensive stances.

A misty drizzle brought a damp chill to the air. It was dark enough for some of the streetlights to come on. I zipped up my rain jacket and pulled the hood over my head. I would still jog the eight blocks from the Chinese martial arts academy near Navy Pier to the restaurant at the Prudential Plaza. The sidewalk and streets were slick with the rain. I carefully avoided the puddles. Didn't want to ruin my soft leather running shoes.

When I arrived at the restaurant ten minutes early, Cheryl was waiting. She was never late and usually early. She had selected a corner table, one of the few not up against the large plate glass windows. I sensed this was not just a session to catch up on each other's lives or relive old times. She was checking her phone as I headed toward the table but looked up when I was a few feet away. A slight squint and hooded brows opened into a warm smile as her eyes focused on me. She stood and we hugged. For a moment, she held me at arm's length looking me over with an approving shake of her head.

"It's been too long since we last got together," said Cheryl, frowning.

I agreed.

"You look wonderful, positively glowing," she said with an admiring smile

"I just came from an invigorating workout and run."

I noted her trim figure and bronzed skin. "You don't look too bad yourself."

Cheryl chuckled. "Well, that's surprising. I've had little time to exercise or do my regular bicycling regimen."

"Not surprising. I read about your involvement in that gene patenting case. It sounded very complicated and sad given the suffering the disease must cause."

Cheryl harrumphed. "That's not even half the story."

I realized that was why she set up this meeting. She

was good, my crafty friend. She got me to open up the topic she was interested in. This ability to seduce to her way of thinking got us out of many a jam in college. I guess I loved her for it.

"Let's hear it. What's going on?"

My curiosity was piqued, but it would have to wait to be satisfied. The gum-chewing, multi-pierced, young waitress stood over our table, pad in hand. When Cheryl noticed her, she clamped her mouth shut.

"What can I get for you, ladies?" said the waitress, pencil poised.

We gave the tabletop menus a cursory glance and ordered cappuccinos and paninis. The waitress nodded, scribbled, and headed toward the next recently occupied table.

Cheryl watched her go, waited two beats, and began, "You've probably read about the murder of Dr. Alan Scanlon last week."

"Yesss. Oh wow! Wasn't he one of the defendants in your feraxia case?"

"That's right. The patent at issue was applied for in his name. His death throws everything into turmoil. But that's still not the most troubling part."

"You've got me on edge here. Give."

"My client, Golda Merino, is president of the local feraxia support group and mother of a child with the disorder. She's the chief suspect in the murder," said Cheryl, grimacing and shaking her head.

My eyes widened in sympathy. "That's terrible. And you're pretty sure she didn't do it?"

"I'm positive she didn't. You'd have to meet her. The salt of the earth."

I couldn't help slipping into detective mode. "Why

is she the prime suspect?"

"Because she was particularly distraught about delays in research on feraxia and Scanlon's role in those delays." Cheryl looked down sadly. "Her daughter had just taken a turn for the worse and she was desperate. She went to see Scanlon, against my advice, argued with him, stormed out of his office calling him a murderer and saying she would be back to deal with him. She did return early the next morning about seven a.m. Apparently, the security guard was out of the kiosk when she arrived since the time wasn't recorded. She left around seven thirty a.m. and was logged out. Institute doors were unlocked and the security system did not seem to be on when she got there. Scanlon was alone in the lab and dead. She obviously touched the body, possibly the gun, and other things in the lab. She left not seeing anyone else around. She called me from her car in a panic. I told her to call the police and report finding the body but not to say anything else. She didn't call the police for another half hour."

"How was Scanlon killed?"

"As far as I can find out from one of my police contacts, he was shot in the right temple with a small caliber weapon. It sounded pretty messy. My client said there was a lot of blood." Cheryl hung her head, shaking it, and looking very glum.

"Have the cops found the weapon?"

"I believe so."

"On your client?"

"Thankfully, no."

"Witnesses? Security footage?"

"Again, I don't know yet."

"Is your client in the slammer?"

"Not yet, but I've heard the Cook County State's Attorney will be filing an information momentarily. They had a warrant to search her house and found the clothes she had worn on the day of the murder. Scanlon's blood was on them."

"What a disaster! Who's handling the criminal case?" I asked, although I thought I knew the answer.

"I told Golda that my experience was primarily with civil matters, although I have done some white-collar crime, but that I could recommend a top criminal lawyer. She wouldn't have it. She insists that I represent her. We developed a good rapport during the patent case. I couldn't refuse."

"Are the police following up on other suspects?"

"No."

"As usual when they think they have an easy target. It looks like the only way out for your client may be to discover who really did it. You want Korb and me to take on the investigation?" I was pretty sure of the answer to this question too.

With tightly compressed lips, Cheryl nodded. "I'm really sorry to presume on our friendship. But Golda does not deserve what's happening to her. She, and I, need the kind of help that only you and Marko Korb can give. She can pay but will need some kind of installment arrangement. Her husband's a CPA with Burns & Marwick. I will reduce or waive my fee if necessary, but I can't waive expenses."

I looked out onto the rain-swept street. The dark, dreary day mirrored my feelings about Korb's likely response. A "tsk" of sympathy escaped me as I shook my head.

"Well, Cheryl, I am ready to help, but I can't speak

for Korb. I'll do what I can to convince him. He only takes cases if they interest him and if they pay. I'm hoping he will at least talk to you and your client before making any decision."

I didn't know what else to say. I couldn't meet Cheryl's eyes with a hopeful look. Korb would be hard to convince. Fortunately, the food arrived providing for a few moments of pensive silence.

Chapter Five

KELAN SU

When I arrived home after lunch with Cheryl, Korb was in the office sitting in his favorite overstuffed wing chair reading a book. He still wore his scuffed leather slippers and bright yellow pajamas. *It was three p.m.!* He pushed the reading glasses to the end of his nose and glanced over the top of the lenses as I entered but immediately pushed the specs back and returned to Hamid Ismailov's, *The Railway.*

Closing the door behind me with a little extra force, I stood, still watching my boss. After about five seconds, I cleared my throat. Finally, Korb looked up with a tight smile, placed the book open over his knee, and took off his glasses. "Is there something you want?" he asked, cocking his head to the right.

"Well, you know there've been no new paying clients for over two weeks," I began after a slight hesitation.

"Yes. I consider it a welcome respite."

Korb was lazy between cases, although a bulldog once he got his teeth into an investigation. Money was important to him, but not always as important as his time for reading, reflection, gourmandizing, or playing bridge.

"Our operating accounts are guttering. There may not be enough next month to pay Des's and my salaries and Mickey D's retainer."

"If necessary, I can replenish the accounts with personal funds. All will be paid."

Korb was loaded as a result of his renown as an investigator and some very prudent investing. "Oh, I'm not really worried about my salary. I know you're good for it. But…"

Korb looked down and shook his head slightly as he interrupted me. "Kelan, stop beating around the bush. You want us to work for your friend, Cheryl Dain, who is representing the woman accused of murdering the scientist who patented the gene and test for feraxia, do you not?"

My mouth opened soundlessly for a moment. I finally managed to sputter, "How did you know that?"

A loud "harrumph" came from deep down in Korb's chest. "The conclusion was obvious. I read the papers. The development of the case has been front-page news and fodder for several letters to the editor. You told me yourself that you were to meet with Dain today and mentioned that you hadn't seen her for quite a while. Your little diversion about our accounts didn't put me off the scent. Can she pay, or is this another one of your *pro bono* projects?"

I closed my eyes, contemplating how to put it. "She can pay, but an installment arrangement will have to be set up. Dain will cover expenses as they occur."

"If we do this, and I'm not committing to it, I will need to talk first to Dain, Merino, and Merino's husband and daughter. Our contractual agreement will have to be with Dain, so we are covered by attorney-client privilege and Dain will be liable for our fee.

"As much as I hate to travel to the suburbs, the

initial meeting should be at Dain's office to bolster any privilege or work product claim. See if you can arrange this for Monday afternoon. Make sure the car is ready for a trip to Marshfield." Korb put on the glasses he had been holding in his right hand and picked up the open volume. "Well, does that conclude the business for which you interrupted my immersion in this excellent novel?"

I nodded. Korb made the fifty-mile I-90 jaunt to Marshfield seem like a daylong trek in the wilderness. I couldn't think of anything else to say. It was too early for a thank you as Korb might still refuse the case. Somehow, I knew he wouldn't. The publicity had made this case a heater and showing up the police and state's attorney in a high-profile matter was just the thing to goad him into action. He would be driven to prove, once again, that he was the world's most astute exposer and analyst of criminal behavior.

Best to quit while I was ahead. Without a word, I turned and left the office.

Chapter Six

KELAN SU

I would have preferred that Korb sit in the back
and read his book to his taking the front seat and trying
to direct my driving. He was not a good traveler.
Marshfield was a straight shot west from Chicago on I-
90 – flat, no deviations, and not much scenery. It should
have been an easy drive. At ten a.m. on a Monday
morning, the traffic in our direction was light. Most
traffic was eastbound into the city. With Korb's
constant admonitions to slow down, however, the fifty-
mile trip took seventy minutes instead of the forty-five
minutes at my normal cruising speed. I could feel the
tension build in my shoulders.

We arrived at Dain, Ross, & Klyberg's Victorian
office building just after eleven a.m. and made our way
to Cheryl's sunlit office. Cheryl was at her desk. There
was a haggard and rumpled woman already there,
seated in a chair opposite and toward the right side of
the attorney's desk, balancing a cup and saucer on her
knee. Must be Golda Merino. Cheryl sipped her coffee
from an Illinois Bar Association mug. She put down the
cup and stood when we entered, circled her desk,
stepped up to Korb, and shook his hand. We hugged.

"So good of you to assist us. Let me introduce you
to my client, Golda Merino," said Cheryl, turning to the
seated woman. "Golda, this is the renowned detective,

Marko Korb, and his colleague, and my dear friend, Kelan Su."

Golda placed her coffee on Cheryl's desk and stood up hesitantly, trying to smooth her granny dress. Korb put out his hand, palm down. "Please sit, Ms. Merino," said Korb.

Golda sat down awkwardly. I stepped up to her and took her hand, giving it a squeeze. "So pleased to meet you, Ms. Merino." Golda looked up at me and smiled slightly. I could see why Cheryl could not believe Golda was a killer. Despite her sunken eyes, even her half smile conveyed to me warmth, trust, and goodwill.

Korb wedged himself into an oversized chair that Cheryl had specially brought in. He turned the chair so he could see both Cheryl and Golda without turning his head. I took a seat to the right of and slightly behind Korb so I could observe all the interactions and took out my notepad and pen.

Cheryl asked if we wanted coffee. When we declined, she began as we had agreed. "Golda, I have asked Mr. Korb and Ms. Su to be my investigators in this case. They want to speak with you before beginning their inquiry. Please feel free to answer their questions as you would mine. What you say to them is protected by our attorney-client relationship." Cheryl looked at Korb.

Nodding to Cheryl, Korb turned to Golda and smiled broadly. I was impressed by how reassuring he seemed.

"Ms. Merino, I was sorry to hear that your daughter had taken a turn for the worse just before you talked to Dr. Scanlon that last time. How is she doing?" asked Korb, looking very concerned.

Golda looked grateful for Korb's sentiment. "We were able to get her stabilized quickly. She is doing as well as can be expected. She is finally walking confidently."

"I'm glad to hear that. This must be a grueling experience for you and your family. It's clear they need your full attention. Difficult to give under the circumstances. I hope we can do something about that."

Golda nodded.

Korb's expression became piercing as he got down to business. "Now, Ms. Merino, can you tell me how many times you have met with Dr. Scanlon since your organization started working with him?"

Golda's brow furrowed. "Let's see. He came to us with his research proposal the first time. We were interviewing several researchers, mostly academics. We had put out notices in medical journals about our interest in supporting feraxia research."

"When was this?"

"About two years ago."

"How did he strike you at that meeting?"

Golda shifted in her chair. "Well, he was well-prepared–better than most of the others we interviewed. Most of our board was very impressed, but I wasn't. He struck me as too slick. Nor was I impressed with the work of the Shabel Institute. It seemed well-funded, but we were not aware of any research achievements that had furthered health care. I had hoped for academic researchers."

"And did you make these feelings known to the board or Dr. Scanlon?"

"Yes, I told the board about them, but I realized they were only feelings with no real basis in evidence.

Dr. Scanlon's lab was well-equipped to do the research we wanted. The board chose him in a six to three vote. I didn't express my feelings to Dr. Scanlon in the interview, but he might have read some doubt in my mind from my questions and body language."

Korb's eyes narrowed. "Would you say that your doubt reached the level of hostility?"

"No, no."

I was trying hard to read her demeanor. Was she bitter about not having her feelings vindicated by the board? Resigned, maybe, but not bitter or convinced that the board had decided wrongly at the time.

Korb followed up with, "How was the fact that the board had chosen Dr. Scanlon's institute conveyed to him?"

Golda shifted in her chair and thought for a moment. "As president of the group, it was my job to tell him his lab had been chosen, why, what we could offer in terms of support, and what we expected. We met at his office. I thought I was very cordial and encouraging and he seemed extremely pleased to be working with us."

"And did you report back to the board about this meeting?"

"Yes, and I told them that the meeting had gone well and that I had every confidence that Dr. Scanlon would work hard on our project."

Korb cleared his throat. "What other meetings did you have with Dr. Scanlon up to the time when you heard he had isolated the feraxia gene?"

Golda looked up to the ceiling, then squinted into the distance as if trying to read her calendar off the far wall. "I think I met with him three or four times after conveying the board's decision to him and before I heard about his success."

"How did those meetings go?"

There was a knock at the door. Cheryl gave us a "sorry" grimace and said, "Come in." The interruption was welcome. I relaxed and flexed my shoulders. Golda's head dropped low as she exhaled. I didn't realize how much tension had mounted in the room.

Rosalie came in and whispered something in Cheryl's ear. Cheryl nodded. "I'm sorry, I have to take this call. I'll be back in a moment. Rosalie, can you ask everyone what they would like for lunch? We'll have it brought in from The Oaks. Also, refresh any drinks. Thanks."

Rosalie nodded and asked us our preferences. The tension in the room eased a bit. To keep it down, I made some small talk, commenting on the great weather we'd been having and how Cheryl's office was flooded with sunlight. Golda merely nodded her agreement while Korb steepled his fingers under his chins, eyes closed. Rosalie returned with our drinks and we all thanked her.

When Cheryl reentered, Korb's eyes flashed open, and he leaned forward with his elbows on his knees, ready to resume his questioning. However, Cheryl had an announcement. "I'm sorry to say that the state's attorney has filed the information charging Golda with first- and second-degree murder."

Golda gulped, hung her head, and started to cry. Both Cheryl and I went to her. I rubbed her back and Cheryl kneeled and held her hands. "You know we expected this."

"Will I be going to jail?" sobbed Golda.

"The state's attorney asked that you turn yourself

in at the 2nd District courthouse in Skokie Wednesday morning. Let's be glad it's not that hell hole at 26th and California. You won't be going to jail."

Golda, eyes wide, searched Cheryl's face for reassurance.

Cheryl squeezed Golda's hands and smiled slightly. "I have requested an immediate bail hearing. The SA has agreed not to ask for money bail, but there will be some restrictions. Better bring your family so the judge can see your ties to the community. I'll call Teri's medical team and ask them to fax or email Teri's diagnosis and treatment plan indicating the need for constant care on your part. I'll try to get one of them to come to the hearing. The court will ask for your passport, so get it if you have one. At the worst, they may ask you to wear an ankle bracelet monitor."

I saw a box of tissues on a credenza and brought Golda several of them. She dabbed at her eyes and struggled to compose herself. Korb was looking away. He was embarrassed at weepy shows of emotion. I'd bet that he was also frustrated because of the break in his interrogation rhythm.

Cheryl regarded Korb. "Can we continue this interview at a later date? I think Golda needs some time to collect herself."

Korb frowned. But before he could answer, Golda broke in. "Oh no. Mr. Korb and Ms. Su have come all this way to help me. Let's go on."

I could see she was fighting for control. I admired her courage.

Korb's frown dissipated. "Thank you, Ms. Merino. I am most anxious to start working on this case and I'll need some more information from you before I can begin. You are being very helpful. Kelan, where were we?"

Korb often relies on my memory, which is almost photographic. Furthermore, I had taken some notes as a backup. "You were asking Golda about her meetings with Dr. Scanlon after she had relayed the board's decision to engage his laboratory. I believe she said there were three or four further meetings prior to learning of his success in isolating the gene. Is that right, Golda?"

"Y-yes, I think so."

"You wanted to know how those meetings went?" I continued.

"Excellent, Kelan. Thank you. How did those meetings go, Ms. Merino?"

Golda sucked in her breath. "At the time, I thought, very well. At the first meeting, he showed me around the lab and introduced me to the staff members working on the feraxia research, in particular his chief collaborator, Dr. Elaine Sessions. Several other research assistants were working on the project, but I got the impression that Dr. Sessions was the one really in charge of the operation. I thought she was bright and committed."

Korb pursed his lips. "And the next meeting?"

"Well, that was totally with Dr. Scanlon. I was disappointed as I felt that Dr. Sessions would be more frank about the research progress. Dr. Scanlon was very encouraging about how the work was going, but he also asked about increasing our group's financial contribution. We knew that the research would be costly. We made a substantial initial grant of a hundred thousand dollars. But we had selected the institute on the assumption that its financial backing was very strong and that they already had the necessary staff and equipment in place. I told him I would bring the request to the Board. With the care of our afflicted children, we would be hard-pressed to contribute more."

Korb's eyes half closed. "Did you have an inkling then that Scanlon was planning something underhanded?"

Merino looked down and shook her head. "I had a bad feeling in the pit of my stomach after talking to him. It never translated into a conscious thought. I convinced myself that his optimistic view of the progress was true. I guess it was mostly true. In fact, his dishonesty was in underplaying the nearness of success. I even complimented Dr. Scanlon on the rapid progress he and his team were making."

"Did you report this meeting to your board?"

Merino nodded.

"And did you convey your feelings to them?"

Merino shifted in her seat. "No. I said that Scanlon was optimistic about forthcoming results."

Korb nodded, one eyebrow raised. "And the next meeting, when did that take place?"

"In early April, the third, I think."

"Who was present at that meeting?"

"Dr. Scanlon and Dr. Sessions. They were both almost jubilant. They said the gene had been isolated and a test would soon follow. I was overcome. I didn't ask enough questions. I just thanked them profusely and took the good news back to the board." Golda let out a long sigh. "I feel guilty that I let our group down. I should have exercised more supervision. Was I lax because I thought this discovery would not directly help

Teri? I don't know." Merino covered her face with her hands and sobbed.

Cheryl broke in, moving to Golda and putting her arm around the sobbing woman's heaving shoulders. "Golda, you did all you could. Because of you, this discovery was made very quickly. You couldn't have known what Scanlon was planning. You have nothing to feel guilty about."

I understood only too well that hollowness in the pit of the stomach that came from letting down those who counted on you. In my case, it was my brother, killed while doing my shift in my parents' store, and my one true friend on the force who had died before I could get to him. I closed my eyes tightly to hold back tears. To no avail.

Korb had maintained a patient, sympathetic smile during this emotional break. The only thing that betrayed his impatience at the interruption of his questioning was a slight tapping of his fingers on the arms of his chair.

To get things going again without taking responsibility for insensitivity to Golda's feelings, he turned to me. "We should probably let Ms. Merino go home and get some rest. She needs to be in court on Wednesday. Do you have any further questions, Kelan?"

My eyes snapped open. There was more I needed to know, but I didn't want to press Golda now. "Let's wrap this up. We have enough to get started on. Golda, I'll text you questions. Cheryl can help you with them. For now, go home, get some rest, and hug your husband and children, and leave the worrying to Cheryl and us."

I did have a lot of questions: I needed a list of the

dates of Golda's meetings at the institute and of the people associated with Scanlon and the institute that she encountered with particular attention to the day before, the day of, and the day after the murder. How did she make her way to the murder scene? What did she see and touch? Who did she see or hear? Who might have seen or heard her? Did she notice anything unusual? What exactly did she do in the hour before she reported the killing to the police? Why did she delay?

If Korb was upset with my move to terminate the interview while important questions remained, to hell with him. This tortured woman needed a break. I looked at Korb out of the corner of my eye. He had his fist to his mouth, nodding in what I hoped was agreement.

Chapter Seven

KELAN SU

During the long, congested drive home, Korb's eyes were closed and his breath whistled in and out between his teeth–a sure sign that he was plotting strategy. At least he wasn't criticizing my driving. I knew that he would be giving me my marching orders for tomorrow. As I edged between cars crossing two lanes to the exit ramp, Korb's eyes snapped open. He was disoriented, his eyes wide and unfocused as he grabbed the armrest.

"We're just about home," I said. "Will you be briefing me on my assignment for tomorrow before dinner?" I knew that mentioning dinner would settle him. "I'm sure Desmond will have something special, knowing you've been out working all day."

A sigh shook Korb's belly and a slight smile crossed his face as he contemplated Des's artful cuisine. "I think the briefing can wait until tomorrow morning," he said as he leaned back in his seat and looked out the window.

****

I pulled the armored Lincoln Town car into the garage next to my Ford Escape hybrid. Turning off the engine, I looked over at my boss. He was staring at the door to the kitchen. I was sure he envisioned his dinner.

I got out of the car quickly and ran around to the

passenger side back door. Opening the door, I pulled Korb's eagle-headed cane from the back seat. He had already opened the right front door and was struggling to turn his sixth of a ton toward the opening. Between grunts, he grabbed the cane I extended to him. Placing it between his legs and leaning on it with both hands, Korb pushed himself to a standing position. Letting out a long breath, he said, "I guess I earned my dinner."

As I hit the garage door button and the door descended, Des looked out of the entrance to the kitchen. He pursed his lips in a mock pout. "You're late. Glad I made gumbo. The longer it simmers, the better it gets," he exclaimed in his British-tinged, Caribbean lilt.

I always felt safe at home when I saw Desmond St. Clair. It wasn't just his dazzlingly warm smile, his darkly handsome face, and his six-foot, four-inch chiseled body, although those things certainly helped. It was what he did for us. The smells of his creole cooking always warmed my heart. He was also our super-efficient housekeeper/valet. But best of all, he was my partner in keeping Korb safe. He was a former elite British SAS commando. Korb had met him in 1997 in Bosnia at an Operation Tango briefing session concerning the arrest of Serbian war criminals.

After Des left the army, he opened an Afro-Caribbean restaurant back home on Tortola. Although the restaurant was moderately successful, it was devastated by Hurricane Irma in 2006. Rather than rebuild, he took a job with a security firm in Chicago. He had missed the excitement of special ops. Corporate security didn't fill the bill either. He reconnected with Korb, whose investigative career was renowned and whose cases seemed much more edgy. Working for Korb allowed Des to indulge all of his specialties.

"Whassup, Des?" I asked. "How was your day?"

"Well, aside from the gumbo prep, I refocused some of our security cameras, and changed our passwords–you'll find an encrypted message in the usual place. I also did the background checks for Tiedermann Industries. Mostly routine, but you'll find one intriguing result. The report is on your desks."

"You lazy boy."

"Oh ya, I did a wee bit of research on the Shabel Institute staff and directors. I think you'll find the funding sources very interesting. That's on your desk too."

What a wonder! I wanted to kiss him, but instead, I shook my head and merely said, "Thanks." My only worry was that Korb would realize that, with Des, he didn't need me.

Korb was at the stove looking into the gumbo pot with a wooden spoon in one hand and a potholder and the cover in the other hand. He breathed in deeply, savoring the pungent aroma. His eyes closed and a smile lit up his bulldog face. As he lowered the spoon into the pot, Des grabbed his hand.

"Not yet, mon. Need to add the last of my secret spice and more bone broth. S'posed to be over sticky rice."

Korb frowned, pursed his lips, and slowly put back the lid and spoon. "When will it be ready?"

"Soon as you shower and change. I've laid out your clothes."

Korb nodded and moved with uncustomary alacrity to the elevator. I followed. I was anxious to get comfortable and savor Des's signature dish.

Chapter Eight

KELAN SU

At nine a.m. the next morning, I was seated in the large library on the main floor, which was also Korb's office. My office was next door. When open, French doors between the two rooms allowed me to see and listen in on clients seated before Korb's oversized desk as well as see Korb's mountainous profile. When the doors were closed, three CCTV cameras allowed me to monitor any goings-on in the library.

I heard the whirr of the elevator signaling Korb's descent. He had briefed me before his breakfast so I could get moving on the case. We had read Des's report. Earlier this morning, Golda, through Cheryl, had sent us a list of people at the institute with whom she had had contact. I was pretty sure Korb would tell me to start at the institute, and that's just what I wanted.

Korb entered, still wearing his bright yellow silk pajamas–the rising sun. He squeezed himself into his oversized, well-padded desk chair with a nod to me. He held up one finger to forestall any questions I might have and picked up the desk phone, punching the kitchen intercom button. "Desmond, I'll have my usual breakfast in the office in twenty minutes."

I heard a crisp "Yessuh!" as Korb clapped down the receiver.

The bright yellow rondure put both hands down on

his desk and looked at them. Slowly, Korb raised his massive head and gave me a hard stare. I stared back.

"We need to jump-start this investigation. You'll be going to the institute today. I want you to find out everything you can about their security system, how and why it wasn't operating the night Scanlon was killed and get to Elaine Sessions. We need her take on Scanlon, the patenting scam, and who else might want him dead. She seems to be sympathetic to Ms. Merino."

"Right, Boss. Should I go as myself or be creative?"

"Let's keep it above board for the time being. Since we are working for Cheryl Dain, we are officers of the court. If we need subterfuge, I'll bring in one of our freelancers, possibly Seminoff."

"Right." I hesitated, wondering if there would be further instructions. Korb looked down at his desk, seeming to search it for a mislaid document. What was he looking for? Something for me? I leaned forward to see if I could help. He looked up, brow wrinkled.

"Well, what are you waiting for? Get going."

Chapter Nine

KELAN SU

It was a clear, bright, stifling September day. The lakeshore parks and beaches were starting to fill up despite the workday. The waters of Lake Michigan sparkled in the sunshine, but heat waves radiated off the pavement on the Outer Drive. Heading north to Peterson on the Drive in the morning wasn't too bad. Going west to Lincoln was slower. It gave me time to think about my strategy. I'd be totally upfront–ask for Dr. Sessions, wait or get an appointment if necessary. In fact, a wait would be beneficial. Give me time to befriend the receptionist or secretary.

I arrived at the Illinois Science & Technology Park in Skokie at ten a.m. checked in at the gate. I gave the guard my business card and asked for directions to the Shabel Institute Rare Disease Genomics Lab. I was somewhat surprised that the guard didn't ask me about my business at the institute or call ahead. He just entered my name, plate number, destination, and time of entry into a computer log. *I'll need to get a gander at that log for the day of the murder.* He told me to take the second right onto Mulberry Lane. The institute would be the third building on the right.

The park, established on the former G.D. Searle pharma company sight in 2009, had been the home of the Rare Disease Genomics lab since 2012. The lab shared the site with several other technology companies. Most of the buildings were occupied. The park seemed to be thriving although there was still some space for expansion. The landscaping was spectacular. The grass was a lush green. Flowering bushes in a huge variety of colors were artfully located around the property. A waterfall continued to burble as the water fell into a small brook that meandered through the property. At one point, the stream was dammed to create a stocked fishpond. Several people were enjoying their coffee breaks lounging on the grass—an idyllic setting that seemed to belie the violence that had occurred there. Of course, being in Skokie, there was a tasteful sign at the entrance wishing that everyone have a good new year: *L'Shanna Tovah*!

I decided to tour the Park's perimeter and note points of access. Along the eastern border, there were railroad tracks and a rail siding with a tall cyclone fence separating the tracks from the park grounds. Skokie Boulevard, U.S. 41, ran north to more remote suburbs and Wisconsin and south into Chicago where it became Cicero Avenue. Surrounding the rest of the grounds was a high berm, also topped with a cyclone fence. The fence was adorned with flowering, climbing vines. Neither railroad tracks nor cyclone fences were major deterrents to those determined to enter the compound surreptitiously. I wondered if there were other security devices monitoring entries. Certainly, each of the establishments in the park would have some more sophisticated systems around their sites. It was clear to me that someone could easily enter the property bypassing the guard.

I wanted to get a closer look at the fence at the rear

of the property and see the surroundings from a higher vantage point. Pulling over to the side of the road, I got out of the car. When I opened the door to exit the air-conditioned car, a blast of hot, sticky air engulfed me. I had to traverse up the steep, grassy berm. I was sweating pretty heavily by the time I reached the top. I looked back toward the buildings. Someone entering from here could not be seen by the guard. Furthermore, there were no windows in the loading areas to the rear of nearby buildings. While there were loading docks and garage doors facing this spot, they would not be in use in the wee hours of the morning.

Finding a gap in the vines entwined through the fence, I could see the parking and loading areas of industrial buildings just outside the science park. Some of these businesses had night shifts, so a car parked in the rear opposite the fence would not attract attention. Someone might have noticed a fence climber. I didn't see any breaches in the fencing, although one might have been repaired since the murder.

I'll need to check.

Well, time for the scene of the crime.

I traversed slightly, going down the berm to the car so as not to slip on the recently watered grass. I saw some skid marks and scraped-up grass from someone who had not made the descent without incident.

I reached the car, happy to know it would still be cool from the AC. Having almost circled the perimeter, Mulberry Lane would still be the second street from the guard post, but now it would be a left turn. The institute was a single-story structure, a flat-roofed square about 100 feet on a side. It was faced in a yellowish brick with small windows just under the roof line. It would be impossible to see in through those windows without a ladder, and they seemed too narrow to allow access for any reasonable-sized person. There was parking in the front. A driveway large enough to accommodate semis led around to the back of the building. I'd check that later.

I parked and spent a few minutes letting the AC dry up my sweat. Turning off the engine, I went to the entrance of the lab, which was surveilled by two CCTV cameras. I entered through a revolving glass door. On the side of the revolving entrance was another interior-opening double glass door with a keypad and a fingerprint scanner—probably the after hours access point.

Straight ahead of me as I entered was a semicircular steel and light wood desk behind which sat a young, bespectacled, African-American woman. She was typing ferociously on her computer. As I approached the desk, she looked up, fingers poised over the keyboard. She gave me a sheepish smile, as though she had been caught doing something sketchy.

"Uh…may I help you?"

"Yes. I'm looking for Dr. Elaine Sessions."

"I'm afraid Dr. Sessions is not in and I don't expect her today. She won't be in until Thursday. Did you have an appointment?"

I pulled out a business card and handed it to her. My strategy was to lay it all on the line as Korb had suggested. "I am an investigator working for Golda Merino's attorney. I was hoping to see Dr. Sessions and anyone else who might have worked on the feraxia project or had any contact with Ms. Merino. You know she's been arrested as a suspect in the murder of Dr.

Scanlon."

The young woman pursed her lips and nodded. "We were all shocked and frightened by the murder. The police swarmed around here for a couple of days. That was reassuring. But we haven't seen hide nor hair of them lately. I hope they catch the killer soon. I'll feel a lot better."

"My boss, Marko Korb, and I want to help the police find the real murderer. That will make everyone safer."

"I really can't believe Ms. Merino had anything to do with Dr. Scanlon's murder. I've met and spoken to her on the phone several times. She was always so nice to me, asking me about my family and such. When I heard what Dr. Scanlon had done restricting the research on the feraxia gene, I was disgusted." The woman shook her head, her disappointment evident.

"I would like to help, but I can't discuss it here. Why don't I make an appointment for you to see Dr. Sessions Thursday at ten a.m.?" She looked up at me, eyes wide in a questioning look.

"That would be good," I said with a welcoming smile. "Possibly I could take you to lunch today, somewhere off-site? Where can we meet?"

The young woman hesitated, closing her eyes for a moment. "I usually take lunch at twelve-thirty. But I don't want to meet too nearby. There is a little restaurant called the Golden Lantern. It's about four miles from here."

The receptionist reached for a sticky note and scribbled quickly. I must have looked a little bewildered as she wrote the directions down and handed it to me. I read, "South on Skokie Boulevard, right at Touhy Avenue, left at Niles Center. It's on the right at the southwest corner of Niles Center and Devon." Nodding my thanks, I folded the note and slipped it into my pocket.

She smiled, and I got the feeling she was relishing this as an adventure. I hoped I could enlist her aid. "By the way, what's your name?"

"Carolyn Macready."

I stretched out my hand to her. "I'm Kelan Su. It's nice to meet you, Ms. Macready." I said with a broad smile. She took my hand in a firm shake and returned my smile.

"Please, call me Carolyn. You know, I never met a real private detective before. It's kinda exciting."

I nodded, narrowing my eyes, raising one eyebrow, in a knowing look that I hoped would be worthy of Sam Spade or Philip Marlowe.

Chapter Ten

KELAN SU

With some time to kill before meeting with Carolyn, I stopped at the guard kiosk. Pulling over to the side of the road, I made my way through the thick, hot air to the glass door of the station and knocked. The guard came to the door with a No Entry To Guard Station sign.

I flashed him my warmest smile and held up my investigator's license to the glass. The guard pursed his lips and nodded, opening the sliding glass door. "I don't know about this," he said, shaking his head.

I moved through quickly before he could change his mind. The conditioned air seemed frigid after being outside in the sun. I again flashed a smile that I hoped was seductive. "I'm Kelan Su," I said holding out my hand. "And you are?"

For a moment he looked me over appraisingly, but then said, "Jim Czerna. I'm not s'posed to let anyone in." He took my extended hand awkwardly and shook it.

I touched his arm with my other hand. "No problem. I'm investigating the death of Dr. Scanlon at the Genomics Lab. I've already checked in with them. I'd just like a look at your log for the day of the murder."

The guard grimaced. "Weelll, I've already talked to

the police. A murder is not something I signed on for. Is this necessary?"

"Look, we can subpoena these records and require you to come to court and testify. We're only trying to get a handle on who might have seen or heard something concerning the murder."

"Hey, I don't want any trouble."

"Fine. Just let me take a quick look at the log for the day before, the day of, and the day following the murder. That would be September seven, eight, and nine. Don't worry. I've no need to tell anyone how I came by the information."

As Czerna still hesitated, wrinkling his brow, I tacked in another direction. "Hey, you don't want to be a rent-a-cop forever. I was a Chicago police officer and I can tell you it's more interesting than sitting in this kiosk. I'm giving you a chance to help with a major murder investigation."

His eyebrows raised and I could tell he was getting interested. I moved in for the coup de grâce. "Look, you help me out here and I will put you in contact with Gerald Lanscombe at Loyola. He's the head of the grad criminal justice program. He was also a Chicago cop for many years and an assistant superintendent. He's a very good friend of mine—my mentor. He has contacts in big city police departments around the country and just about every department in Illinois."

"Do you think he'd help me?" Czerna was hooked.

I nodded and smiled. I knew Professor Lanscombe would at least talk to him if I asked.

While the guard was bringing up the log on his computer screen, I asked him if there were cameras or other security measures for detecting breaches in the cyclone fence circling the property. He said there was a security patrol car on the perimeter road every half hour from dusk to nine a.m. The landscaping company for the development also maintained the fence. There had been no breaches reported for the year and a half that he had been working there.

"Here's the log for the seventh," he said, pointing at the screen.

I put my hand on his shoulder as I bent down to see. My face was close to his.

He leaned a little toward me and our cheeks touched momentarily. I let it linger. Then straightening up, I asked him if I might sit to get a better view. He stood up reluctantly, moving behind the chair. I scrolled through the names looking for ones that were familiar or listed the institute as the destination.

Three cars had lined up at the kiosk and Czerna had to deal with them. I took the opportunity to use my phone to quickly photograph the relevant screens for the three days. As September eight was a Saturday and the ninth a Sunday, there had not been a lot of traffic.

The guard turned back toward me just as I was turning away from the computer. He looked relieved. "Jim," I said, "were you on duty on these dates?"

He looked back at the computer screen, scrolled to the seventh, and said, "Friday, Saturday, and Sunday it was me only until midnight. From midnight to eight a.m., on those days, it was Donna Walsh."

"Did you notice anything unusual while you were on duty?"

Czerna frowned, pursed his lips, and shook his head. "No. They were slow days. A weekend and very hot. I was happy not to have to open the slider much.

Allows the AC to keep it cool in here. Otherwise, it can be brutal."

"And Donna Walsh, when will she be on duty again?"

"She left the job last week. Said she needed to go down to Florida to take care of her mother. Didn't think she'd be back. She didn't much like all the police questioning after the murder. Don't blame her for that. I didn't like it either. But I think she failed to check out some folks who were leaving the park that night."

I got up and thanked him, handing him my business card.

"Look, Jim, if anything else occurs to you, please give me a call. Give me a buzz, too, if you would like to meet with Professor Lanscombe and I'll arrange it."

He looked down at the card in his hand, looked up, and smiled in a way that made me suspect he might be calling for other reasons. "Thanks," he said.

"Take care, and don't forget to sign me out," I said over my shoulder.

Chapter Eleven

Korb was ensconced behind his huge, dark mahogany desk, sitting in an oversized leather swivel chair that had been custom-made to accommodate his girth comfortably. However, the assumption that his bulk would remain stable had been unwarranted. As a result, though lost in thought, his huge posterior wriggled. He would, of course, deny any discomfort caused by increased avoirdupois and any need to restrict his gourmandizing.

Korb's fingers were steepled under his chin, his lips rounded as if whistling a tune, and his eyes half closed. On the desk lay Golda Merino's list of Shabel Institute contacts and Desmond's report on the institute's funding. Korb trusted Su to ferret out the contacts and get as much as could be gleaned from them. The funding was what set his antennae vibrating. It was convoluted, unusual, and highly suspect. The institute itself had three directors: Alan Scanlon, Jack Colter, and Tracey Gould. Colter and Gould both were listed at the address of the law firm Bryan, Swayze, and Colter. Colter was the managing partner and Gould was on the administrative staff.

The CFO of the institute was a CPA named Stanley Vrdoliak. The name had a familiar, if sinister, ring for Korb. He'd have to have Desmond or Kelan check him out in more detail.

While the foundation had several respectable individual and foundation donors, the vast majority of the funding came from two corporate sources. One source, MedTech Innovations, was a U.S. corporation whose directors were members of a Brazilian law firm. The other source was a Cayman Island corporation whose major stockholder was an American financier who had spent some time in prison for operating a Ponzi scheme. Some of the minority stockholders were food service and restaurant supply companies. The directors of the Cayman Island corporation, besides the financier, were two lawyers, one from Chicago and one from Miami, both of whom had been disbarred.

Contemplating this strange lineup, Korb massaged his forehead with the fingertips of both hands. A conclusion was forming slowly as the intercom on his desk buzzed.

"Yes, Desmond."

"Your lunch is ready, sir."

"Would you bring it to my desk with a glass of the *Commanderie* rosé? I've been going over your report on the Shabel Institute finances. Excellent job. It's giving me some ideas that I'll want you and Kelan to look into."

"Right. I'll be there in a tick."

****

After finishing Desmond's excellent *salade niçoise*, half a loaf of crispy French bread and a second glass of the chilled Provençale wine, Korb daintily patted his lips and wiped his fingers. Pushing the dishes aside, Korb opened a desk drawer and pulled out an extra-large burner cell phone. The size accommodated Korb's fat fingers. He laboriously tapped in a text message to a Washington, D.C. number.

Let's see, 2 p.m. here, 3 p.m. in DC. Have to wait a couple of hours until Axel leaves work before the return call.

At four-thirty p.m. Chicago time, Korb's desk phone buzzed. He picked it up, noted the number, and pressed answer. "Hello, Axel," said Korb. "Smart of you not to use your regular phone. If you had, I wouldn't have answered."

"Your cryptic message from a burner phone seemed to demand that," said Axel Boardman, chuckling. "What's up? Why the intrigue?"

"I need your expertise as former head of the DOJ organized crime division."

"You know I can't speak about ongoing or even past cases."

"I wouldn't put you on the spot by asking about specific cases. I just need an expert opinion on some underworld trends. You know I first established my reputation on pharmaceutical fraud cases and I seem to remember that my information helped advance your career too. Might even be able to help you again."

Axel chuckled humorlessly. "Okay, Marko. No need to remind me that I owe you. Shoot. What do you need to know?"

"If I mention to you a medical research non-profit linked to MedTech Innovations and Medicamentos Illimitados Corp., what organized crime figures might be maneuvering behind the scenes?"

"The non-profit wouldn't be the Shabel Institute by any chance."

Korb hesitated, pursing his lips. "I can't say yet, Axel. But I will inform you once I have investigated further."

"Marko, be very careful on two points. I think you might want to check out Victor Crosetti and Piers Vorland. These are cold and calculating killers."

"And the second reason to be careful, Axel. Might that be an ongoing federal investigation into Crosetti and/or Vorland with links to the Shabel Institute? A political heater and possibly an insider informant?"

"Marko, sometimes you are too clever for your own good. I can say no more."

"Thank you. I'll keep you posted on what I find."

"I expect no less. *Ciao*, Marko."

The phone beeped as the call ended. Korb pried open the back of the phone and ejected the SIM card. He pulled a black box from his desk drawer and plugged it into a socket on his desk lamp. He opened the cover of the box, placed the SIM card inside, and closed the cover. After about ten seconds, the green light turned red. Korb removed the SIM card, dropped it on the floor and stomped on it.

Chapter Twelve

KELAN SU

It took me twelve minutes to get to the Golden
Lantern. Parking seemed a problem at first until I
spotted a supermarket a block away. The restaurant was
doing a brisk lunch business, but most of it was texted
orders for pickup. The eatery seemed to be a favorite
with workers from the offices and small industrial
concerns that dotted the neighborhood. I arrived early
and found an isolated booth where I could see the door.

Carolyn arrived a few minutes later. She looked
around nervously for me and for anyone she might
know. Seeming satisfied with her anonymity, she
headed toward my booth. She looked a bit harried and
was out of breath. We nodded to each other as she slid
into the seat opposite me with her back to most of the
dining room.

"Whew! I ran from the supermarket lot. I had a
last-minute letter to type and got away late." She ran
the back of her hand across her glistening forehead.

I liked that she was anxious to be on time for our
meeting. "Do you want to wash up first?" I offered.

"No, they'll bring a glass of water and we can
order."

"Thanks for rushing over. How much time do we
have?"

"About an hour and a half. I told them I might have

to run an errand before returning and there's an intern who will fill in at reception."

"Excellent." I was developing a fondness for Carolyn. She really seemed excited to assist with my investigation. How much help would depend on how knowledgeable she was about the institute's operations and whether she could give me relevant information rather than telling me what she thought I wanted to hear.

I needed to know more about three things: the character of Dr. Scanlon, Dr. Sessions, and others involved with the institute; the security system; those who came and went on the day of the murder.

The waitress, clicking her gum, came over with water and menus. "Y'know what you want, girls?"

Carolyn didn't need to look at the menu. "I'll have the turkey club on wheat bread, light on the mayo, no fries, and a diet coke."

"Same for me. Coffee, black, instead of coke."

The older woman nodded, picked up the menus, and turned sharply away. Not a stiff blond hair on her head moved.

Carolyn gulped down her water. Took two napkins from the dispenser on the table and wiped her mouth and then her brow. She leaned forward and said, "What do you want to know?"

"Thank you for this, Carolyn. Do you mind if I record our conversation?

She bit her lip. "Welll."

"That's okay. I don't need to record. I have a very good memory and I'll take some notes." I took out a small, ruled pad and a pen from my purse. Carolyn looked relieved.

"What can you tell me about Dr. Scanlon? What was he like? Was he a good boss?"

Carolyn's mouth made an O. "Wow, the million-dollar question! Don't get me started. He was a stuck-up sonovabitch and secretive–woooeeeee. Considered himself god's gift to women. Hardly anyone at work he didn't hit on although he was seeing Dr. Sessions regularly. She's beautiful, smart, nice. Couldn't see why she put up with him. No tellin' these things."

"Did Dr. Sessions, any of the women at work, or their significant others confront him on this–say or do anything threatening?"

"Well, I know that two of the women and I told him in no uncertain terms that we weren't the least bit interested. He fired one of them–a lab assistant, Janie Cummings. Didn't fire me. Maybe 'cause I know too much."

I noted the lab assistant's name and interrupted her narrative. "About what?"

"Aside from the sex stuff, he was getting some interesting telephone calls from what sounded like a pretty tough customer. He often told me to say he was on another line. It seemed to me he needed a chance to pull himself together."

I was intrigued. "Do you know who this caller was?"

"No. He always called himself a major benefactor. He sounded more like a hoodlum. I did once hear a name that could have been Kober or maybe Kovar."

I quickly scribbled the names. "How often did he call?"

"At least once a month, but three times in the week following the service of papers regarding the feraxia support group's lawsuit and twice on the day before the murder. Each time Scanlon seemed more jumpy."

"Did this caller ever leave a number, or was the number registered on phone records?"

"No. The number always came up as 'restricted.'"

"After Scanlon received these calls, do you know if he did anything in particular?"

"Well, he almost always called his lawyer, Jack Colter, right after he talked with the benefactor. By the way, Colter is also a director of the institute."

Just then the waitress came with our orders on a small tray balanced on one hand. With her free hand, she placed the drinks down and then slid the sandwiches expertly in front of us.

"Do you folks want anything else?"

"Not right now," I said, and Carolyn nodded in agreement.

The food looked great–triple deckers loaded with turkey and bacon, the bread toasted to perfection. With mutual nods, we each took a bite of the club, followed by a sip of our drinks. The coffee was good too.

After several more bites and some thoughtful chewing, I asked, "How does your security system work?"

"I'm afraid I can't give you too many details. It's pretty sophisticated. I only have badge access to the front door."

"Well, what company provides it?"

"It's called En Garde. Must be high-end, huh? With a French name. We pay two hundred and fifty dollars a month. The tech comes in monthly to test and update it. Wasn't there when it was installed so I don't know the upfront cost."

"Do you know what its components are?"

"There's a shitload of cameras and CCTV monitors at the guard station, in Vrdroliak's office and Scanlon's office. There are motion detectors in every room and sensors on all windows and doors. Access to the building after hours is from the outside by keypad, badge, and fingerprint ID–all of 'em, not just one. Access to the lab is by badge and thumbprint. Scanlon's office also requires a retinal scan. Only Scanlon and Sessions can open the lab when all restrictions are set. And only Scanlon can open his office. Other employees have badges, but these only work when Scanlon or Sessions have suspended the other access controls. The master controls are in Scanlon's office. There is also a security safe that contains master controls. I think Dr. Sessions also has the combination for this."

I was impressed. "Wow. You are observant. Thanks. This is really helpful."

"What can you tell me about who was around on the day before the murder?"

"Oh yeah, I brought you a printout of the appointment schedule that day. I made a few marginal notes about each person." Carolyn reached into her large, brown leather messenger bag and retrieved a manila envelope. She handed it across the table to me, nearly knocking over her diet soda. She laughed.

"Thanks." She was really getting into this investigation. It made me wonder if there was some ulterior motive here. But the help was welcome.

"Everyone on that list showed up for their appointment and none of them, except the tech guy, stayed more than twenty minutes. The tech guy was there for about an hour. He checked things out and then talked to Dr. Scanlon in his office."

"Do you remember the tech's name?"

Carolyn smacked her lips in thought. "Greg, I think."

I nodded. "So who came after the tech?"

"Mr. Colter came in just as I was packing up for the day–around five o'clock. He had no appointment but usually didn't need one to see Dr. Scanlon. Don't know when he left. Dr. Sessions was the only one left in the lab. The cleaning crew had just arrived from Jenkins Janitors. They're usually done by seven-thirty." Carolyn frowned, trying to recall more.

For a while, we ate silently. My incredible informant looked at her watch and grimaced. She quickly wolfed down the rest of her sandwich and took a long draw on her drink. "I'd better get going. I should come back with a package of something to justify the errand I mentioned," she said.

I couldn't help smiling. She was into undercover work. "Oh sure, Carolyn. I don't really have any more questions now. You've been great. Do you have a PI license? You should have. If you don't mind, I may contact you again to follow up on what you've told me. If anything else occurs to you, please give me a ring."

We both stood up and looked at each other for a moment. "Kelan, I really hope you find out who did this. As much as I disliked Dr. Scanlon, I sure don't like the idea that there may be a murderer at the lab."

I gave her a look that was more reassuring than I felt. "That's just what we intend to do and your help has been key."

Carolyn's expressive face slowly broke into a wide grin, which I couldn't help responding to. We stepped into each other's arms for a warm hug.

Chapter Thirteen

Korb put down the book he was reading and took off his reading glasses. He put one of the earpieces in his mouth, leaned back in his padded chair, and squinted into the distance. The real nature of the institute's activities was becoming clear. After a contemplative moment, he slammed the glasses down on the desk decisively. They bounced up and onto the floor. Korb scowled but he didn't retrieve them. Instead, he picked up the desk phone and pressed the intercom button.

"Suh?" came Desmond's clipped, military response.

"Desmond, as soon as Kelan gets back, I want you two here in the office."

"Right, guv."

Korb grimaced. He did not like sobriquets, be they American or British, but he was resigned to overcoming this annoyance as both Desmond and Kelan were wedded to them.

Grunting, he laboriously bent down to pick up the glasses and placed them back on his nose. Korb reached for his book, sank back against his chair, and sighed as he returned to his reading.

****

The murmur of voices pulled Korb from his novel. He heard the deep, calypso lilt of Desmond and the singsong inflections of Su as they came through the kitchen and down the hall to his office. He couldn't make out the words, but the tone was of friendly banter. At a level of consciousness he would never admit to, Korb knew he was lucky to have these two brilliant associates.

Desmond and Su were sharing a laugh as they entered the office, but they both made an effort to wipe the grins off their faces when they neared Korb's desk. Korb nodded to them and they seated themselves in two of the chairs opposite the desk.

"Shall I report?" asked Su.

"Naturally," responded Korb, raising an eyebrow. "Was your day well spent?"

"I would say yes. While I didn't get to see Dr. Sessions, I do have an appointment with her on Thursday. However, I did get a good look at the external setup of the industrial park where the lab is situated. I also talked to the guard at the entrance kiosk and got copies of the entry and exit logs for the relevant dates. You'll note that Scanlon's car left the park after Scanlon was dead. It seems obvious that this was the killer. Unfortunately, the guard on duty, Donna Walsh, is no longer employed and is somewhere in Florida. She had a history of laxity on the job. The police did question her before she left. I'll have to locate her. I also had a long interview with Carolyn Macready, the secretary/receptionist for the institute and got an appointment list for the day preceding the murder. She was sympathetic to Golda and very helpful."

"Excellent. Proceed," said Korb nodding.

Su looked first at Korb, then at Des, who smiled encouragingly, and finally back at Korb. She recounted in detail the events of her day with an almost verbatim narrative of the conversations with Carolyn. She handed Korb a manilla envelope with the written material she had received and printouts of the photos she had taken of the entry and exit log. When she finished, Korb stared steadily at her. Slowly, a smile spread across his face.

"And inferences you may have drawn from all of this?"

"Well, first, Scanlon was a man who could have many enemies with sufficient motivation to do him in. He was in no way well-liked. Those motivations seem to fall into the categories of sex and money. Second, there was likely some kind of financial hanky-panky going on at the institute which might involve some powerful and unsavory characters. Third, it would seem that several insiders would have been able to turn off or breach both the lab's security system and avoid the recording of their entry and exit into the industrial park. This could all be beneficial to Golda's defense."

"Vvvery good. This meshes with a suspicion that Desmond's excellent, but preliminary, report about the institute has raised." Korb tilted his head in a sideways nod to his Tortolan associate.

Des gave Korb a tight smile, acknowledging both the praise and its limits. Su leaned forward, eyes wide, awaiting a hint of Korb's suspicion. For what seemed a full minute, Korb stared at a corner of the ceiling. He ignored the pregnant silence that he was expected to fill.

Su and Des were holding their breaths. They glanced quickly at one another. Des noted the roll of Su's eyes. They returned their gaze to Korb, who was still staring absent-mindedly at the ceiling.

Korb looked down and cleared his throat. "Aren't you curious about my suspicion?" he said, raising his eyebrows. Des couldn't stifle a short snort and Su rolled her eyes once more. Korb could be a drama king.

"Of course, Chief. We just wanted to be sure you were ready to tell us. I know you often like to keep unsubstantiated suspicions to yourself until you can support them with hard evidence," said Su in a singsong tone, which did nothing to hide her feeling that his reluctance to share hindered their investigations. Implicit, however, was her respect for the awesome accuracy of Korb's apparently off-hand suspicions.

Korb nodded approvingly, taking full cognizance of the implication. "It seems to me that the Shabel Institute is little more than a money laundering operation for organized crime, specifically the family of Victor, THE COBRA, Crosetti. Did you not hear something like 'Cobra' from Ms. Mcready? Note also the shady off-shore and domestic corporate funders of the institute and the presence of CFO Stanley Vrdoliak, Crosetti's CPA of choice for many of his most shady businesses. Scanlon's research and actual success, I believe, came as a surprise to his 'connected benefactors'. And the patent lawsuit was an extremely undesired development, bringing unwanted attention to the institute."

"You think Scanlon's killing was a mob hit?" asked Su, frowning.

"Not so fast. Although that may be a beneficial specter to raise on Ms. Merino's behalf, I am not convinced that Scanlon was killed by the mob. I do think, however, that the mob connection to the institute may relate to why Scanlon was killed."

Su nodded. "So what are our next steps?"

"Desmond, I would like you to run full database and newspaper checks on the institute and all the folks who may be connected with this case. We're talking here about Scanlon, Sessions, Merino, Donna Walsh, Colter, CFO Vrdoliak, Crosetti, Vorland, Gould, the Bryan, Swayze, and Colter firm, MedTech Innovations and that financier heading the Cayman corporation, Walter Karlakis."

"Yes, suh!" said Des, flashing a grin.

Su smiled at Des's evident enthusiasm. "And my assignment?" asked Su, turning toward Korb.

For a moment, Korb squinted at her. "Tomorrow we're due at the courthouse in Skokie for Ms. Merino's arraignment. We will also report to Attorney Dain about the results of our investigation so far. We can hope that the State's attorney will begin some of the required disclosure which might point us toward other witnesses. In particular, I would like to see as much information about the crime scene as possible so that we can recreate it."

"What time do we need to be there, boss?"

"The arraignment is scheduled for ten-thirty. Ms. Dain said she'd be there by nine-fifteen, so we could brief her."

Su thought for a moment. "Okay, let's leave at eight a.m. You never know about traffic, although it shouldn't be terrible in that direction."

Korb frowned but nodded his assent. He didn't like waking up earlier than ten a.m., although he accepted the need for early rising in this case. He also didn't like to be the one who had to travel. His preferred method of reporting or interviewing was to have the clients or subjects come to the office at a reasonable hour in the afternoon after he had a decent interval to digest lunch.

"What else is on my agenda, sir?" asked Su, fearing, rightly, she was breaching a dam.

Korb closed his eyes and rubbed his forehead. "Primarily, locating and interviewing involved parties. You'll need to find Donna Walsh, the security guard on duty at the kiosk on the day of the murder, and the financier, Walter Karlakis, as well as anyone else who had an appointment on the seventh, eighth, or ninth. Get to En Garde technology and find out more about the security system. Of course, Sessions and other lab staff and Tracey Gould. See if you can use any of your police contacts to find the officers and technicians who investigated the crime scene and, if possible, get their reports. We'll have to see what Attorney Dain can get tomorrow at the courthouse. I want Vrdoliak and Colter here to interview. Think about how we might do that. I'll figure a way to get to Crosetti."

"And what should I do with all the free time that will leave me?" said Su under her breath.

Korb heard or guessed her response. "I shall have to think of what other tasks are necessary to make sure you won't get bored," he said, raising an eyebrow. "Anything else?"

Su and Des shook their heads, taking the cue that they were dismissed. They rose together and gave each other a tight-lipped, eyes wide, look of commiseration. They exited and headed toward their offices.

Chapter Fourteen

KELAN SU

I pulled the Lincoln town car up the semicircular drive in front of the glassed-in atrium at the center of the Skokie 2nd district circuit courthouse. I slid out of the seat and went around to help Korb exit from the rear passenger side. It was a gray day–not too warm, but high humidity. I could smell the rain coming.

Korb unwedged himself from the car using handles on either side of the rear door. There were already beads of sweat on his forehead from the effort. Once upright, he leaned heavily on his cane with both hands. He was resplendent in a charcoal gray, pin-striped, double-breasted suit, light pink shirt, tie with blue and red color splashes on a silvery background, and charcoal gray fedora. I don't know why Korb loved double-breasted suit coats. They made him look even wider than his sixth-of-a-ton girth.

It was good that we had left home at 8 a.m., despite Korb's constant grumbling on the ride up to Skokie. The traffic was heavier than expected going North on the Drive and then Edens expressway. It was 9 a.m. when we arrived at the courthouse. Cheryl and Golda were already there. I could see them waiting for us through the glass doors at the entrance. I pointed that out to Korb, who harrumphed that he could see them for himself.

I said, "I'll meet you inside the first-floor waiting area just past the security checkpoint." As I returned to park the Lincoln, Korb laboriously caned his way toward the atrium.

****

Even though they knew me well, the Cook County Sheriff's Deputies on the security detail were surly and officious as usual. I had been careful not to have anything metal on my person–no jewelry, belt buckles, hair clips, etc. I removed my jacket and emptied the pockets, as well as emptying my purse. I didn't want to give them an excuse for the pat down that their leering expressions convinced me they hoped for. I wondered how Korb's heavy walking stick with the golden crouching lion handle had fared at the checkpoint. That cane was what used to be called an "equalizer" and Korb knew how to effectuate that eponym.

When I reached our group, Korb was still standing, leaning on his cane. When she saw me, Cheryl rose and gave me a hug. Golda stood too and held out her hand. I took it and gave it a squeeze. Her red-rimmed and deep-set eyes told me she had spent a sleepless night. My half smile was meant to be both concerned and reassuring.

Cheryl said, "I've reserved the attorney conference room next to felony prelim courtroom 105 where the arraignment will be held. This way." She led us down the tiled, high windowed hallway to an oak door which opened to reveal a cubicle that had a round table whose surface was scarred with deep scribbles and six thinly padded wooden chairs. I wasn't sure the chairs could support Korb's ponderous derriere. Nor was there much room between the table and the chair-gouged, off-white walls made even less inviting by the harsh fluorescent lighting. It was clear to me that the building's exterior and common areas were designed to impress, but the working spaces suffered from little concern for comfort and less than conscientious upkeep.

Korb picked a chair at the corner of the room where he could back it up far enough to attempt gingerly lowering his bulk to the seat. He kept his feet firmly planted and leaned forward on his cane. We all scraped our chairs back from the table and sat.

Cheryl spoke first. "I have explained to Golda what will happen today. She will be asked to plead to murder and voluntary manslaughter and will plead not guilty. The State's Attorney, just one of the assistants here, will not ask for money bail continuing the recog, but Golda will have to surrender her passport. I have prepared and will present a preliminary motion requesting a bill of particulars specifying the acts constituting the offense. I'm also moving for the production of police reports, crime scene photos, autopsy results, physical evidence, and a list of witnesses. Finally, I'll make a Brady motion asking the SA to turn over any possibly exculpatory evidence. I don't expect quick results, Mr. Korb, so you may have to pursue this information by alternative methods."

Korb nodded. "What about the civil lawsuit over the patent?"

"We are holding that in abeyance for the time being. Now that Scanlon is out of the picture, the institute seems ready to settle favorably."

"I suggest you go slow on the settlement. We may need the threat of the lawsuit and discovery to get certain information and witnesses to cooperate for the criminal case," said Korb.

Golda leaned forward, looking at Korb. "Uh," she began timidly. The others had to strain to hear her soft, cracked voice. "I can't hold up work that may only begin once the patent is released or reasonably licensed. I won't stand in the way of lifesaving research that might help my Terri and the other feraxia families, even to save myself."

Korb couldn't mistake the pain and anxiety in Golda's face. He lowered his eyes, nodding sadly. "I fully respect your feelings, and of course Ms. Dain must follow your instructions. I withdraw my suggestion." Korb cocked his head sideways to look at Cheryl, who nodded.

Cheryl's phone gave off its chiming ring. She fished it out of her briefcase and looked at the caller ID. She frowned, held up one finger, and said, "I need to take this."

"Hello, Cheryl Dain here." She listened and said, "Yes, I'll have to confer with my client. How long do we have?"

A slight pause. "That's not much time. Will I be seeing you at the arraignment?"

Another pause. "I see. She's here. I will confer with her now, but I can't promise an immediate answer. Yes. Later." Cheryl tapped the 'end call' button and put down her phone. She looked down at the table, frowning, and rubbed her forehead. Then she looked up, taking in all of us. Her gaze shifted to Golda. "That was the State's attorney," she said. "He has made a very interesting offer. Plead guilty to involuntary manslaughter and he will recommend two years' probation. No jail time. He says he recognizes there was extreme provocation given Teri's situation and that your family obligations are overwhelming."

Golda's hands went to either side of her face as she shook her head spasmodically. "W-w-what? I don't understand."

"Golda, the SA wants to end this matter quickly. I'm not sure why, but it also indicates that their case is not particularly strong."

"Are you t-t-telling me I should take this offer?" Golda stammered.

"Golda, I can't tell you to take it or not. It is an extremely good offer if they have any case. I am not sure why they are in such a hurry."

"But I didn't do it. I didn't shoot Dr. Scanlon."

"If you are telling me that you are not guilty of any action that could be construed as resulting in Scanlon's death, I cannot represent you in a plea of guilty."

Golda sobbed. "I do so want to end this torture and get back to Terri and my family, but I can't say I killed Dr. Scanlon."

"Okay, I'll tell the SA that you will be pleading not guilty and asking for a preliminary hearing. At the prelim we may get a better look at the State's case," said Cheryl, nodding to Korb and me.

I felt as bewildered as Golda. Why was this moving so fast?

Korb took Cheryl's nod as a signal for him to continue his exposition. He launched into an extremely concise account of what we had done so far and some of the inferences drawn from this information. He emphasized the possible mob connections to the institute. This emphasis told me that Korb was still hoping Cheryl could walk the tightrope, stalling the settlement while assuaging Golda's conscience, so that he could deal with those who might be reluctant to reveal the funding and money laundering activities of the Shabel Institute. *Good luck on that*! I thought.

During this presentation, Golda's eyes grew larger and larger. It was hard for her to believe what a complex and melodramatic situation she had fallen into. Even my worldly friend Cheryl looked stunned. I found it hard to believe myself. *Was this real or a cinema noir plot?*

****

We exited the conference room and entered the courtroom next door. Courtroom 105 handled preliminary matters in felony cases. Since there were no full trials and no jury box, it was small. The blond wood décor and off-white walls were an improvement on the conference room. The spectators' area, already crowded and buzzing with attorneys, nervous clients, and families, had wooden pews and beige tile while the area in front containing counsel tables and the judge's bench had non-descript and worn beige carpeting. The unoccupied bench, offset into the left-hand corner of the room, reached a height of six feet off the floor and was flanked by a witness box and a clerk's desk, also slightly raised. There was a plexiglass-fronted gallery to the right—also packed. I recognized some of the reporters there. Given the number, I assumed that there might be some other newsworthy cases. Windows high up on the back wall brought in some morning sun, but the main source of illumination was recessed fluorescents.

Korb and I seated ourselves at the rear, where there was barely ample room for him to squeeze in. It was just after ten-thirty a.m. Proceedings often didn't start on time and there were also several cases that had been scheduled for the same time slots. I knew that the judge had been doing video arraignments for prisoners held by the Department of Corrections.

Cheryl and Golda continued on through the swinging gate to the long counsel table on the right, which seated three other attorneys and their clients. Cheryl helped Golda to her seat and moved to the clerk's desk to check in. She then conferred briefly with someone at the left-hand counsel table, presumably the Assistant State's Attorney handling the case. That lawyer immediately pulled out her cell phone and held an animated discussion with whoever was at the other end. She then went up to the clerk and back to Cheryl and Golda. Cheryl whispered something to Golda, who slumped back in her chair.

At ten-thirty-five, the clerk looked up and stood. The door behind the bench opened. The black-robed judge, a petite woman with a stern, thin-lipped face framed in short gray hair, stepped behind her chair. The clerk intoned, "All rise, the Circuit Court of Cook County District Two is now in session, the honorable Doris Fitzsimmons presiding." The courtroom hubbub quieted. I had to assist Korb to a standing position. The judge's ice-blue eyes peered over her half glasses at the full courtroom. Judge Fitzsimmons nodded to the clerk and took her seat. She pushed the glasses back up her nose as she looked down at the docket printout. The clerk, sitting down, said into her microphone, "You may be seated." The pews creaked as we all sat.

The judge addressed the gathering. "This court handles preliminary matters in felony cases. Today we will be arraigning persons charged with felonies, informing them of their rights, and accepting pleas of 'guilty' or 'not guilty'. If you or your attorney have not checked in with the clerk, please do so now."

The judge paused. There was some murmuring between attorneys and clients. No one moved to check in.

The judge nodded. "Good. It is assumed for the record that everyone scheduled for arraignment this morning has checked in and is within earshot."

She then began her recitation in a singsong voice. I wondered how many thousands of times she had done this.

"Ladies and gentlemen, it is very important for you to pay close attention. I will be explaining our procedures, but more importantly, your statutory and Constitutional rights. When the clerk calls your name, please rise and come forward with your attorney. You will first be apprised of the charge or charges against you. This is a criminal arraignment docket. It is an opportunity for you to hear the charges against you and enter a plea of either guilty or not guilty to those charges. If you choose to plead guilty this morning, you need to understand what you are doing by entering a plea of guilty to the charges.

"When you plead guilty, you are telling me you are guilty and that your guilty plea is free, voluntary, and knowing. You are also telling me that you understand that pleading guilty can have unforeseen consequences, such as a loss of scholarship opportunities, housing, and possibly result in enhanced penalties should you be convicted of this same type of charge again.

You also are telling me that you understand that

you are waiving your constitutional rights. Those rights include the right to a preliminary hearing, to have a jury or a bench trial, the right to call witnesses on your own behalf using the subpoena powers of the Court and the right to cross-examine witnesses called against you.

"You have the right to have the State's attorney prove her or his case beyond a reasonable doubt, keeping in mind that you are innocent until proven guilty. Today the State is represented by Assistant States Attorneys Walker Graebel and Janet Kosinsky seated at the table to my right." Judge Fitzsimmons indicated the prosecutors with a nod and a lifting of her hand in their direction. Both the assistants swiveled their chairs toward the opposite counsel table and then to the crowd seated in the pews.

The judge went on. "Should you plead guilty, before I accept the plea, we will hold a 402 conference this afternoon. This conference requires that the State present me with facts, including a pre-sentence report, justifying the guilty plea and the recommended sentence. Remember that the sentence the prosecutor has said he or she will ask for is only a recommendation. Pursuant to the relevant statutes, I have the final say in your sentencing."

There was some nervous shifting of position and glancing at lawyers following this statement. The lawyers reassured their clients with nods, smiles, and whispered comments.

"For those pleading not guilty, I will schedule a preliminary hearing in the next ten to twenty days, where the state must present sufficient evidence to justify binding you over for trial. If you wish, on the advice of your attorney, the preliminary hearing may be waived and a trial date will be set."

The judge paused again and looked around the courtroom. "If you do not understand anything I have just said or have a question, please bring this up when the clerk calls your name and you approach the bench." The petite jurist let out a deep breath. Turning to the clerk, the judge said, "Ms. Bracknell, you may call the docket."

The clerk called "Deshon Roble." A short, bald, swarthy man in creased chinos and a blue polo shirt rose with his lawyer, a young, bearded, dark-haired man in a rumpled gray suit. The judge's brow wrinkled as she watched them approach the bench. She did not turn on her microphone as she addressed the defendant. It was hard to hear, but it seemed she was asking if they had received a written copy of the charges. She held up a paper, probably her copy.

From prior courtroom appearances, I assumed that she asked them if they needed to have the charges read– to which the lawyer shook his head and must have said "No." Turning to the defendant, the judge probably asked if there were any questions regarding the plea procedure. The defendant also shook his head. The judge nodded and directed an emphatic question at the defendant, which I assumed to be "How do you plead?" The defendant seemed to mumble something that the judge couldn't hear. She frowned and tilted an ear toward the defendant, who cleared his throat and said loud enough for me to hear, "Not guilty, your Honor." The judge noted something down in her docket sheet and consulted the laptop computer on the bench to her left. Assistant State's Attorney Kosinski approached the bench. The colloquy that followed must have concerned setting the date for the preliminary hearing or accepting a waiver.

Four more defendants were called up. They all had attorneys. Neither the clients nor the attorneys were particularly well-dressed. From what I could glean, two of them pled guilty and two not guilty. I recognized two of the attorneys and one of the clients as courthouse regulars. You don't see too many well-heeled clients and high-end attorneys in the criminal courts. The role of top criminal lawyers who represent wealthy clients was to forestall charges being filed in the first place. And they were highly successful in doing this–further skewing the criminal legal system against the poor and minorities.

With such a rote and inaudible performance, it was hard for me to get a sense of the judge's personality. During my policing years, I had little contact with suburban Cook County judges. I had heard that she was tough and fair, but few lawyers were willing to criticize a sitting judge to an outsider. In any case, she would only be in charge of the preliminary hearing and motions in our case. I was sure that Cheryl would be better informed on what to expect from her.

As people connected with the already arraigned defendants left the courtroom, I asked Korb if he wanted to move up so we could hear the proceedings. He shook his head. I slid out into the aisle and found a place in the front row of the spectators' seating. Murmuring, "Excuse me", I edged past two people sitting next to the aisle. Just as I sat down, the clerk called, "Golda Joanne Merino." Cheryl and Golda rose from the counsel table and went to stand before the judge.

Chapter Fifteen

Golda was nervous. She made a slight misstep on the worn carpeting and almost stumbled. Cheryl caught her arm. The judge's eyes widened as she tilted her head toward Golda. It seemed to me that she was evincing a sympathetic look. She raised the charge sheet and asked if Golda and her attorney had received and read a copy. "Ms. Merino, do you understand the serious charges against you? Would you like to have them read aloud?" Golda shook her head.

"Ms. Merino, you must answer yes or no. Your gesture will not be recorded."

"No, your Honor," Golda replied softly.

"Do you have any questions before you enter a plea to these charges?"

"No, your Honor."

The judge compressed her lips. "And how do you plead to the charge of murder and the lesser included charge of voluntary manslaughter?"

Golda looked at Cheryl, who nodded and gave her an encouraging half smile. A heartened Golda answered strongly, "Not guilty to both, your Honor."

A satisfied smile flitted across the judge's face. The judge looked at her computer as the Assistant SA Kosinski approached the bench. "Your Honor," she began, "May I have a moment to confer with Attorney Dain and Ms. Merino?"

The judge gave Kosinsky an exasperated look. "No more than five minutes. You may use the clerk's anteroom."

Cheryl, Golda, Graebel, and Kosinsky exited quickly behind the clerk's desk. Golda gave Cheryl a questioning frown. Cheryl shook her head slightly and shrugged her shoulders. They both turned to Kosinsky.

The Assistant pursed her lips, shaking her head. "I have received instructions to dismiss the charges at this time. In addition, if you agree to settle your civil lawsuit immediately with the Shabel Institute granting free access for research and clinical purposes to the feraxia gene and test, the State will make the dismissal of the murder charges with prejudice."

Golda was about to grab this lifeline enthusiastically when Cheryl cut in, shutting her down. "Of course, we'll have to give this some consideration and verify the settlement offer you mentioned. It was not brought to us by the defendants as yet."

"Okay," said Kosinsky with a slight scowl. "Let's go back in and get this over with. Please let me know your final decision by Monday."

The quartet reentered the courtroom and Assistant States Attorney Graebel told the clerk they were ready. The judge called them up to the bench. "Has anything been resolved?"

Kosinsky, after an embarrassed hesitation, said, "Your honor, I have been instructed by the State's attorney to ask for dismissal of these charges without prejudice to the State."

The judge's eyes widened and her jaw dropped before snapping shut in a tight-lipped stare at the ruffled Assistant SA. The judge was clearly taken aback.

"I don't understand why the State went forward with the information charging Ms. Merino if you were going to dismiss the charges at this time. Are you playing games with the defendant and this court?" said Judge Fitzsimmons, clearly miffed.

"Your Honor, I am sure States Attorney McGovern had good reasons for his actions, but I am presently not privy to them," said the embarrassed assistant.

"Well, I see no reason not to grant the dismissal and let Ms. Merino get on with her life," said the judge. "Ms. Merino, the charges against you are dismissed and you are free to go. The personal recognizance bail order is quashed and the administrative fee will be returned to you. I am sorry for any inconvenience the State has put you through."

"Th-thank you, your Honor," said Golda. Cheryl acknowledged her thanks with a nod to the judge.

Chapter Sixteen

KELAN SU

Cheryl explained to us what happened. I was bewildered. Korb, however, nodded knowingly. "This case and your lawsuit are 'heaters', that is politically sensitive," he explained. "I believe there is already a federal probe and there are some highly influential citizens who have supported the institute. They either already knew or are beginning to suspect that some of their donee's activities may not be entirely aboveboard and don't want any dirty laundry exposed in public proceedings. They are probably already disengaging from the institute and trying to quash or at least delay any legal proceedings. You can be sure they have the ear of State's Attorney McGovern."

We left the courthouse immediately. The media crowd from the visitors' gallery had dogged our exit and were firing questions at all of us. Korb was well known to them. Cheryl took Golda by one arm and I took her other arm. We drove head down toward the rear parking area door of the courthouse. Korb, unable to match our pace, plopped down on a bench in the hallway, scowling and waving away the relentless questioners.

Golda needed to calm her nerves after the unexpected dismissal and tense atmosphere of the courtroom. Cheryl was going to take her out for a drink and lunch and then drive her home.

I asked Cheryl if the dismissal meant that we should discontinue our investigation. She glanced at Golda, who had heard my question. Golda frowned. Our work would cost her money that she might not be able to afford. On the other hand, Cheryl had explained that the dismissal might only be temporary. The SA could refile charges at any time. The onslaught of the press as we had exited showed that Golda would always be regarded with suspicion unless Scanlon's killer was caught. It looked as if the powers that be were happy for the matter to dissipate, leaving the cloud over Golda. We were all still uncertain about why things had moved so fast to charges and then dismissal. I couldn't help thinking that part of the motivation was our investigation and what we might turn up. I caught a whiff of corruption.

"Stay with it for the time being," Cheryl said, and Golda nodded her agreement.

I pulled our car around to the front and went back in for Korb. I wasn't looking forward to the mood he would be in, being left behind with clamoring reporters. He hated to be out and about in the world and wanted to get home asap. I had to put up with his pouting when I told him that we would need to stop at the Skokie Police Department on Niles Center Road.

"I assume we are to go on with the case," he said with a scowl. I nodded. His resigned acquiescence, accompanied by a deep frown and a grumbling noise from the back of his throat, told me that he knew it was a good move.

****

We took Edens back to the Touhy Avenue exit.

The southbound traffic on the expressway was heavy as delivery trucks were heading into Chicago. The acrid smell of their exhausts filled the still air. It was good to get back onto the less traveled Skokie streets as we turned north on Niles Center Road. The Skokie police headquarters always astounded me. I had been given the ten-cent tour a couple of years ago. It was in an award-winning building—a repurposed factory/warehouse facility. The one-story above-ground building with enclosed courtyards and walls of windows was extremely light and airy—not your typical cop shop. It had four below-ground levels, including a shooting range, swimming pool, workout room, and a small, very secure lockup. Even Korb was taken aback by the building's elegant exterior.

I had a good friend in the department—a former lover. Fortunately, we had remained close after ending the intense affair. Neither of us had found someone new. He and I still accompanied each other on occasions that called for a guest or a significant other. Sometimes we both regretted the ending. The sex had been great.

Ron was head of the Homicide Division in Skokie. A job he took after twelve years as a Chicago homicide detective. He would likely be directly supervising our case. Whether I could wheedle information out of him was the question. He suspected that my continuing friendship had something to do with the help he could give me on Korb's cases. He was not entirely wrong about that. Mostly, however, I enjoyed his company and he was one of the few people who understood my feelings about the Chicago police and detective work. We would commiserate about how our professions gave us an unfavorably skewed view of human nature. *Yes, even in Skokie.* I admired the fact that he could fight this off and remain a warm, compassionate, fundamentally optimistic person and an honest, ethical police officer.

I parked in the small lot in front of the station. I asked Korb if he wanted to go inside. He grumbled a "no." I left the engine on for the AC.

I hesitated when I reached the door of the station and bit my lower lip. Seeing Ron always gave me a disconcerting jolt. One, he was drop-dead gorgeous. And two, when he looked at me, the rest of the world faded into non-existence. As my hand touched the door handle, I straightened up and assumed my professional face.

The tiled entry was well-lit by skylights. Facing the door was a long counter topped by thick glass. Behind the glass was a heavyset, middle-aged woman in civvies. I remembered her from previous visits.

"Hi, Jocelyn. Is Lieutenant Sager in?"

The woman pursed her lips, trying to stifle a smirk. I guess she knew about me and Ron.

"I think so. I'll buzz him to come out."

"This is business. I'd like to see him inside."

"Okay. I'll check."

She picked up a desk phone and pressed three keys. "Detective Sager, Ms. Su is here. She says she needs to speak with you on police business. May I let her in?" She nodded. Jocelyn waved her hand toward the door at the end of the counter. She buzzed it open.

"You know the drill. Empty your pockets and step through the metal detector."

I did so. No beeps. I picked up my phone, wallet,

keys, kerchief. Jocelyn nodded toward the door at the rear. I thanked her.

As I reached the door, it opened and Ron stood, holding it with a wide grin on his rugged face. The usual unruly strand of curly black hair had slipped down above his right eye.

"Kelan, it's been too long. Miss ya. I guess you didn't have any Skokie cases to pump me about."

I exhaled and grimaced. Didn't want to admit that he was right. But I also thought it was safer not to see him too often. "Ron, it's good to see you." I stepped up to him and gave him a peck on the cheek. He put his hand on my shoulder as he ushered me in. I felt an electric charge down my back.

He directed me to his small, cluttered office. At least it had good natural light and a nice view of Laramie Park to the east. He pointed to a chair for me and went around to sit behind his desk. I sat down and leaned back, assuming a casual pose. Ron rubbed his chin, looked down at his desk, then up at me, and asked, "To what do I owe this 'official' visit?"

When his intense, dark eyes met mine, I couldn't suppress a quick intake of breath, belying my attempt at nonchalance. *Why did we break up? Of course, I knew the answer. We loved our careers and couldn't see how they would mesh.*

I held Ron's penetrating gaze for a long moment prior to speaking. I needed to regain my composure. I leaned forward and put my hands on his desk.

"You must know that Korb and I are working for Golda Merino's lawyer regarding the Scanlon murder," I began.

Ron nodded slightly without breaking his eye

contact.

"But did you know that McGovern dropped the charges?"

Ron was only slightly taken aback by that news. "Well, in truth, I was surprised and annoyed when the SA moved so quickly to bring charges against Ms. Merino. Our investigation was just beginning. We did not recommend charging. Frankly, I found it hard to believe that Ms. Merino was a murderer. But you never know for sure what someone will do under extreme stress. I've been wrong before."

There was something more Ron was not saying. "And did you think that there was something unsavory going on at the institute?"

"I didn't say that."

"But your cop instincts did?"

Ron raised his eyebrows and pursed his lips. I took that as a 'yes'.

"How is your investigation progressing?"

Ron was again silent for a long moment. "It's not," he said, almost too softly for me to hear.

"So the dropping of charges was no surprise to you. Do you suspect that there is something big political or federal going on behind the scenes? Have you been warned off?"

Ron leaned back, looked up at the ceiling, and exhaled deeply. "I am not at liberty to say," he said with a crooked smile on his lips.

Again, it was a tacit yes. The good cop that he was strongly resented being aced out of the inquiry and having to bow to politicians and the feds. This gave me the opening I needed.

"Well, we are still on the case. Golda fears later

charges and wants to clear her name. What can you tell me about your investigation so far? Can I look at your file? I would really like to see any reports and pictures from the crime scene, information on the weapon, autopsy reports, time and cause of death, physical evidence, info on Scanlon's car that exited the industrial park after his death."

"You know I can't give you all of that. Now that there are no charges against your client and no court case, you aren't entitled to that stuff," Ron said, cocking his head to the right and turning up his palms.

Again, I read the gestures as meaning "Let me see what I can do."

He thought for a moment, pulled a file from under the stack on his desk, opened it, nodded and dropped it back on the desk. "Would you like a cup of coffee?" he said. "Excuse me for a few minutes. I think I'll need to brew a fresh pot." He got up, took a long look down at the file on his desk, and left the office, closing the door behind him.

As soon as the door banged shut, I grabbed the file and opened it. I laid out as many of the pages on the floor as I could get within the focus of my phone camera and snapped. If someone came in, I would say that the file slipped off the desk and the pages spilled out. I did another layout and then another. That pretty much covered the entire file. I thanked God for my almost photographic memory in which I etched a couple of the police reports regarding the vehicle and the weapon. I just had enough time to scoop the pages back into the file folder when I heard a soft knock on the door. I stood to open it as Ron was carrying two coffee cups. I took one.

"Thank you," he said with an inquisitive look.

"No. THANK YOU," I said emphatically.

He smiled. "You might not thank me after you taste the coffee."

I chuckled and sipped the brew. It wasn't good, but it wasn't battery acid. I felt it would be ungrateful if I didn't finish it. We both sat down.

"In the interest of fair play, I hope you'll keep me posted on your investigation."

I nodded over my cup.

"And…"

What was coming now? Was Ron calling in a marker?

"How about dinner and a play at the Theater on the Lake this Saturday? It's the last play of the summer season, a new one called "A Going Away Party.""

"I'd love to," I gushed and then frowned, being chagrined by my too obvious enthusiasm.

"Great. It's not far from you. I'll pick you up at 6pm."

"That's perfect. What a great setting for an end-of-summer outing." I busied myself entering the date into my phone calendar.

"Well, I'm really looking forward to it," he said a bit sheepishly.

"Me too."

Chapter Seventeen

KELAN SU

Korb was fuming when I returned to the car. "I hope you cracked the case by now," he said with a deep frown and a sarcastic tone.

Although I was only gone about twenty-five minutes, I couldn't entirely blame him. When I'm with Ron, I lose track of time. "Of course, I did. It was the butler, or was that Cutler? Oh well, something like that." I searched the moon roof as if trying to remember the true culprit. I looked back at Korb, shrugged my shoulders, and smiled. I figured he'd bite my head off, but instead, he let out a loud "Hmmph," pursed his lips and finally gave me a half smile. I turned back, started the car, and headed home.

****

When we arrived at home, I helped Korb out of the car. He grumbled about having a late lunch. I assured him that Des would have something wonderful waiting for him. Des never fails to serve something that can bring our boss out of a foul mood. When we opened the door into the kitchen, we were greeted with a sweet, smoky aroma that made our mouths water. Des had done it again!

"What is that heavenly smell coming from?" I asked in awe.

"Korean barbecued brisket," he answered, looking

smug. "Started slow cooking at four a.m. this morning. It should be perfect now. I'll serve it with rice, kimchee, and lettuce wraps. I think some Hite Korean lager would go best with it."

I looked at Korb. His eyes were wide and he licked his lips in anticipation as he nodded to Des. Being late was forgotten.

****

When Des had served the lunch and Korb had his first few contented bites, Des asked if it would be alright for Reggie to join us for dinner that night. As his mouth was full, Korb just nodded his assent. He could never refuse Des while eating one of his creations, and he liked Reggie.

After that lunch, I had no idea how I could ever eat dinner. But knowing Des, he would have something that no one could resist. Probably after the heavy lunch, dinner would be much lighter fare. Let's see: Des was a brilliant researcher, a military hero, an award-winning chef, funny and warm, with the carved, muscular body of Adonis. I'd marry him in a flash. Unfortunately for my plan of an idyllic married life with great sex and even better meals, Des had a steady boyfriend who lived in town. This relationship was serious and longstanding, as they had originally met in the army. Reggie had followed Des from Bosnia, to Tortola, and now to Chicago. Des spent what little down time he had from Korb's affairs with his friend and lover.

I had met Reggie several times. Ron and I had double-dated with him and Des twice and Reggie had been to dinner at the house more than a few times. Reggie was a poet who had moderate success. He was able to catch on with Roosevelt University here in

Chicago, teaching creative writing and Caribbean literature. He had a degree in Art History and had been an art critic prior to the army. My impression of him was that he was an extremely thoughtful and incisive man. He did not speak often, but when he did, it was profound and beautifully expressed. Although slim and handsome, he did not have Des's physical presence. What struck me the most was his face. It was smooth and unlined. It belied his age. He was older than Des by five years. When I looked into his striking almond eyes, I saw intelligence, kindness, and compassion. He and Des were an amazing couple.

Chapter Eighteen

The scrumptious lunch settling well in their stomachs, Su and Des cleaned up the dining room and kitchen. As lunch had been late and Reggie was coming for dinner, Des would not have much time to welcome his close friend and prepare dinner. Then there was the report on what Su had learned from Ron to be made to Korb, as well as Des. They worked quickly and efficiently, Su bringing in the dishes and Des stacking them in the dishwasher. Su collected the napkins, combed the crumbs from the dining room table, folded and stored the tablecloth.

Korb had laboriously risen from the table, both hands on his oversized chair's arms, and retired to his office, voicing only a clipped "Report in ten minutes, my office" to Su. She responded in an equally terse manner. "Right. Police file photos on your desk." Su relayed Korb's order to Des, who had already refrigerated the meager leftovers and wiped down the kitchen surfaces.

Su and Des left the kitchen for Korb's office together. She effusively complimented Des on the meal. Des accepted the praise with a sheepish grin. Changing the subject and raising an eyebrow suggestively, he said, "So you have inveigled confidential police files from your erstwhile paramour?" Su shot him a dagger with her eyes, which then softened as she nodded.

"You should give him a little sugar to keep the pipeline open. Besides, you two were good together," said Des, cocking his head and giving her a searching look.

Su shook her head and sighed softly. "We are going to the Theater on the Lake this weekend." Des gave her an approving smile.

Korb didn't look up as they entered the office. He was poring over Su's photos of the police file. He merely indicated their customary chairs with a wave of his hand. They sat, looked briefly at each other, and then directed their attention to Korb, awaiting his royal notice. When he finally acknowledged them, Korb asked, "Have you seen these, Des?"

"Yes, Guv. Some joy there. Scanlon's car was found in the parking lot of Oakton Community College, about a half mile from the crime scene. Unfortunately, it was not a surveilled lot, so there is no record of what cars were there or when they entered. It seems that the killer left the institute in Scanlon's car and that the perp wore a white coat taken from the lab closet when committing the crime. There were some bloodstains on the driver's seat of the car—Scanlon's blood. The coppers searched areas and dumpsters within a mile radius of the lab but didn't find the coat. The gun was Scanlon's. He may have had it with him in the lab for fear of a visit from Crosetti's gang. It makes this look more like a crime of opportunity, not planned. The killer had some kind of confrontation with Scanlon that developed into a provocation."

Korb agreed, "It looks very clearly like the murder was committed by someone Scanlon knew well. Possibly someone he was expecting a visit from.

Someone familiar with the lab, particularly in light of the security system being shut down. Kelan, you will be looking into that with the security company."

"Yes, sir. Have an appointment with them on Friday. Seeing Sessions tomorrow. Some good stuff for Golda. The police were surprised when the SA charged her. The report indicates that Golda's fingerprints were on the gun in Scanlon's blood, but only her thumb and pointer midway down the handle.

"She probably picked up the gun gingerly like this," said Su, raising her hand, thumb and forefinger facing downward. "No pre-blood spatter fingerprints except Scanlon's. Powder residue tests on Golda and Scanlon were inconclusive in that they were done some time after the killing and Golda had washed. If this was opportunistic and the killer did not come prepared with gloves, there were boxes of latex gloves at hand in the lab."

"Did your friend on the Skokie force have any insight into why the SA's office has backed away from the case?"

"He had noted some pressure to put the case on a back burner and possibly to eighty-six it. He thought that some bigwig must have an interest in keeping the institute's affairs cloaked."

"Will you be keeping in touch with Lt. Sager?" said Korb with a raised eyebrow and a tight lip half smile, almost a smirk.

"Y-Yes," said Su, trying to sound matter of fact, but failing.

Korb nodded. Des stifled a chuckle. Su shot him a warning glance.

Su went on. "Okay. Other aspects of the police file:

Time of death–between one a.m. and three a.m. Saturday, Sept. 8. Weapon——.22 Ruger Mark IV bought new and registered to Scanlon on August 18, 2018, less than three weeks before the murder. One shot to the rear right of the parietal area from close range, no more than twelve inches. Slightly downward trajectory. No exit wound, considerable brain damage from bullet ricochet in the cranium. Lot of blood from the entry wound. Entry wound and trajectory exclude suicide. Body lying on the right side next to overturned lab stool. One cartridge case was found two feet north of Scanlon's head.

"The last employee, Carolyn Macready, my informant by the way, left the institute just before six p.m. The cleaning crew had just arrived. Scanlon was still in his office. The janitorial service finished up at eight p.m. They saw no one except Scanlon and Macready. The last security system log was Scanlon leaving his office and entering the lab at five past ten p.m. The security system was turned off at twelve-ten a.m."

"Ahh," said Korb, squinting into the distance. "Would you like to bet that the police techs did not check the HVAC system? I am sure they recorded the ambient temperature at the time of examining the body but did not check the system to see if that temperature was constant throughout the night and early morning hours. Labs have programmed usually cooler temperature settings. My guess is that the time of death was more likely between three a.m. and five a.m. Unfortunately, a later time of death doesn't help our client."

Des and Su nodded uncertainly.

Korb looked at Su. "You're seeing Sessions tomorrow? I'd like you to bring her here."

Su frowned. "I don't see how I can do that."

Korb folded his fingers together and gave Su a steady look. "Tell her that we have some important information to relate to her concerning Scanlon's murder and the danger she might be in. We need to ensure confidentiality. Time is of the essence for her protection. We'd prefer not to do this through the lawsuit. What time were you to meet her?"

"Ten a.m."

"Make it eleven a.m. here."

"I'll see what I can do."

"No, you'll do it. She will come."

Su nodded. Des shook his head in bewilderment.

Chapter Nineteen

At precisely 11 a.m., the doorbell rang. Su checked the video screen. Widely spaced, clear blue eyes in a lightly freckled, heart-shaped face framed by honey blond hair severely cut were frowning into the camera. Su pressed the intercom button and asked, "Dr. Sessions?"

A clipped "Yes" was the response.

"I'll be right down," said Su, heading toward the stairs to the ground floor.

On reaching the front door, Su checked the video screen there to assure herself that Dr. Sessions was alone. She twisted the knobs on two deadbolts and pressed her thumb on the fingerprint pad to unlock the door. A sharp click followed the latter action. She swung open the door.

Elaine Sessions nodded, giving Su a tight smile. The scientist was tall, dressed in a slim, black, thigh-length skirt and light black jacket over a silky, ivory-colored, mock turtleneck. The blouse was adorned by a gold chain and jade pendant.

Su took in her black Christian Louboutin pumps. *Must have cost a bundle*, she thought Su's appraising gaze momentarily betrayed envy of the woman's stylish, sexy, yet business appropriate look. Su looked down at her own black, straight pull-on pants and black running shoes and gave a short sniff.

"I am so glad you were able to come. Mr. Korb rarely leaves the house. But he is very anxious to meet you and discuss with you some developments in the Scanlon case that could bear heavily on your career and even your safety," said Su, glossing over the fact that Korb was most interested in questioning Sessions.

Elaine Sessions did not seem taken in by this ploy. However, her curiosity both about the notorious Marko Korb and what he knew about the Scanlon murder that might pertain to her had driven the acceptance of this meeting. She simply nodded.

The detective led her to the elevator, which stood open. She stepped aside to allow the "guest" to enter first, followed her in, and pressed 2. Noiselessly, the door closed and the elevator ascended. The two women stood silently side by side until the car stopped and the door opened.

"Please follow me," said Su as she exited. In the vestibule, she looked back to be sure that Sessions had complied.

Su led the scientist through her own workspace to the door that connected to Korb's office. Her knock was answered with a terse, "Come." Su opened the door and motioned for Sessions to enter. Korb looked up, smiled graciously, and said, "Dr. Sessions, so good of you to come. Please forgive me for not rising to greet you. My bulk makes that extremely difficult. Please, sit down." Korb motioned for Sessions to sit in a high-backed, burgundy wing chair directly in front of his desk. This was the detective's interview chair of choice. She sat while Su took the seat to Sessions' left.

"First, let me offer my condolences on the loss of your colleague," said Korb solemnly.

Sessions merely inclined her head. She looked at Korb with a tight-lipped stare. The scientist guessed this was but the opening gambit.

Korb continued. "The institute must be in grave difficulty since Dr. Scanlon's passing. He was the mainstay of the institute, both in terms of the management and the science, was he not?"

"Alan often thought of the institute as a one-man show but be assured that I and several of my lab colleagues were more than instrumental in the scientific domain and Stanley Vrdoliak, our CFO, and Jack Colter were key to the management." Dr. Sessions squirmed a bit in her chair and leaned forward, frowning at Korb. "Ms. Su said that you had something important to tell me that may affect my career and safety."

Korb leaned back in his chair and steepled his fingers, flicking a quick glance at Su, who gave him an almost imperceptible nod. "Dr. Sessions, I need to know how much you already know about the funding and purpose of the institute before I give you confidential information that we have uncovered." Korb lifted his head and raised an eyebrow, moving his hands under his chins. He kept his eyes on Sessions, but said nothing more, preferring to let her decide whether to proceed.

The scientist looked down, closed her eyes, and sighed. Her curiosity and uneasiness about Scanlon and the institute got the better of her. "Alan preferred to keep me and the rest of the staff in the dark about the funding and operations of the institute, but I always felt there was something shady in the background."

"So why did you stay?"

"Initially, it seemed like a great opportunity: a

well-equipped and funded lab, a say in hiring lab staff, a great salary." Sessions clasped her hands and grimaced. "Alan was charming and very persuasive. The feraxia research was extremely interesting as well. Right after we isolated the gene, he told me he had booked a week's stay for me at an Antiguan beach resort. He said I should go down immediately, soak up the sun, and relax. He also gave the rest of the team a week off. We'd celebrate when I returned."

"Did you go?"

Sessions fidgeted again and gave a genteel snort of a laugh. "Yes, of course, it sounded more like an order than a reward. But I must admit, I needed the break. We had worked sixteen hours a day in the last two weeks before the breakthrough. I didn't know at the time that Alan would apply for a patent of the gene and restrict its usage."

Korb looked at Su for a moment and frowned. "When did you find out about the patent application?"

"On the third day I was at the resort, I received an anonymous message. It read only 'Feraxia gene patent applied for by Scanlon.' Nothing more. The clerk who had taken the message said it sounded like a male voice, but he could not be sure."

Korb squinted at Sessions. "What did you do then?"

"I tried calling him both at his home and the lab. He was either not in or not taking my calls. I cut my stay short and went home. I went directly to the lab and confronted him in his office. He had applied for the patent of the gene without consulting anyone at the lab who had worked on it. He bragged about how he could now control all feraxia research–how this would prove his stature as a groundbreaking scientist. I was livid. I demanded how he could do that, cutting out those who had really done the work and the feraxia sufferers who had supported the research. He laughed. I felt betrayed. I called him a vicious, greedy bastard whose existence was a curse on the scientific profession and on the world. I left slamming the door." The so recently cool and collected doctor looked down at the floor with a sob and a sniffle.

Korb leaned forward, elbows on his desk, fingers at his temples, and gave Sessions a sympathetic look. Su rose and offered a tissue, which the discomfited scientist took, dabbing at her eyes and nose. "But you did eventually go back to work at the institute, did you not?" asked Korb.

Sessions nodded dejectedly. "Yes, after two days of not being able to get out of bed, I decided to finish up another very intriguing project I and my team were working on. It was the *in vivo* use of customized CRISPR/Cas9 libraries to understand cancer immunology. As cancer cells try to establish primary and secondary tumor sites, they accumulate genetic instability and somatic mutations to avoid being eliminated by the host immune system. CRISPR libraries could enable us to identify regulators of T-cell immunity."

Sessions halted and blushed at her enthusiastic and highly technical response. "Sorry, the science carries me away. I guess that's why I could go back into a hostile and humiliating environment at the institute. When I am working in the lab, I am in another world. And I couldn't just abandon my research team."

Korb nodded. "No need to apologize. I am sure that

your dedication and focus makes you an excellent scientist. But what of the future now that Scanlon is dead?"

Sessions looked up at the ceiling and sighed. "I don't know. I have a modest hope that I can take over as Scientific Director of the institute. But I have to make a case before the benefactors."

"And are you familiar with the benefactors?"

"Not at all. I had left that to Alan, Stanley Vrdoliak, and Jack Colter. They were very closed mouth about them. Jack has said that he would put in a good word for me and set up an opportunity for me to speak with the benefactors after the furor over Alan's death has died down. In truth, given that Alan was murdered, many of the benefactors will probably jump ship. I've prepared my CV to send out to other labs and some academic institutions, but I'd like to keep my team together. That may take some doing."

Korb leaned back in his chair and closed his eyes. He looked up and gave the scientist an intense look. "And that brings us to what I have to tell you. It bears directly on your future and the future of the institute."

Korb paused dramatically, and Sessions frowned, gripping the arms of her chair. Su leaned forward in her chair.

"Based on our investigation to date," Korb went on, "we have reason to believe that the principal benefactors of the institute are persons and organizations connected to criminal activities, and that the institute is primarily a money laundering vehicle for organized crime."

Elaine Sessions gave a quick shake of her head, her eyes wide, and her mouth agape. All she could utter was a guttural, "What? I don't believe it."

Korb tilted his head to the left and nodded. "You said yourself earlier that you thought there was something shady at the institute. We have confirmed it. I am sorry I can't give you more details. You know there is a lawsuit regarding the patent, and much of this information may be brought out in the course of the litigation. However, if you will help us, I can assure you that we will do all in our power to keep your reputation from being damaged by association with the institute and the murder of Dr. Scanlon."

Sessions lowered her head into her hands and moaned. She rocked back and forth in the chair, sobbing. Su went to her again and put her hand gently on the woman's shoulder. "Please try to get a hold of yourself. There are a few questions I need you to answer so we can clear up this matter with the least involvement on your part." Su regretted this disingenuous reassurance, but she had some important questions to ask Sessions.

Chapter Twenty

KELAN SU

Dr. Sessions used the crumpled tissue to dab at her eyes. Her rocking had stopped, but the tears were still flowing. Was this a genuine show of grief over her possibly ruined career or something deeper? I pulled my chair over next to hers watching her intently as she gathered herself together. Korb was looking away. I wondered whether he assumed this was honest emotion or a ploy to hide her prior knowledge of the institute's purpose and backing. Either way, he didn't like crying women.

I waited for a long minute as she dried up her tears. She took a deep breath and looked at me with her eyes red and half closed. I sympathized, but at the same time, I needed to ask questions while she was in a vulnerable state.

"Elaine," I said starting in a friendly tone, "we're so sorry to have hit you with this at such a difficult time, but it will be to your advantage if we get to the bottom of this as quickly as possible."

Sessions sighed and nodded. She gave me a penetrating look. Again, I had the thought that this entire scene might have been staged. I'd start with factual questions that might seem neutral. "What can you tell me about the security system at the institute?" I added, letting her know I could check on her answers,

"I have an appointment tomorrow with the company tech that installed and maintains your system and I would like to have as much information as possible to inform my questions."

"Well, I am not familiar with the technical aspects of the system. I have a magnetic badge and a password to enter the institute building and my thumbprint is registered to allow me to enter the lab. The password is changed every forty-five days and is sent to us through an encrypted message from the security company. All of the office staff had a password and badge and all of the research staff also had their thumbprints registered. To my knowledge, only I, Dr. Scanlon, and our CFO, Stanley Vrdoliak, had another password and an encrypted electronic key that would allow them to turn the system on and off, check the recordings, and possibly modify the parameters."

The recital was precise and to the point. She had obviously gained control of her emotions. *Too quickly?* I wondered. Now I had to venture into more dangerous territory. "Elaine, do you happen to know anything about Dr. Scanlon's family? Who is his next of kin?"

Sessions frowned. Her eyes narrowed momentarily. Then her face assumed a bland look. "I don't think Alan had any close family. At least he never mentioned them. I wouldn't know of his next of kin. Why do you ask?"

"Well, we need to know who might gain from his death. Can you tell me anything about his lifestyle? Did he live well?"

"Yes, I believe he was very well-off. His apartment was on the lake front, high up with a magnificent view, large and expensively furnished. He traveled a lot. His ride was a Jag. He was a regular at some of Chicago's most chi-chi restaurants. Season tickets at the CSO."

"So someone may inherit a substantial estate. Do you know if he had a will or who might be his heirs?"

Sessions hesitated before answering and looked down at her hands clasped in her lap. "No. But possibly Jack Colter would know. He was Alan's as well as the institute's lawyer."

"Did you know Scanlon well, personally? What kind of person was he?"

"He certainly had a charming exterior. He treated me well and fooled me for some time. But apparently he was greedy, vain, and deceitful. I should have sensed something, as he was miserable to most of the rest of the staff."

"Dr. Sessions," Korb cut in, "I must ask you this. Was your relationship with Dr. Scanlon strictly professional?"

Sessions glared at Korb and stood up abruptly. "How dare you? We're done here."

Korb shook his head and spoke in a calming voice. "Please sit down, Dr. Sessions. I am not trying to insult you or pry into anything that isn't already known around the institute. But getting your take on the relationship will be instrumental in profiling Dr. Scanlon. The character and relationships of the victim are an essential element of an investigation. It will be essential to our helping you."

Korb fixed the woman with a hard gaze. It froze her. "Now, Dr. Scanlon was supposed to meet you in Antigua, was he not? But he didn't show up. When you confronted him on your return, you were not only incensed about the patent but also because he made it clear that he was never really romantically interested in you."

Sessions flashed a look of pure hatred at Korb. She turned and strode toward the door.

"Kelan, you had better show Dr. Sessions out," said Korb evenly.

I had already risen and got to the door before Sessions. I opened it for her and let her swish past me. The elevator door was open and we entered it without speaking. I didn't want to look at her or she at me.

Chapter Twenty-One

KELAN SU

Friday morning was gray and damp. There was a bite to the wind that augured fall. As I headed east to the Drive, a light rain began to fall. When I got on the Stevenson, the swish of the wipers began to make me drowsy. Fortunately, Des had filled a small thermos with a double Americano. I sipped it gratefully as the long, flat interstate unwound. I exited at Illinois 171 in LaGrange and wound my way on glistening wet streets through a light industrial area, primarily occupied by trucking companies. No surprise as there was easy access to interstates and a Conrail siding.

The long, single-story, empty industrial building that my friend Phyllis, a commercial real estate agent, had provided the keys and the plans for wasn't hard to find. The journey from the house had taken less than fifty minutes, despite some traffic. It was an hour before the En Garde Security Systems tech was to arrive. I asked for Greg who Carolyn said was the tech working with the institute's system. I gave myself enough lead time to study the floor plan and its representation. I parked the car at the rear of the building, so the En Garde rep wouldn't see it and check the license number. Security people, like detectives, are always curious.

When I unlocked the double glass door at the front

of the building, a blast of warm, dusty air hit me. It made me cough. Phyllis said that the building had been empty for two and a half years without much interest– only occasional showings. By the light filtering through the glass bricks at the front and a long row of translucent factory window panels high on the back wall, I found an array of switches for the fluorescent lighting. I flicked them on, illuminating the vast empty space. About one-tenth of the 30,000 square foot building was divided into office space. The rest was unpartitioned.

The main entrance led into the office space. The loading dock and a nearby doorway accessed the open space at the rear. The ceiling was untiled with beams, cables and ducts criss-crossing the expanse. The floor was concrete in the open space and laid with aging, cracked tile in the office area. It seemed to me that only astronomical pay and extensive remodeling could make working here anything less than soul-sapping. But I guess factory work is rarely inspirational.

I paced the area while checking dimensions on the plans. I was getting into this. It was like really setting up a factory laboratory. I was so engrossed and focused that the loud knocking on the front door made me jump. I turned to see a face topped by a royal blue En Garde baseball cap peering through the glass, both hands shading the face for a clearer view inside. Sketching a wave, I went to open the door.

Greg, the tech/salesman I had spoken to on the phone, stepped in and offered his hand. We shook. He held my hand a bit longer than I liked as he looked me over. "Ms. Cho, I presume," he said.

"Hi, Greg. I'm sorry I didn't get your last name."

"Saunders."

I nodded and removed a card case from my purse, slipping out a business card. I handed the card to Greg. "So you won't forget my name."

With a slight leer, he said, "I doubt I would do that."

I did not like Greg, but his manner made me feel much less guilty about conning him.

He read from the card, "'Jacquelyn Cho, Chief Security Officer, Wedderburn Pharmaceuticals.' Impressive."

"Well, as I mentioned on the phone, we are acquiring a small OTC pharma company here in Chicago and want to move the combined operation to this site. We will be working on cold remedies with pseudoephedrine, which can be turned into methamphetamine, so we need extensive security for the operation." If I were really going to provide security for this business, I would not even have told Greg that much. Security is nine-tenths keeping information to yourself.

"Okay," said Greg, assuming a more professional manner. "What are the dimensions of this building?"

"Two hundred frontage by a hundred fifty depth. Thirty thousand square feet."

"And how many entrances or exits?"

"Three. The front door, the loading dock power overhead door and a rear door to the side of the loading dock."

"Are you interested in security personnel or a patrol?"

"No, just alarms, surveillance, and an access control system. The alarms, including intruder, fire, carbon monoxide, temperature and power outage should go to certain key employees and the local police and fire department."

Greg nodded and slowly toured the perimeter walls and doorways. He had an iPad on which he was writing with a stylus. "How will the space be divided?"

"The front entrance should lead into a small waiting area with space for a secretary/receptionist. Adjacent to the reception area would be a small office for a security guard with monitors. Then five offices, a conference room, a break room, and a corridor leading into the lab/manufacturing area. That will take up about four to five thousand square feet. The rest of the space will be for a laboratory and manufacturing equipment." This recitation sounded authentic to me. From his nods, I gathered Greg felt so too.

This gave me the courage to press on. "I was thinking that we need a magnetic badge and numeric code for the outside access doors, additionally a thumbprint to get inside the office section and a retinal scan for the lab area. Individual passwords for three of the offices. At least eight CCTV cameras and several motion detectors inside and outside the building and monitors in the guard's office and in the Lab Director's and Plant Manager's office. Also, climate monitoring is very important for the lab area."

"Sounds reasonable. I'll have to send you specs and a quote, but the ballpark will be twenty K for equipment and installation and monthlies of two hundred fifty to five hundred dollars. Do you need cybersecurity?"

"No, we handle that internally. You understand that we are asking for quotes from several companies."

"Of course, we expect that. Can you tell me who else you're considering?"

I avoided answering and went directly to the key question. "Look, I understand that you handled the system at the Shabel Institute where that Scanlon guy was murdered. Despite several recommendations for your service, that worries me more than a little. What was the problem there?"

Greg clenched his teeth and exhaled sibilantly through them. "That was not a system failure. The system was turned off and video storage was deleted."

"You mean by someone with authorization to do so?"

He hesitated. "Y-ycs. At least with someone who had access to codes, passwords, and an authorized party's cell phone. You know that security is only as good as the people who use it. We changed passwords and codes every forty-five days and sent them by encrypted text messages to those authorized to have them. We visited the institute monthly to check the equipment and we conducted random checks to be sure people were keeping their access authority secure. They weren't, and Scanlon was the worst offender. His office and the lab were regularly left open, and he kept his cellphone, security badge, and often a sticky note with codes and passwords in an unlocked desk drawer. We warned him and the rest of the staff to be more security conscious. We sent them training videos every year and registered who viewed them. It was not a good scene security-wise. I hope your crew is more careful." He shook his head disgustedly.

That answered my question, but not in the way I had hoped. It meant that almost anyone on the staff or who was in the office area could have manipulated the security system. No narrowing of the suspect list.

"Well, thanks, Greg. I await your quote and we will let you know one way or the other by the end of next month. Shall we go?" I headed toward the front door.

"Uh. Is there any chance we could go for a coffee somewhere?" His appraising leer had returned.

"Oh, sorry. I'd like to, but I have an important appointment back in Chi. Maybe some other time." I should have bitten my tongue before giving him even the least encouragement, but I didn't want to antagonize him. Might need more info.

He gave me a resigned nod and followed me to the door. I let him out and stayed behind until his van had pulled out of the parking area.

Chapter Twenty-Two

KELAN SU

Korb would want a report but, at the moment, he was discussing dinner with Des. That was good as I needed a shower to wash the factory dust from my body and hair. After the shower, I put on some sweats and sneakers and tied back my hair, hoping I could also squeeze in a workout. Luck was with me as Korb was surveying the fridge and freezer for meal ideas. Dissatisfied with the inventory, he picked up the phone. Calling our butcher, I presumed. He did not even look up as I slid past him to the basement stairs. Descending, I heard him ejaculate "*magret de canard*, yes!" into the phone. His stentorian response might have deafened the butcher but our meat man probably knew Korb and his enthusiasm for food well enough to hold the phone away from his ear. I must admit that my mouth started to water. After all, I hadn't had lunch.

Des was lifting weights in our basement gym and had already worked up a sweaty sheen that gave his muscled body a glistening, god-like aura. *Whew!*

I started with some *Qui Gong* breathing, stretches and meditation, then moving on to a slow-motion Tai Chi workout. I used the heavy bag for punches and kicks and ended with a series of flips and falls on the mat. I finished up with two miles on the treadmill. I hoped I had developed my own goddess-like aura as

Des was watching me with an approving half smile.

I smiled back and said, "Guess we have earned our dinner. It's going to be *magret de canard*. Korb ordered some on the phone. Do you have a good recipe for it?"

Des smiled broadly. "*Bien sûr, mon petit chou.* I'm always ready to satisfy Korb's last-minute culinary whims. But thanks for the heads up. Let's see. How about the duck grilled with honey and anise, a starter of heirloom tomato salad, and sides of roasted potatoes and braised red cabbage?"

"*Oh la la*!!!" I faked a swoon. Almost didn't have to fake it.

****

After another shower, I finally caught Korb in his office and reported on my meeting with the En Garde security tech. He was mellow after his lunch of *vichyssoise* and a *salade frisée aux lardons* accompanied by a fresh, bright, white Menetou-Salon. I was glad there was some being held for me in the kitchen. Damn, I was hungry.

Surprisingly, Korb asked no questions. He merely lowered his forehead to his steepled fingers. When he lifted his face, he nodded with a raised eyebrow and a knowing look.

"Okay," he said with an almost jolly smile, "that means we must look more closely into Colter and Gould."

"I don't understand. What about the others at the lab, Sessions, Vrdoliak? And Crosetti?"

"Yes, I see. Of course, we must pursue all avenues and we will. But I am beginning to discern a pattern. However, please locate Donna Walsh, Karlakis, and anyone else with appointments up to the time of the murder."

I nodded. "Uh, sir. Just wanted you to know that I have plans for tomorrow night and Sunday. I'm going to see Ron Sager Saturday night and go to my *kwoon* on Sunday and then to my parents."

Korb gave me a wry smile. "You know you don't have to explain your weekend activities to me unless, of course, your date with Sager is in the line of duty."

"N-n-no," I stammered. "It's not."

"Is the following visit to your parents of special significance?"

"I thought I didn't have to explain my weekend activities," I said, frowning deeply at Korb's prying, or was it because of my ambivalence about Ron?

Korb, chastised, wiped the playful smile off his face and merely nodded.

Chapter Twenty-three

KELAN SU

I was in a funk after the colloquy with Korb. Even the marvelous dinner Des had prepared didn't lift my mood. Korb, absorbed in the food, seemed oblivious to my silence. Des kept looking at me questioningly, concerned. I focused on the food in my plate.

The mood had only partially dissipated by Saturday morning. By then, I knew it wasn't Korb. It was me. My relationship with Ron had passion and deep friendship—a solid basis for the long term. Yet, we both loved our work and could never ask the other to give theirs up.

I decided to immerse myself in work until I saw Ron this evening. I fired up my computer. To gather more information about Donna Walsh, my first step was to conduct an online search. Her listings were dated and only reflected her Chicago addresses. I located her mother's Florida address and phone number in White Pages. It looked like her mom was in a nursing home. I then went to TLOxp, a TransUnion product and the most frequently updated of the investigative databases. There, I found a Florida address and phone number for Donna. That information matched an earlier address and phone number for her mother. My guess was that Donna was living in her mom's old house or condo. TLO also came up with a cell number for Donna.

From the reports that Ron had let me see, I knew that the police had asked Donna about her stint at the guard kiosk on the Saturday midnight to 8 a.m. shift. They were particularly interested in who she might have seen exiting in Scanlon's car. Apparently, she had been talking on her mobile with a boyfriend and two girlfriends for most of her shift. She had not been paying close attention to vehicles entering or leaving the industrial park. There had been at least one car entering and one leaving that she failed to identify and log and she did not notice who was driving Scanlon's car when it departed around 5 a.m. I needed to question her, although over the phone was not what I would prefer. Her answers and tone would let me know if I needed to fly down to Tampa where she was staying near her mother. It was also possible that Korb would want me to bring her back to Chicago so that he could pose the questions. That would be a challenge.

I tried the home phone number first thinking that she would be more relaxed at home. If I got her cell, she might be on the road or where she couldn't talk freely. The phone rang four times and then a raspy, halting old lady's voice said simply, "Please leave a message." I tried the cell.

It rang three times and a husky voice answered with a clipped, "Yeah."

"Hello, is this Donna Walsh?"

"Yeah. Who's this?"

"My name is Kelan Su. I am investigating the murder of Alan Scanlon. I need to talk with you."

"I already talked to the police."

"The Skokie police have been preempted by a higher authority." I thought that was a good characterization of Marko Korb, at least for me. "I have been instructed to ask you some questions. If the answers are unsatisfactory, I will have to come down to Tampa and bring you back for more intense questioning."

A heavy sigh came over the phone. "Okay. Ask your questions."

"As I understand it, you were on duty on Saturday, September 8, 2018, from midnight to eight a.m."

"Yeah."

"Was this your regular shift?"

"Yeah. I had that time slot from Wednesday to Sunday."

"And how long had you been working security at the kiosk?"

"About a year and a half."

"I would guess that your shift was rarely a busy one until the end when people start arriving for work."

"For sure, especially on weekends."

"So, there were very few cars in or out during your shift on September 8."

"Yesss."

"How many?"

"Well, I guess the police have told you that I wasn't really paying much attention. I was texting and talking to friends. It was the only way I could stay awake. I don't drink coffee."

"What did you notice?"

"I did see Dr. Scanlon's car leave the park at five a.m., but I only saw a white-coated figure in the car."

"Male or female?"

"I'm not sure. The car zipped past."

"Did you notice anything at all unusual about

Scanlon or the car?"

She hesitated. "Hmm. Scanlon never wore a lab coat and he usually sketched a wave as he passed the kiosk. This driver didn't even look my way."

"Think hard," I encouraged her. "You may remember something important."

"Hmm," said Walsh. There was a pause. "Oh, yeah. The driver was tall. The head was partly hidden by the roof of the car."

There was a buzz on the intercom, which I had left open in case Korb had wished to listen in. "Just a moment, Donna. My boss has buzzed me. Stay on the line."

Korb's voice rasped, "Kelan. I'm sure you are going to ask about the cars Ms. Walsh did not log in or out. I'm going to listen in. Please inform Ms. Walsh that your 'Superior' will be in on the conversation."

I took a breath. "Right, Chief." I knew the sobriquet would reinforce the official appearance of the call and annoy Korb.

I cleared my throat. "Donna, my boss is on the call with us. He has directed me to ask you about what else you may have noticed, but not logged, during your shift."

"Well, just after I arrived at the kiosk, a car passed. I was busy getting settled and firing up the computer. It was not a car I recognized, but I didn't get a good look. I figured I would see it on the way out and also log it in at twelve-ten a.m. When it left the Park, I was busy texting and didn't notice any details. It did seem like the same car that I had missed earlier, but I'm not sure. All I can say is that it was a small sedan with an out-of-state plate. It was dark both times so I can't even be sure about the color except that it was dark."

"What time did the car exit?"

"About four a.m."

Korb broke in. "Ms. Walsh, you expected to see the car again before the end of your shift. Why is that? Over your year and a half of service at the industrial park, did you notice regular entrants around midnight who exited around three or four a.m.?"

Walsh hesitated.

"Donna, are you still there?" I asked.

A sharp exhale indicated she was. "I just don't want to get anyone in trouble."

"Don't forget," said Korb, "this is a murder investigation. Not answering fully is not an option."

"Well, during my first sixteen months on the job, Dr. Sessions was often an early morning visitor to the lab. More recently, it has been a woman who calls herself Tamara Grodin. And a funny thing, she seems to drive a different car each time, often with out-of-state plates."

"What does this woman look like?" Korb asked.

"Blonde, big glasses—she seemed short as her face only just cleared the wheel."

"And how often has this woman been coming during your shift?"

"About twice a month."

"Would you recognize her if you saw her face to face?"

"I don't know. She usually had a sweater or coat collar up around her face."

"Anything else you can think of out of the ordinary that might help us?" I asked.

"No. I hope I won't have to come back to Illinois.

My mom needs my help," said Donna in a plaintive tone.

"Not for now. You have been most helpful, Ms. Walsh. If you do think of anything more, please call Detective Su," said Korb and disconnected his phone.

"Thank you, Donna," I said. "You have my number. Good bye."

"Yeah. Bye," she said sounding relieved, and hung up.

****

"Soooo," said Korb, pursuing his lips, "Tamara Grodin. We can go about this two ways. You can go back to the industrial park kiosk and get a look at the Tamara Grodin log entries for the license plates. Different car, often out-of-state plates, spells rentals. Then you can check the rental places. However, we could short-circuit that."

"How do we do that?"

"Come on, Kelan. Use your imagination. Tamara Grodin–TG. What TG do we have in relation to this case?"

I looked at the ceiling and exhaled. "Of course, Tracey Gould. She's one of the incorporators of the institute and works for the institute's law firm. I don't know yet what she looks like, but I bet she fits Tamara Grodin's description."

"So do you want to check the security kiosk and car rental places, or bring Tracey Gould in for an interview if she fits the description?"

"Let's go directly to Gould. I'm going to check out her apartment while she's at work. I think I can get enough leverage to bring her to you."

"Satisfactory. Get her here at two p.m. Tuesday. Meanwhile, enjoy your weekend."

Chapter Twenty-Four

KELAN SU

My mind had been active all day thinking about how to approach Tracey Gould. It was now 4 p.m. It was beyond time to get ready for my evening with Ron. It had been a warm day, but in mid-September by the lake, it would cool down quickly. I showered and brushed my hair–fifty strokes. I chose dark blue yoga leggings and a light blue embroidered cotton/chiffon tunic. For the cool of the evening, I'd take my merino shawl. Shoes, let me see. How about my cross-strap ballet wedges? Didn't want to be too tall, although Ron was an even six feet. I left the underwear selection for last, trying to judge how I was feeling as the evening approached. Sexy, but understated. That's the ticket.

When I finished with my preparations, it was five-forty-five. I checked myself in the mirror. Not bad. Better than my usual black and white blah, but nowhere as intense as the fantastic red outfit that Korb had bought for me in Venice. It would do.

The doorbell rang at six p.m. on the dot. I checked the monitor in my room and spoke into the intercom. "I'll be down in a flash. Do you want to come in?"

"Not necessary. It's a fine night. But the fog is starting to roll in on the lake."

"I'm prepared for late summer lakefront vagaries." I heard Ron chuckle as I shut off the intercom and headed for the stairs. As I passed through the entrance hall, Des gave me a whistle and a thumbs-up. I sketched a wave. "Would you lock up behind me?" I asked as I undid our security bolts and opened the door.

"No problem. Give my regards to Ron."

The night was damp with the soft, velvety air that follows a perfect late summer day and presages a foggy night. Ron was waiting on the driveway–navy dockers, navy turtleneck, gray Donegal tweed sport coat, raised eyebrows and a sexy smile. I couldn't help returning the smile.

"Hey, girl, you look fine."

"As do you."

He bowed slightly as he opened the passenger side door of his metallic red Mustang convertible and helped me in. I was halfway in when I felt a soft kiss on my cheek. It was electric. Naturally, I suavely banged my head on the car roof. Ron couldn't fully suppress a chortle.

I joined him in a laugh. It helped hide the frisson.

The ride up the Drive was short, about a mile. The theater's open, prairie style building was ablaze with lights, the lake and the sky were darkening and the fog was coming in waves. The moon was a "ghostly galleon." It was a thrilling sight.

I heard the deep bccc-oooo of a foghorn which always comforted me. It reminded me of my childhood vacations with my parents in South Haven, Michigan. I slept in a room with my brother and two other kids on the third floor of an old clapboard cottage near the beach, while our parents had rooms on the floor below. The foghorn of the old South Beach Lighthouse would sing me to sleep.

Inside the theater's high-beamed, oak-floored restaurant pavilion, the warm lighting, the clink of glasses and silver, the spectacular view of the fog-bound lake, and the pungent aroma of garlic and herbs were elegant delights.

The hostess walked us to a table near one of the panoramic windows. Ron pulled out my chair and I sat, I hoped, gracefully. He took the chair opposite me, leaned forward, and looked into my eyes for a long moment. Just before I dissolved into a puddle, he leaned back in his chair and said, "You look wonderful. It's been too long since we were out together. Let's celebrate."

I nodded my approval.

"No business talk," he said with a wry smile.

I nodded again. "What shall we celebrate with?"

Ron picked up the wine list and handed it to me. "You're the expert, pick something festive and mellow."

"How about a bottle of the Morey Bourgogne Aligoté?" It's a favorite of mine.

Ron smiled and nodded

The waiter appeared at the table. "Hello, I'm Ben. I'll be your server tonight. Can I get you something to drink?"

"For sure," said Ron. "We'd like a bottle of the Morey Bourgogne Aligoté and water."

"Bottled or tap?"

"Tap is fine. We're right here on Lake Michigan. Seems like an insult to drink imported water."

"Right you are. Do you wish to order now?"

"We'll order when you bring the wine."

The waiter smiled and turned away.

"What are you thinking of having?" Ron asked.

I had been studying the menu and getting hungry. "Whew. I think I'd like to try the elote tostadas for a starter and then the brisket chili. Unfortunately, if I do that, I'll have to skip dessert. So I might opt for a salad as the main. How about you?"

"Well. I don't mind skipping dessert here. Back at my place, I have a quart of Black Dog goat cheese-cashew-caramel gelato. By the time the play is over, we'll be ready for dessert, I'm sure."

"Mmm. Dessert at your place. Sounds very enticing."

"I should hope so."

The bus boy brought us a pitcher of water and filled our goblets. He also set up a wine cooler next to Ron. The waiter returned with the bottle of wine and two wine glasses. He set down the glasses and showed Ron the wine label with a flourish.

Ron nodded. He gave me a wry look which said, "Who needs this rigamarole?"

The waiter uncorked the bottle with his jointed corkscrew and poured a sip for Ron. Ron swirled the wine, inhaled it deeply, tasted it, and looked at the waiter, who was waiting expectantly.

"It's wine all right," Ron said with a serious look.

The waiter relaxed and entered into the spirit of the joke with a smile. "I'm so glad. Our sommelier has been known to send over a bottle of salad dressing by mistake."

"No worries of us wasting this on a salad," said Ron

The waiter filled both our glasses and placed the bottle draped in a napkin into the cooler. "Are you ready to order?"

Ron looked at me and I nodded.

The waiter turned toward me and asked, "For the young lady?"

"I'll have the elote tostadas as a starter. Since we are going to the play, I'll also order the brisket chili now."

"Very good." The waiter turned to Ron.

"I'll have the ceviche and the hanger steak. Do you know the term 'Pittsburgh?'"

"Nooo."

"It means seared almost black on the outside and very, very rare on the inside. It's an old steelworkers' term for when they brought raw steak to work for lunch, put it on a pallet, and shoved it into the blast furnace for just a few seconds. Do you think your chef can prepare it that way?"

"He's very good although we don't have a blast furnace. We do have a high heat brick oven. That might do it."

"Okay then." The waiter turned toward the kitchen.

"That was interesting," I said. "I'll have to quiz my gourmet boss on that method of cooking."

"Yeah. I had an uncle who was a steelworker. He told me that story."

Ron picked up his glass and again gave me intense eye contact. "How about a toast?"

"Sure, to what?"

"How about? May our lives be full of love and laughter."

"Sounds wonderfully poetic. I'm impressed."

"Ah, yes. There is much you don't know about me, but I hope you'll want to learn more."

I felt unsettled. "Ron, let's enjoy the moment."

"I certainly am. I hope you are."

"Definitely." I smiled brightly.

The waiter arrived with our starters. I was relieved as we both turned our attention to the delicious concoctions.

Chapter Twenty-Five

KELAN SU

The dinner was superb. Keyanna Khatiblou's *A Going Away Party Play* was interesting, not great. In any case, I was distracted by the scent of Ron's cologne and his thigh pressing into mine. We each had a brandy and soda at intermission while enjoying people-watching the milling crowd. Ron identified some of Chicago's top politicians and their wives or girlfriends—several aldermen and a deputy mayor. I pointed out a few local tycoons and journalists. We watched them schmooze with each other. Not much chance they were discussing the merits of the play. The spouses and dates stood idly by, smiling perfunctorily, looking around to see who else was there. Ron received covetous looks from some of the women.

After the play, Ron said, "My place for dessert?"

"Your place definitely." My place was closer, but privacy was a limited quantity with both Korb and Des living there. They were good about trying to stay out of the way, but accidental encounters couldn't be avoided. It just never felt right.

Ron had a spacious two-bedroom condo on Arthur, not far from Sheridan Road and the Loyola campus. It took us about 15 minutes up the Drive from the theater. We were both pretty quiet on the trip–immersed in our own thoughts about where our relationship was going. I couldn't keep from sliding my hand onto his thigh. He covered it tenderly with his big mitt. I exhaled sharply and he stole a glance at me. He wore a sheepish smile.

As soon as we entered the apartment, he turned to me, took my face in his hands and kissed me deeply. It took my breath away. He dropped his sport jacket and my shawl on the couch. Then he took my hand and led me to the master bedroom. I was already woozy with passion. We kissed again, our bodies pressing hard against each other. His hands slid down to the bottom of my tunic and he lifted it over my head, bending to kiss my neck. Gently, the camisole was slid off my shoulders, and it dropped to the floor. He kissed and caressed my breasts, tonguing the nipples. I was panting. I pulled his turtleneck up over his head. For a moment, it caught on his chin and we both had to laugh. The comic relief only heightened the sexual tension.

I kissed his nipples, running my hands over his rippled midsection meanwhile tugging at his belt. He helped me unbuckle and unzip his pants. His erect penis created a turgid bulge in his gray briefs. I kicked off my shoes and slid down his briefs as he pulled down my yoga tights and bikini underwear together. For a moment, we admired each other's nakedness. Then we embraced. I could feel his tumescence pressing against me. My knees were beginning to buckle.

Ron took my hand and kissed it, leading me to the bed. I lay down and closed my eyes as he grasped one of my feet, massaging it and kissing the sole and each toe. Then he did the same to the other foot. He knelt on the bed beside me, slowly massaging my legs and thighs and covering them with kisses. When his mouth finally reached my juicy center, I was moaning deep in my throat. His incredible foreplay had reduced me to pudding.

With the little strength I could muster, I pulled him toward me and helped him enter me. He moved slowly, gently. I rose to meet him. He showered my face and neck with kisses and I returned as many as I could. Our thrusts deepened and the pace quickened. We were both breathing like steam engines. As his hands went behind my back pulling me to him, I couldn't resist grabbing his firm buttocks. I screamed as waves of orgasm flooded over me. I felt his back arch with a last deep thrust and a guttural groan escaped him as he too climaxed. His body fell heavily on mine as he swept kisses across my face from ear to car. I was a puddle and could only lie still absorbing the warmth and tenderness.

Gently, he rolled onto his side caressing my belly and breasts. I turned to him and finally returned his kisses. We lay exhausted for several minutes. Not speaking, staring at the ceiling and caressing each other's bodies. Then we looked at one another. Both of our faces had that after-sex, rosy glow, but our looks also shared a certain lasciviousness.

I kissed Ron, sliding my tongue in deeply. He responded in kind. Then I rolled away. Looking at me, he grinned and said "Wow!"

"Likewise," I responded.

We were sticky with sweat and bodily fluids. "How about a shower?" I asked.

His grin widened and he nodded enthusiastically. "I'll get the water ready. Sometimes the water heater is slow," he said. He rose a bit stiffly and padded to the bathroom. I stretched luxuriously and closed my eyes almost dozing off. *Gonna sleep well tonight,* I thought.

I got up slowly and made my way to the bathroom. Ron was already in the large glassed-in shower, eyes closed, the hot water streaming hard down his back. For a moment, I admired his hard, sculpted body and marveled at his gentleness. His penis was slack and undemanding, but started to pulse when I opened the shower door and stepped in. He greeted me with a soft kiss and moved so I could get into the stream.

The stinging streams of hot water were wonderful. Ron began soaping my shoulders and back, working his way down to my rump where he spent some extra TLC and a few suctiony kisses. Squatting, he soaped my groin, thighs, and legs and then turned me around. I took the soap from him and he turned so I could repeat the process for him.

Finally, after shampooing and rinsing, we dried each other, kissed, and headed back to the bed hand in hand. Once comfortably settled, he spooned me. I felt so completely fulfilled, warm and safe that I fell asleep instantly.

When I woke in the morning, the sun was streaming in. Ron was gone, but his indentation in the bed was still warm. I heard clinking in the kitchen, and the aroma of dark roast coffee wafted in. I grabbed last night's tunic and slipped it over my head. As I entered the kitchen, Ron was pushing down the plunger on a French press. He was just wearing boxers this morning. Though loose, they did not hide his muscled butt and thighs. I slid my arms around his middle and rested my head on his shoulder. "Delicious," I said.

"Me or the coffee?"

"Both."

"I was thinking that the gelato would be great for breakfast."

"Oooooh, yes!"

"We should talk," he said seriously.

"We should," I responded without enthusiasm.

Ron poured coffee and dished out the creamy, buttery gelato. We sat at his terrazzo bistro table and looked at each other without speaking. I took a spoonful of the gelato, savored it until it melted and slid down my throat. "Whew. So good. The Black Dog never fails to please."

Ron took a spoonful and nodded, without smiling. We each took a sip of the coffee.

"Kelan, I want you with me," he said, searching my face for a reaction.

To escape the intensity of his gaze, I shifted my focus to the table. "We've talked about this before. There would be too many times when our professional interests conflict and too much need to keep information from each other. Neither of us is ready to give up our work, and living together would require that for one of us."

"If you moved in here with me, you wouldn't have to give up your work. Just modify the terms somewhat. Des could see to Korb's security. You wouldn't be far away."

"Yes, but I love my work, including the security, and I would be shortchanging you responding to Korb's beck and call at all hours. By the way, your work is the same."

As if to prove my point, Ron's cell blared out the cavalry charge bugle call.

"Oh shit." He shook his head, grimaced, and went

to pick up the cell from the kitchen counter.

"Yeah. Sager." His shoulders slumped and he said, "I'll be there in fifteen."

I raised my eyebrows and cocked my head.

"I've got to go. An armed robbery in progress– shots fired."

"Okay, Ron. Look, I want to see you much more and I plan to stay over often. That will have to do for now. Oh yeah, I'm meeting my folks for lunch. I'll give them your regards. Call me tonight. I do love you." The last words surprised me but rang true. I stood and embraced Ron hard and kissed him longingly. "Be careful out there," I said.

Chapter Twenty-Six

Korb liked to linger over the Sunday papers–Trib, Sun-Times, NY Times. As he was a late riser, this would take him until mid-afternoon. He started his day with an orange shandy and a large mug of black French Market coffee made with chicory. Des was busy frying up codfish fritters and plantains. On the table before Korb was a tellicherry pepper grinder and a carafc of coffee. Korb was attired in midnight blue silk pajamas. Wire-rim reading glasses perched on his nose. As he read, Korb kept up a running commentary on articles that interested him. Des would periodically grunt his interest and occasionally pose a question. Korb scanned the pages quickly and only rarely stopped to read an article more fully. He ignored the Sports and Style sections of the papers. He would save the New York Times magazine and Book Reviews for later reading.

Des placed the plate full of fritters and plantains before his boss with the appropriate cutlery and a large plaid dish towel instead of a napkin. Korb tucked the towel into the front of his pajamas. He inhaled the bouquet of this traditional Caribbean breakfast, closed his eyes, and nodded appreciatively. *"Bon appetit,"* said Des.

Korb ground a copious amount of the pepper onto the fritters and dug in. He savored the first bite of fritter and then did the same with a forkful of plantain.

Washing them down with a draught of coffee, Korb licked his lips and returned to the newspapers. He alternated mouthfuls with the turning of the pages.

On page five of the Trib, Korb read carefully a story about the US Attorney's office investigation into Victor Crosetti and mob money laundering. There was a hint that certain non-profits and philanthropists might have been duped into supporting these activities. The notables had not answered any of the reporter's questions, referring him to the law firm of Bryan, Swayze, and Colter. Korb summarized this for Des, who moved to read over Korb's shoulder.

"Think that we should be talking to Crosetti?" asked Des.

"Exactly," said Korb.

"Won't be easy."

"But distinctly possible. Crosetti and I have a history. However, getting to him will require some planning. We'll discuss it tomorrow after Kelan gets back. Even more pressing may be to follow up on Tracey Gould. She is the Administrative Assistant to Jack Colter. It is my feeling that she holds the key to this mystery."

"You think she killed Scanlon?"

Korb carefully put down his fork and knife and half turned toward Des. "Of course it's possible, but more likely she has a strong inkling of who did and why."

Korb turned back to his plate and papers.

Des squinted hard at his boss's back, nodded to himself, and went to begin the kitchen cleanup.

Chapter Twenty-Seven

KELAN SU

I pulled the SUV up to my parents' apartment building on Pratt near Sheridan Rd. They had been living there since I left for college. It was smaller, but much nicer and in a better neighborhood than the Uptown apartment on Winnemac where we had lived during my childhood. The day was sunny, but not too warm. I was five minutes early, but, of course, my folks were already outside waiting for me. I double-parked on the crowded street and got out to help them in.

"*Qīnài de bàbamāmā,*" I said as I hugged my mother and then my father. I caught the familiar aromas of Chinese spices and Old Spice aftershave. My mother held me at arm's length for a moment looking me over. "*Qīnài de nǚér,*" she said, smiling. "It is so good to see you. You are looking well. Mr. Korb is not working you too hard, I hope?" My father looked on smiling slightly more at my mother than at me. Then he patted my shoulder. I almost teared up at this unusual display of tenderness.

Dad helped Mom into the back seat and then came around to the front passenger side and got in. "So, what's going on in your life?" he asked.

They both wanted to hear that I had quit Korb and gone to work at a big law firm and was dating a Chinese boy from a good family. Foolishly, I tried to impress them with, "I'm working on a big industrial espionage case for a Fortune 500 firm. It's about to break. Can't talk about it, but you may be reading about it in the papers soon."

"Interesting," was all he said.

My mother added, "I hope it's not dangerous."

"No, just a lot of surveillance and computer work."

"Are you seeing anyone?" mom asked.

"Well, I did go to dinner and a play at the Theater on the Lake with Ron Sager last night. We had a great time. By the way, Ron sends his regards."

My mother nodded and my father just looked straight ahead. Although Ron wasn't Chinese, when they had met, my parents seemed to like him. They had a long discussion of the changing neighborhoods in Chicago and the suburbs. Ron's Jewish grandparents shared many of the same immigrant experiences as my parents. In fact on his father's side, Ron's grandparents had owned a small grocery store in Albany Park. My mother was now desperate enough to hope I would soon marry anyone nice, even if not Chinese, and have babies.

We were headed for Kaufman's deli in Skokie. I always found it an interesting reversal of stereotypes: Jewish people like Chinese food and Chinese people, at least my folks, like Jewish delicatessen. *Who knew?!*

I was lucky enough to squeeze into a space in the deli's small parking lot on Dempster. I guess the Sunday morning takeout crowd was munching their kosher delicacies at home. We were also very lucky to have a choice of tables as the eclectic mix of chairs sometimes resulted in uncomfortable seating. My folks would have a problem eating comfortably in the plastic

Adirondack chairs. We seated ourselves at a round bistro table that was surrounded by three red, 1950s Naugahyde and chrome kitchen chairs. *How kitsch it is!*

The aromas of fresh baked bread, smoked fish, onion rolls, coffee, and half dill pickles mingled in an enticing way. I picked up a menu. My folks didn't need to as they always ordered the same thing.

The waitress came over. She recognized my parents right away. She greeted them with "Hello, dears. Do you want your usuals?" The usuals were: For my mother, Nova lox and cream cheese on a lightly toasted garlic bagel with all the trimmings–sliced tomato, onion, cucumber rounds, and black olives. For my father, it was a special sandwich called the Trustee– turkey pastrami piled high, a schmear of chopped liver, cole slaw and a dollop of Russian dressing.

"How about you, sweetie?" asked the waitress.

"I'll have the David's CJF." That was smoked sable, tomato, onion, cucumber slices, and veggie cream cheese piled high on a pumpernickel bagel. I wondered what CJF stood for: *Cold Jewish fish? Classic Jewish food? Calories just fade? Can't just finish? Cross-dressing Jewish Female?* I should have asked but didn't want to seem like a greenie.

"Anything to drink?"

"Hot tea all around," I said. Here it was served Russian style in glasses with handles.

The waitress smiled and said, "Be back in a jiff."

"So how have you guys been? How's your blood pressure, Dad?"

"Under control. My doctor was amazed at the results from the Chinese herbal concoction I am taking. Down over twenty points. It's good to see that many of the younger American doctors are open to trying herbal remedies and acupuncture."

"That's great. I was worried as your readings seemed to be climbing in the last year. I hope you're also reducing your work time at the store. How is that new woman you hired working out?"

"Fine," said my mother. "We are able to trust her running the store by herself when we're out. We can take more time off. It's especially nice for me as we can talk to each other about our families during the day. She's joined our Mahjong group too. By the way, she has a very handsome younger brother about your age who's an accountant."

I couldn't help wincing at the last comment. I quickly returned to the subject of health. "Has more time off helped with your back pain, Mom?"

"Yes, that and acupuncture."

"How is Mr. Korb?" asked my dad. "Has he and your colleague Desmond tried any of the Chinese recipes your mother sent?"

"Mr. Korb is fine although busier than he likes. His reputation has grown so that we must turn down a lot of work that's offered. Yes, he and Des have made some of the recipes, but I must say, despite their gourmet cooking credentials, the dishes have never come out as good as when Mom makes them. Of course, I don't tell them that."

My mother chuckled at this. My father said, "That's why we never go out for Chinese food. No one in Chicago can make it as good as your mother."

"What have you heard from our family back in China? How are Aunt Cho and Uncle Wei and my cousins?"

"The business is going well, but the young folks are chafing at being tied to it and also a bit at the more authoritarian turn the government has taken," said my father.

"Is Cousin Huwa still pursuing a fellowship to study in the States?"

"Yes, but it has been confusing with both US and Chinese policies seeming to change on a daily basis. He may contact you to make some inquiries for him."

"Tell him I'll do what I can. I still have some contacts at UChicago and Harvard. Mr. Korb knows many State Department officials. I can ask him for some leads."

We cleaned our plates and leaned back in the chairs contentedly. As we sipped our tea, my mother used one of her pet English phrases. "Well, that was an elegant sufficiency," she said smiling and daintily dabbing at her mouth with a napkin.

When the check came, both my father and I reached for it. He was still very quick from his championship ping-pong days. As we both pulled the check, it tore in half. We looked at each other for a moment and laughed. "Please, let me," I said. He nodded once and handed me his half. I took out my wallet and placed three twenty-dollar bills on the table.

"Why don't we go to a movie, on me?" Dad said. My mother nodded.

"Sounds great. You pick."

My dad suggested *The Green Book* while my mom chimed in with the mother-daughter coming-of-age film *Lady Bird*. I hadn't seen either. "Both sound great."

"Well, Dad, as it's on you, I guess you should pick. *Lady Bird* does sound a bit like a chick flick."

"Check what's playing nearby," he said.

I took out my cell and thumbed in "movie theaters Skokie."

The AMC Regal close by had *Lady Bird* but not *The Green Book*. Not much farther on a multiplex had both. Choosing what would please my mother the most while saving face, my father said, "Let's go to the closest and soonest. After all, it's two chicks to one rooster."

"Well, *Lady Bird* it is and the showtime is in twenty minutes. Perfect," I said turning north on Niles Center Road and we all lapsed into a comfortable silence.

****

It was 4 p.m. and still light and warm when we left the over air-conditioned theater. I think both my parents were a little put off by the movie. The hyper-critical mom struck too close to home as did the financial struggle to pay for elite education. I was uneasy about what was coming next. In fact, I was surprised it hadn't been suggested earlier. During the movie, I was hoping that the weather had taken a turn for the worse.

"We have time to go to the cemetery before it's dark," said my mother with an anxious smile. My father nodded tight-lipped.

"Can we stop at the florist near the entrance? They stay open on Sundays."

I nodded. "Of course."

The grave of my brother, Li Jie was in the nearby Memorial Park Cemetery. He had been tending the store for my parents when two ten-year-old kids tried to hold him up. He joked that he knew karate and his hands were deadly weapons and the kids fled. He chased them out to the street with a twenty-dollar bill in his hand. I think he wanted to give it to them. He was hit by a car ten feet from the curb. The hit-and-run driver was never found. It was the kids who came back to him and yelled for someone to call an ambulance. They stayed with him until it came. I think they knew him and had been to the store before and the robbery business was a little game. They had pegged him correctly–tough and smart, but a marshmallow on the inside.

I was fifteen at the time. After that, I took on all my parents' aspirations for both of us. It was a heavy load that I have never been comfortable with. At times, I blamed him for dying. So my heart was heavy as we approached the cemetery.

Chapter Twenty-Eight

KELAN SU

It was a very emotional weekend, so I was glad to get back to work on Monday. I arrived outside Tracey Gould's Sheridan Road high-rise at four-forty-five p.m. There was a guest space just outside the entrance to the residents' garage–an excellent vantage point to observe her arrival. My database research had given me Gould's address, make of car, and plate number. I wanted to catch her right after she returned home from work. I hoped she wouldn't be burning the midnight oil today. While I waited, I considered my approach. I was pretty sure I had the leverage to make her come to Korb's office. I had the feeling that she was something of a pawn in whatever shenanigans were going on at the institute.

Thoughts of my brother as well as Saturday night and Sunday morning with Ron intruded achingly on my tactical planning. Not entirely unpleasant, but unhelpful to the business at hand. This reverie was interrupted by the appearance of Gould's bronze Cadillac XT4 SUV coming toward the parking garage. I slumped down in the seat as she passed. I'd give her about ten minutes to get up to her apartment on the seventh floor. *She'd have a pretty good view of Lake Michigan at that level,* I thought.

I buzzed her flat from the panel in the covered

entrance portico. There was a camera lens embedded in the panel. I assumed that it would transmit my image to the resident's apartment. A voice crackled over the intercom. "Who is it?"

I looked up and smiled, holding up the business card I had prepared. "I'm Kelan Su from Lakeside Real Estate Management. We're conducting a survey of residents' needs and satisfaction with the maintenance of the building and apartments. I'd like to ask you a few questions. It will only take a few minutes." The door latch went *bzzzzzzz-t* and I entered the building.

When the elevator doors slid open on the seventh floor, I was facing a plaque indicating that 704 was down the hall to my left. I knocked at the door and saw the peephole darken. The door opened partially to the length of the chain. I handed Gould the card. She glanced at it and frowned clearly reluctant to open the door fully.

I gave her a nervous smile trying to look harmless. "Ms. Gould, I am only here to be sure you are finding your residence in our building satisfactory and get any suggestions you have for improving our service. If you don't wish to speak with me, I can leave the questionnaire with you and have my boss pick it up tomorrow. But I'd appreciate it if you would answer the questions for me. My boss gets cranky if I have to send him around to complete a survey."

Gould chuckled. "Bosses are like that."

I had made a connection.

Gould opened the door. I stepped into the vestibule and she ushered me into a bright, airy living room with large windows overlooking the lake. The sun slanted over the water, causing a rippling light show. The room was done in off-white–walls, rugs, and furniture. It was impressive.

"Thanks for letting me in."

"Please, sit down," said Gould, indicating a white cushioned chrome and leather chair facing a sectional sofa and chaise against a windowed wall.

"I was just about to get myself a glass of wine," she added. "Would you like some?"

I grinned. "Anything light and white."

Gould nodded and smiled. She stepped over to a drinks table with a small fridge below and pulled out a stoppered bottle of Kendall-Jackson Chardonnay. The blond woman decanted two good-sized pours of the light amber liquid into stemless glasses. She handed me a glass and took a sip of her own before sitting down on the couch opposite me and leaning back. Gould took another long taste. Kicking her shoes off, the petite, blonde woman curled her legs up under her. "I hope you don't mind if I make myself comfortable. It's been a long day."

I commiserated, feeling guilty about my deception and the pressure I would bring to bear. I took a long draw on the wine, leaning forward and giving the legal secretary a hard-eyed stare. Her brow wrinkled, and she looked puzzled and then alarmed. "I'm not with Lakeside Real Estate, Tracey. I'm investigating the death of Alan Scanlon."

She shook her head convulsively. "I was told that the police didn't seem very interested in pursuing the matter."

"You're well informed. But there are higher authorities than the Skokie police interested in this case."

"W-what do you mean?" she asked, leaning toward me. She put her wine down clumsily, spilling a few drops on the glass coffee table in front of her. She clasped her hands tightly together.

"I work with Marko Korb, of whom you may have heard," I began. "He consults with the FBI, many other law enforcement organizations, and insurance companies. We have been asked to look into the Scanlon murder and the activities of the Shabel Institute. The institute has a key person insurance policy for two million on Scanlon with Continental Marine & Casualty. That's an awful lot for a non-profit." *Thought I would let her think that was my connection for a while. I always liked Hammet's Continental op.*

Gould's hands unclenched. She picked up her glass and leaned back, almost finishing the contents in one quaff. "I'm not really familiar with that policy although I knew it existed."

"You are the secretary of the institute's Board of Directors. Didn't the Board have to approve the policy purchase?"

"Yes, but we more or less acquiesced to Scanlon's and Sessions's opinions of his high value to the lab."

"Okay, Tracey. My boss, who rarely leaves the house, would like you to come and answer some questions." I tried to sound offhand in mentioning this.

"I don't think I can do that. At least without my attorney, Mr. Colter, there."

I pursed my lips and shook my head. "Tracey, we know you were with Scanlon until early in the morning of the day he was killed. That information may well cause the police to reopen their investigation. On the other hand, Mr. Korb just wants to find the killer and is known for his discretion in protecting bystanders. But you need to be open and convince him you are a bystander."

Gould put her face in her hands. I heard a short sob. But when she looked up, her face was composed. "I'll come after work tomorrow, say six-thirty."

"Tracey, I think you should come now. By tomorrow, we must assume you would have contacted Mr. Colter and that whatever you say to us will be scripted. Then you'll need Colter's advice after we contact with the police."

Gould sighed. "All right, let me change my clothes." Her work blouse and skirt were rumpled and creased. She had spilled some wine on them.

"No calls. Convince us of your sincerity."

"I know." She got up a little unsteadily. I rose and made a move to help her, but she shrugged me off and toddled toward her bedroom.

Chapter Twenty-Nine

Once back at the Buxton Place townhouse, Su parked in the drive, opened the door for Gould, and ushered her in through the front door. They ascended to the second floor in the elevator. The woman had been very quiet on the trip to the detective's house. Su hoped that Tracey hadn't decided to stonewall. She knew Korb was an expert at breaking through a target's obduracy, but he would blame her for the extra effort that entailed, particularly if it delayed dinner. Korb was fundamentally lazy.

Gould was gazing with interest at the beautiful, yet utilitarian, townhouse. Su knocked on the door of Korb's office. A gruff "Come" sounded from the interior. Su opened the oak door and stepped to the side to allow Tracey to enter.

As usual, Korb did not rise. He motioned for Gould to sit in the leather armchair placed before the massive desk. Gould sat, pulling her skirt down, crossing her ankles, and clasping her hands in her lap. Her eyelids twitched slightly showing her nervousness.

Korb began graciously. "Thank you for coming. Your help is most appreciated to bring a satisfactory resolution to this sad case. Would you like some tea or coffee?

Gould shook her head.

"Water?"

Gould nodded and Korb looked up at Su, who was still standing by the door. She went to a drinks table under a window at the side of the room and poured water into a crystal goblet from a cut glass pitcher. She picked up a small silver tongs and dropped two cubes from an ice bucket into the goblet. She handed it to Gould, who silently nodded her thanks.

The woman took a sip of the water and turned toward Korb. Her eyes were opened wide, her mouth slightly agape, and her face was pale. Her hands clutched the goblet which she held in her lap. The petite young woman was plainly apprehensive of what was to come.

"One thing very important in a murder investigation is to profile the victim. We know you had both a business and a personal relationship with Dr. Scanlon. That makes you particularly able to inform us of the type of person he was." Korb moved to assure Gould that she was not the target of the investigation, but rather an important asset whom he would go far to protect. But he still let her know he was aware of Gould's affair with Scanlon. This was Korb's velvet glove barely concealing the mailed fist.

Gould leaned forward, jaw clenched, eyes wide intensely focusing on Korb. "W-what would you like me to tell you?"

"First, tell me your impressions of Dr. Scanlon as a scientist and institute head."

Gould pursed her lips and peered into the distance. "Well, I thought he was a brilliant man. He was arrogant and had a very high opinion of his scientific expertise and his managerial skills. As head of the institute, he seemed to run a tight ship. I think the staff was afraid of him. I was too–a little. He didn't seem to hold the directors in high regard either. He was often short with them or very condescending. Jack Colter, of our firm and also an incorporator and director, was the only person he seemed to confide in."

"And as a lover?" Korb could be both the good cop and the bad cop in the same interview. Starting with an avuncular concern for the target and asking open-ended questions but becoming suddenly a hard-eyed interrogator shifting to skewering the target with penetrating queries.

Gould felt the probe viscerally. She couldn't stifle a sob. "He overwhelmed me. He was very attractive and dominating. I couldn't believe he was interested in me. I knew he had been seeing Dr. Sessions for some time. She is gorgeous and brilliant, whereas I am basically a mouse. But I would have done anything he asked. At first, he seemed very attentive and he was a smooth and powerful lover. But I think he was primarily interested in getting me on his side on the Board of Directors and pumping me for information about Jack Colter's dealings with the other board members and benefactors. I got the feeling that he was planning some kind of break with Colter and with the institute."

Korb's fingers went to his temples as he looked down at the desk. He exhaled noisily. "Hmmm," he said mostly to himself. Then he looked up at Gould with an intense stare. "Weren't you worried that the affair with Dr. Scanlon would damage your very beneficial relationship with Colter? And I am referring not just to your employment but also to your niece's and nephew's elite education and your luxurious living conditions."

Gould closed her eyes and her head sagged. "That's how obsessed I was. I would have dropped everything and gone with Alan if he had asked. I was bitterly disappointed when I realized he was going to leave without me."

Korb and Su locked eyes for a moment. Then Korb turned back to Gould. "Tell me everything that happened the night and early morning of Scanlon's murder."

Su leaned forward in her chair and looked at Gould with extreme concentration. Gould pushed back on the arms of the high-backed chair and let her head rest momentarily against the leather. Her eyes were tightly shut and a soft whimper escaped her lips.

Korb continued. "Tracey, we know that you got to the institute about twelve-ten a.m. and left around four a.m. How was your meeting with Scanlon arranged?"

Gould gave a little shiver and seemed to collect herself. "I was working late at the office when Alan called around eleven p.m. He said he had to see me right away. He was trying to work, but he kept thinking of me. I didn't quite believe him but I was flattered and it made me—well, aroused. I told him I could be there in about an hour. 'I'll be waiting,' he said in a low tone."

"Did you go right from the office?"

"Well, I left as soon as I could log out on the computer and put the hard copy files away. I also stopped by my apartment to change into some sexier underwear and top." Gould blushed deeply.

"Did anyone at the office know where you were going?"

"Jack Colter and some of the young associates were there working on the same case that I was. I was organizing and transcribing some of their notes. I had to tell them I was leaving, but I said I wasn't feeling well. I thought a migraine might be coming on. Jack looked at me funny and asked if the telephone call had anything to do with it. I said no but felt his eyes following me as I left his office. I didn't think he suspected anything nor did I think he would care. We'd had a brief fling a few years ago, but I thought it had ended amicably. He was still helping my niece and nephew with their schooling."

"How closely do you work with Jack Colter?"

"I am his administrative assistant. We work closely together. As an incorporator and Secretary of the institute, I am closely involved with Jack's relations with the Board. He had recruited most of the Board members and institute benefactors. He relies on me to keep in touch with them."

Korb gave Su a satisfied glance. Su's brow wrinkled. She wondered what Korb had gleaned from the interview so far.

"Okay, Ms. Gould, let's get back to what happened when you arrived at the institute."

"Well, I was going to check in at the security kiosk as Tamara Grodin. I had rented a car earlier that day. I guess you already know that I used that alias and used a rented car for our rendezvous."

Korb nodded. "Go on."

"I slowed at the kiosk and noticed that the guard wasn't even facing in my direction. She was on her cell phone and had swiveled her chair away from the street side. So I just went ahead. I parked the car on the drive next to the office side of the building so it would not be visible from the street. There is a side entrance and

Alan generally leaves it unlocked when he is expecting me. However, this time it was locked. I knocked softly but no one came to the door. I didn't want to make a loud noise in case it attracted unwanted attention. There was a regular security patrol and possibly someone else was with Alan. I called his office phone from my cell. He didn't answer, but he must have seen the number on his screen because he came to the door and unlocked it. He apologized. I embraced him and kissed him to show I wasn't upset and was ready for love. He led me to his office. We usually used the couch there. Instead, he sat me down and took off his lab coat. He seemed preoccupied. I noticed several documents were on his desk."

"Did you notice what the documents were?"

"No. I was intent on making him forget work and concentrate on me. I stood, kissed him, and fondled him. I started to unbutton his shirt. He lifted me and carried me to the couch at that point. My erotic efforts seemed to have worked. We made love several times. He seemed nerved up and insatiable. But after a couple of hours, he got up, kissed me, and put his clothes back on. He said, 'I've got some lab work I must finish. You can let yourself out when you are ready. Sorry, love.' He kissed me again. I was disappointed, but so tired that I dozed off. I didn't see him again. It was about four a.m. when I let myself out the side door where I came in."

"Did the door lock behind you?"

"I don't think so. At least I didn't hear a click or anything like that."

Su caught Korb's eye with her raised finger. "Tracey, did you see or hear anyone else around the institute or laboratory while you were there?"

Gould blanched and hesitated before responding. "Well, at one point I thought I heard a door close somewhere nearby in the building. But I was absorbed in passionate sex and neither listened for nor cared about outside noises."

"Did you see other cars near the building?"

"Just Alan's car."

Korb resumed the questioning. "Earlier you said that Dr. Scanlon had been pumping you for information about Jack Colter's dealings and that you felt Scanlon might be making some kind of break with the institute. What information did you give Scanlon? Can you specify what made you feel he was contemplating separating himself from the institute?"

"He was asking me what I knew about how Jack Colter had recruited the directors and contributors, what were their backgrounds, and whether they had strong international connections. He also wanted to know what had convinced these people to get involved with the institute."

"And what did you tell him?"

"I couldn't tell him too much. I said he should ask Jack, Colter that is. I did think that there were several foreign investors and several associated with pharmaceuticals. I had my suspicions about some of them being shady, but I didn't tell him that."

"Why did you suspect they were shady?"

"Well, Jack was always very close-mouthed about them. But I just naturally suspected foreign law firms and drug companies of being involved in illegal off-shore operations. I didn't have any specific information though."

Korb raised an eyebrow and looked at Su. She nodded. The wordless communication indicated their mutual interest in enlisting Gould in obtaining further information.

"Tracey," asked Su, "would you be willing to send us any information on the directors and benefactors that are in the firm's files?"

Gould had turned her head toward Su. She dropped her gaze to her hands and shook her head. "I can't do that. It's too much of a breach of confidentiality. Many of the directors and contributors are clients of the law firm in other matters besides the institute. I'd definitely lose my job and put Jack and the firm in ethical jeopardy. And my kids, uh, niece and nephew, would lose his support."

Su gave Gould a sympathetic smile. "I understand. For our purposes of protecting you in the murder case, it is probably better that you don't know details about any illicit activities. Could you at least tell us where those files are kept?"

Gould grimaced. "All I know is that Jack has a safe-like file cabinet in his office. It opens with a keypad. He is the only one with the code. He seems to go to it whenever any question comes up about the institute." After several seconds, she said, "Can I go now?" She was clearly weary of the grilling.

"In a moment," said Korb with a reassuring smile. "Did Scanlon ask you about the key person insurance policy when he was pumping you?"

"Oh, yeah. That was another thing that made me think he was planning to leave. He asked whether the policy paid off if the key person left of his own accord or was fired. I told him it was essentially a life insurance policy payable to the institute. Only the death or physical incapacity of the key person triggered it. He seemed a bit taken aback at that."

"Did you tell anyone at the institute or your law firm about Scanlon's questions or your feeling that he was planning a departure?"

"I did mention the insurance question to Jack Colter to be sure I had given Scanlon the correct information."

Korb gave her a slight seated bow. "Ms. Gould, thank you so much for your cooperation with our investigation and answering our questions. As I promised, we will do everything we can to shield you from any embarrassment or legal entanglement as a result of our work. Ms. Su will take you home." Korb nodded to Su.

She stepped to Gould's side and patted her shoulder. Gould rose a little shakily but steadied herself and allowed Su to guide her out the door.

When the door closed behind them, Korb massaged his temples. He mused, *Interesting, but not the whole story. We need to find out more about the directors and benefactors of the institute, particularly Crosetti, and we need to suss out where Jack Colter fits into this.* Slowly, a sly smile parted his lips and widened his bulldog face. *I have an idea how to do each of these things.*

Chapter Thirty

When Su returned, she went immediately to Korb's office. He wasn't there. Of course, the large detective was in the kitchen looking over Des's shoulder while he prepared dinner.

Korb edged up close to Des's left arm, craning his neck to see what Des was stirring. Des shrugged him off.

"Boss, the antipasto is on the table. Please, go and eat that while I finish preparing the truffle pasta dish. It will be ready shortly. I'll bring it right in. You'll want to eat it while it is still hot. Then I'll cook the veal piccata. It won't take long either. I can't get all this done correctly with you crowding me."

Korb sighed. But the thought of the delicacies to come quickly buoyed his spirits. He clapped Des on the back and headed to the dining table. He couldn't resist a last comment, however. "Be sure the pasta is al dente, Desmond."

Des shook his head.

Su whispered, "Nice work" to Des before she followed Korb to the table. She was anxious to get her assignment from Korb, but realized it would have to wait until the dinner was eaten. Korb wouldn't let business interfere with his appetite.

****

Korb leaned back in his chair with a wide, satisfied

smile. He wiped his lips and his chin daintily with his damask napkin and crumpled the soiled serviette next to his plate. He rasped out a guttural "mmmm" which served as high praise for the meal. Then he clasped his hands under his nose and leaned forward looking from Su to Des.

"Des, I would like you to check on Ms. Gould's niece's and nephew's birth certificates. Find out who the father is. We need to get more information on the involvement of Colter, Crosetti, and some of the other so-called benefactors. I have some plans for this. I think you'll find them interesting. I welcome your feedback on them as well since you'll both be involved. Let me explain."

Chapter Thirty-One

KELAN SU

Korb's explanation of his plans was bare bones. Des and I would have to improvise. For Colter's office, I was thinking of checking out the cleaning crew and seeing if I could insinuate myself into that group. I was going to stake out the office building and see what cleaning companies were involved and what the crew looked like. For Crosetti, Korb's plan was complex. It entailed getting into the Crosetti's Club Victor security system. Fortunately, with his SAS training, Des was an expert on circumventing cybersecurity.

My mind was racing as I headed down the Drive to Chicago Avenue and then west to Ogden Avenue, one of the few diagonal streets in the Chicago grid. *How would I make my entrance into Colter's office?*

It was still light on Tuesday at 5 p.m. after a dreary day as I parked on the top floor of a garage across from the Bryan, Swayze and Colter law office. The firm had two floors in the glass and steel high-rise Tyng building on West Lake Street. There was a coffee shop on the ground floor of the garage structure that faced the entrance of the office tower. Seemed like a good vantage point for the stakeout. Office workers were starting to stream out of the building. Many headed across the street to the parking garage. Others went down the street to a local pub. I saw some Uber and

Lyft pickups as well. I noticed Tracey Gould leaving and crossing the street. I ducked my head down hoping she wouldn't look into the coffee shop. She didn't.

I hung out at the cafe until dark, tapping on my computer as if I were finishing my day's work or FaceTiming with friends. At 8 p.m., there were still a few lights showing on the fourteenth and fifteenth floors where the law firm's offices were. I decided to go up to my car, which was parked facing the building. I didn't want to attract too much attention as the coffee shop had emptied out.

I checked emails on my cell and then listened to music. There was a folk festival on WDCB. At nine-fifteen, I was singing along with Buffy Sainte-Marie, "Seeds of Brotherhood" when two school buses painted white pulled in front of the law firm's building. On the side of the bus was printed "Daisy's Janitorial and Commercial Cleaning Service" with the slogan "Always Fresh as a" followed by the logo of a yellow Shasta daisy. From the front door of each bus, about twenty figures exited, mostly women, clad in white coveralls with bright yellow bandanas or do rags on their heads. *Right in line with the logo—cute.* Each cleaner had an ID badge on a lanyard around her neck. Probably with a memory chip that unlocked office doors. From the rear exits of the buses, ramps were pulled down and several cleaning carts were wheeled out.

I raced down the corner stairs of the garage. As I exited, the buses were already pulling away. My guess was the company offices were not far and they would be picking up another load of cleaners for a nearby office building. I crossed the street diagonally, surreptitiously videoing the gaggle of cleaners. I heard banter in Mexican Spanish as the workers ambled into the building in groups. Once someone swiped their badge, several of the workers entered together. I could see security guards eyeing them very casually. The shapeless coveralls and hidden hair didn't attract much interest from the guards.

I continued down the sidewalk as if heading toward the bar down the street. I concentrated on my cell phone, keeping my head down. Dressed in business attire and running shoes, I looked like so many of the young professionals who hung out at the bar after work. I was checking the address and phone number of Daisy's. As I thought, it was not far, an address on North Halsted. By the time I reached the door of the bar, the cleaners were out of sight. I crossed back to the other side of the street to my car.

I listened to music until, at about eleven-thirty p.m., the buses returned. The cleaners were apparently already in the lobby. They filed out and into the buses, again without much scrutiny. They were nowhere near as animated as they had been on arrival. Their heads were down and their shoulders sagged. Fatigue was written on their faces. The carts were delayed as the guards checked them for anything that might have been taken from the offices. I took more video. When the buses finally pulled away, at eleven-fifty, I headed home.

****

I didn't sleep well that night, thinking of the things I had to do that day. I had two case reports to write. One was a major industrial espionage case in which I had worked undercover at the victim company. Korb had correctly surmised how a highly complex textile coating formula, which only the plant manager had access to, was reconstructed from invoices and inventory accounts by a chemical purchasing agent for the company. The purchaser then peddled the information to a rival company. Korb had also negotiated an outstanding confidential settlement between the companies, ceasing the illicit use of the formula, transferring another important formula from the perpetrator to the victim, along with cash in the tens of millions of dollars. The settlement prevented any negative publicity for the spying company as well as keeping several executives and the purchasing agent out of jail.

The other report was for the Polish Central Anti-corruption Bureau concerning the tracing of a fugitive witness to a major opioid distribution syndicate involving Russian mobsters and several Warsaw city government officials. The difficulty here was not locating the witness but separating him from the "protection" of Russian mob affiliates in Chicago.

Next, I called Daisy's Janitorial and Cleaning Service, saying I was Tracey Gould from a law firm in the Tyng building. I wanted to find out on what days the cleanings were scheduled. Not wanting to let on that I didn't know the regular days, I asked about the schedule for the Thanksgiving holiday week. I was told that the regular Thursday cleaning would be canceled for Thanksgiving, but the Saturday cleaning would take place. So it seemed that the Tyng building cleaning schedule was Tuesday, Thursday, and Saturday nights.

My chores included shopping for white coveralls, a bright yellow do-rag and skin darkening makeup for transforming myself into a Filipino janitorial worker. With the darkened skin and my Asian features, I might pass as Filipino which would explain my non-Mexican Spanish accent. I printed up and laminated a Daisy's ID Badge and hung it on a lanyard. It couldn't be swiped successfully, but, from what I'd seen, I could slide through the entrance and the office doors, with someone else. Fortunately, my mother would not let me leave home before I learned excellent sewing skills. I was able to embroider a reasonable facsimile of the Daisy's logo on the coveralls.

Finally, I texted an order for two dozen croissants to the coffee shop across from the law firm's offices. These were to be delivered to the fifteenth floor the next morning.

Chapter Thirty-Two

KELAN SU

By 7 p.m. Thursday evening, my face, neck, and hands were darkened. The coveralls were on up to my waist and I had my yellow do-rag. I had left the top parts of the outfit down so I could cruise by Daisy's and check out whether I could slip onto one of the buses. I figured there would be some sort of role-taking as the cleaners were allowed onto the buses. I wanted to avoid that.

Sure enough, there was someone with a clipboard at the front door of each bus. They checked off each person who entered. However, I noticed that no one was observing the people who were loading the cleaning carts through the back entrances. Presumably, they had already checked in.

I quickly parked out of sight. I pulled up and slipped my arms into the top of the coveralls, zipped them up, and put on my yellow headdress. I was able to make it to the rear of one of the buses before all the carts were loaded. I helped push one up the ramp and quickly took a seat at the rear of the bus. My seatmate only glanced at me and nodded. So far so good.

Fortunately, the woman next to me was not talkative. She had a drawn and tired look. Conversation would be too much of an effort. Best to save one's energy for the intensive two plus hours of cleaning that lay ahead. I put my head down as if I were trying to catch forty winks before our janitorial ordeal. I maintained that pose for the fifteen-minute ride until the bus stopped in front of the Tyng building and my neighbor tapped me on the shoulder and said, "*Vamanos.*" She jerked her head up and toward the aisle.

It was all women on my bus. I followed them out and attached myself to a group of three who were heading toward the door. This was the moment of truth. One of the women swiped her card and pulled the door open for the rest of the group. The last of our group held the door open for the next gaggle of Daisy's. As we entered, we all held up our ID badges which the guards hardly glanced at. *Whew! I was in. Next test would be getting access to Colter's office.*

The law firm had offices on the fourteenth and fifteenth floors. I assumed that the partners would have the upper floor. One of the women swiped her ID card on the elevator and I followed a group into the car. It stopped at almost every floor and one or two cleaners got out. I figured that there were two cleaners per floor and the carts would probably come up with the freight elevator at the end of the hall. I noticed that no one had punched the twelve button. I reached over and pushed it and stepped back. There was no thirteen, a traditional superstition. I could get out at twelve without attracting attention and make my way up to fifteen by the stairs. I would only have to climb two flights.

When the door opened, I said, "*Fuera, por favor.*" edging past the ladies in front of me and nodding to them. I looked both ways down the corridor and headed to the stairs without being noticed.

At fifteen I saw that a cleaning cart had been delivered. One of the office doors was open. Someone had already arrived to clean on this floor.

The open door was two down from Colter's office. His door was locked. I looked down the corridor again. Another woman was exiting the elevator. She walked toward the cleaning cart. She didn't see me as she was texting on her cell. I stepped toward her and cleared my throat. She looked up. "*Hola. Puedes ayudarme?*" I explained that I was a trainee and they sent me up to her floor to help. She shrugged. "*Ven conmigo.*"

Her ID tag read Isabela Suarez. She looked to be about nineteen or twenty. She was overly made up–heavy on the mascara and bright red lipstick. She also had layered on the foundation, trying to hide acne but mostly worsening it. Piercings with metal studs adorned her nose and ears. A wisp of dark curly hair had escaped her yellow bandana. She continued tapping on her cell as we walked to the entrance to a conference room.

Pointing me toward the open door, she yelled over her shoulder to another woman in the room. "*Bisoño, Marta,*" she called and turned back to the hallway.

Marta turned and looked me over, shaking her head. She was an older woman in her fifties. Something about her radiated authority and I found myself straightening to attention.

"What's your name?" she asked in barely accented English.

"Ana Malbina."

"You're not Latina. Where are you from?"

"The Philippines."

"You speak Spanish?"

"*Si.*"

She continued in rapid Spanish. "I thought there was little Spanish spoken in the Philippines these days."

I responded in Spanish. "In Manila, I went to a school run by Spanish Catholic nuns and when we arrived in Chicago, we lived in Pilsen." While a German/Czech neighborhood beginning early in the twentieth century, Pilsen became the home for many of Chicago's Mexican-American families.

"Have you done office cleaning work before?"

"No. But I have been a maid in a hotel."

She walked up to me. Her head was level with my chest and she was looking at the logo on my coveralls. She exhaled heavily and looked up at me. "You're not with Daisy's. What are you here for?"

I sighed. My considerable efforts were for naught. "I thought I had done a good job on the logo."

The woman laughed. "That's the least of it. Your Spanish is too academic. They don't send trainees straight to an office job. And you don't look either Filipino or like someone who needed to take a cleaning job."

"Wonderful! What are you going to do?"

"Well, first I would like you to answer the question of why you are here."

I hesitated. *Should I lie, tell the whole or partial truth?* This woman was too shrewd to buy a lie. "Okay. I'm a detective. I'm investigating the murder of a client of this law firm. I need to get some information about possible criminal activities he and his lawyer, Jack Colter, were involved in."

Marta rubbed her forehead. "You're not a cop?"

"No. Private. I work for Marko Korb. Have you heard of him?"

"No. I don't know. If I turn you in, the security guards will know you just waltzed in with the crew. They'll start checking IDs closely and want security checks on the cleaners. Many of the girls here can't stand that–illegals, or criminal records. If I don't turn you in and you're busted, Daisy will lose the contract for sure—even if they only discover later you were here. We all need this job. Daisy's rep will be trashed."

I tried to look sympathetic. "Look, let me into Colter's office for twenty minutes. I won't take anything and I'll leave everything as it was. No one will know I was there. I'll leave with the gang and disappear. I'll even clean the office for you." I hoped the last didn't sound too flip. "Otherwise, I'll have to say I am doing a security check of the building and found out how easy it was to enter under cover of a Daisy crew."

Marta rolled her eyes and grimaced. She nodded. "Twenty minutes. I'll do the cleaning. And stay away from Isabela. She's not as unconscious as she looks."

Marta led me down to Colter's office and swiped her card. She entered first and looked around. I think she memorized how everything was arranged so she could restore it if necessary. She motioned with her head for me to enter. The office was at the corner of the building with windows looking south and east. A fantastic view: the downtown skyline, Lake Point Tower, former Sears Towers, Grant Park, and the lake. *Don't get sidetracked, Kelan.*

Before she turned to leave, she commanded, "Twenty minutes. Take nothing. No damage." Each point was emphasized with a finger jabbed in my direction.

I nodded. "*Accuerdo*." The woman gave me one hard look, turned and exited, closing the door firmly behind her.

I was in. I slipped on latex gloves.

Turning on the bright recessed lights, I studied the office deciding what to do first. There was a large teak desk with several drawers none of which appeared to be locked. The desktop was bare except for a large flat-screen monitor. A matching teak credenza cum file cabinet was set along the length of one wall. It was locked but had easily pickable drawers. In a corner, behind and to the left of the desk was a Honeywell keypad document safe. My guess was that the document safe held what would be of most interest.

I was happy to note that there were some croissant crumbs on the rug behind the desk. Buttery fingers would make for clearer prints on the keypad. I zipped down the coveralls and slid the tiny spray bottle of luminescent fingerprint powder from a pants pocket. I misted the keypad of the safe. Turning off the overhead lighting, I pulled the mini forensic light source from another pocket. I set it at UV390 and flicked the switch. When I aimed it at the keypad, the powder glowed green with the heaviest concentration on the numbers one, six, eight, and nine.

I pocketed my tools and turned the lights on. Now for the order. I tried ascending and descending. No luck. It looked like the nine had the least powder. For no very good reason, I assumed that was the last number. I tried one, eight, six, nine. Nope. If this didn't work, I could try my rare earth magnet on the safe's solenoid.

Six, one, eight, nine. The lock clicked and I pulled the door open. A quick glance at my phone told me I had used up five minutes.

There was a standing file drawer in the safe. I fingered through the tabs. There it was—labeled Shabel Institute. I quickly spread sheets out on the deck and snapped pix with my phone of lists of benefactors and directors, articles of incorporation and by-laws, key person insurance policy and personnel files for Scanlon, Sessions and Vrdoliak. At the back of the folder was a copy of Scanlon's will and a document assigning the patent to the institute. The will had a hand-printed sticky note attached stating only "Change of beneficiary requested." I returned the papers to the file and the file to the safe. I closed the door and the lock clicked into place. With my pocket handkerchief, I wiped off the keypad.

My phone showed I had five minutes left before the return of Marta. My picks and 'loids were in a wallet strapped under my shirt. I could work on the credenza, but there wasn't really enough time. I turned to the unlocked desk drawers. In the center drawer was a laptop that was also connected to the desktop monitor. No time to use the fingerprint powder on that. The left-hand drawers were actually one large file drawer. None of the files looked interesting. In the top right drawer, I found a photograph of Scanlon and Tracey Gould embracing amorously and a sticky note that had some cryptic notations. I quickly snapped these.

Marta came in just as I was closing the drawer. She was early. She looked at me. "One of the lawyers is coming up. You'd better get moving. Go into the bathroom and start cleaning toilets. You can always duck into a stall if anyone comes in."

I nodded. She slowly examined the room. She jerked her head toward the door to tell me to leave. She told me I should leave the building with the whole crew to avoid attracting attention. "After the toilets, you can vacuum the hallway. Keep your head down. The noise should prevent anyone from talking to you. If anybody gets inquisitive, send them to me."

I grimaced, but said "Okay," recognizing the wisdom of her strategy. As I entered the bathroom, a very tall man in a leather jacket and tweed cap exited the elevator. I peeked out of the bathroom door as he went into Jack Colter's office. *Whew! If I got out in the clear, I owed Marta big time!*

Chapter Thirty-Three

KELAN SU

I was beat. I had ended up cleaning several toilets and vacuuming the hall. Dragging myself through the lobby made me blend in well with the other exhausted workers.

There was a checker on the bus. Marta again came to my rescue. She pushed me ahead of her telling the clipboard man, "*Es novata. Llegó tarde. Yo me ocupé de ella.*" The man nodded, giving Marta a thumbs-up. She was clearly a personage in this group.

By the time I got home, it was after midnight. No point in looking for Korb. I let myself in and tiptoed to my room. I'd shower in the morning. I stripped down to my underwear and collapsed on top of the covers. I slept like the dead, not stirring until my phone alarm started buzzing at seven-thirty in the morning.

I thought I was in very good shape, but kneeling and scrubbing toilets had strained muscles that I didn't even know I had. There was time for a workout and a shower before breakfast and briefing Korb. I quickly pulled on a tank top, Spandex bicycle shorts, three-inch socks and my soft Capezio dance sneakers–all black.

I ran down the stairs to the basement gym. Opening the door, I reached for the switches turning on the fans and the lights. The lights dazzled my eyes so I turned off the spots. Needed coffee before I could take brightness. After twenty minutes on the stationary bike, it would be a core workout for me today.

In an hour, I had worked up a good sweat. I toweled off ineffectively, turned off the lights, but left the fans on. I draped the towel around my neck and ran up the stairs two at a time.

After a long, hot shower, I carefully reviewed the pix of the documents and photograph I had taken at Colter's office. I felt ready to face Korb and make my report. I sent him my finds with an email saying I could meet him in the office at his convenience. I didn't expect a quick response. Korb was not an early riser and it was only 10 a.m. I was surprised by the immediate reply requesting my presence stat.

On the way to Korb's office, I looked into the kitchen. With a sigh of relief, I saw a French press three-quarters full of coffee and it was still hot!! I poured myself a large mugful. On my way out of the kitchen, I nearly lost my heavenly brew when Des brushed past me.

"Mornin'," he said.

"Thanks for the coffee," I said.

"When you're done with Korb, there'll be one of my special omelets awaiting you, m'lady. I know you haven't had time for breakfast. Then you can fill me in on your exploits." He smiled conspiratorially.

I sighed from the bottom of my gut. "Oh, Des, you are da man."

* * * *

Korb was sitting at his desk, still in bright yellow pajamas. The dishes from his breakfast had been pushed to one side and his laptop was open. The printer was ch-chinging away already, printing out the documents I had photographed.

"I see you had a busy night," he said.

"Yeah, I actually cleaned four toilets. I found a lot of crap."

"Spare me the punishment."

Well, so much for banter with the boss.

"Your pictures look interesting. Did you leave any trace of your work?"

"You mean besides spotlessly clean bathroom fixtures? Not if the woman who helped me keeps her mouth shut. She isn't likely to say anything as it would jeopardize her job and her colleagues many of whom are undocumented."

The printer stopped churning out pages. Korb swiveled his specially constructed, extra-large, padded desk chair and gathered up the sheets. He had skimmed them on his computer but much preferred looking at hard copies and making marginal notes. "The benefactor list is interesting. Two county commissioners and a defrocked, former Illinois Secretary of State as well as some major donors to the political campaigns of certain incumbents including State's Attorney McGovern. May well explain why the charges against Ms. Merino were unexpectedly dropped and the whole case swept under the rug."

"Right, Chief, that and the fact that several of the other benefactors with somewhat shady finances wouldn't want to have their links to Crosetti's laundering scheme exposed," I added.

Only a momentary frown acknowledged that Korb had resigned himself to the use of monikers like 'boss,' 'chief,' and 'guv' by his associates.

"And the patent assignment to the institute and

draft no-fee licensing agreement should make settling Golda's lawsuit easier. At least she'll be getting what she wants. But I'm glad that Attorney Dain is dragging her feet on finally quashing it. The prospect of litigation may still come in handy to our investigation," said Korb.

He raised an eyebrow and asked, "What do you make of the will?"

"It certainly gives Sessions a strong motive for the killing, especially given the note suggesting that Scanlon wanted to make some changes."

"The corporate documents seem to put the financial decision-making in the hands of Scanlon, Vrdoliak, and Colter. To the extent that Colter could count on the support of Tracey Gould, he might have an edge in those decisions. And, of course, Vrdoliak has long been connected with Crosetti. That's where Desmond has come up with much of the money laundering mechanism. The benefactors, including Crosetti, make tax deductible contributions to a non-profit. The institute purchases its equipment, services, consumables and the rent for the premises at inflated prices from companies held by the benefactors, of course with many layers of subsidiaries and affiliates shielding the contributors' ownership."

So far there didn't seem much narrowing down of the suspects. "Boss, what about that cryptic note with abbreviations and numbers?"

"You mean you haven't already sussed that out?" Korb's eyes widened.

I shook my head thinking that this would at least give Korb a chance to massage his ego.

"Well, let's see," said Korb with a condescending

look down his nose. "A. S., hmmm, how about Alan Scanlon?" He closed his eyes and nodded.

"Y-Yess." I said, leaning forward to better absorb his wisdom.

"B.C.I.," said Korb very slowly, emphasizing each letter with a knuckle rap on his desk. "Aha! Bank of the Cayman Islands." He grinned from ear to ear. "The ten digits–an account number. One million–an account balance. And the next, of course, the password."

"Whew, that means that Colter had suspicions about Scanlon skimming from the institute and possibly planning to jump ship. If Colter knew, who else would know? Who would he tell or who told him?"

"Good questions, Kelan. My guess is that Vrdoliak and Crosetti knew, but we'll have to verify that. We'll do that this coming weekend. But then there is the photograph of Tracey Gould and Scanlon embracing. That throws a very different light on motivation and who might know of Scanlon's activities."

"Has any of this advanced our investigation? It seems as if we still have the "usual suspects." I was disappointed. I thought my finds might give Korb a 'Eureka moment' for which he was justly famous. But if he had come to any conclusions, he wasn't sharing them.

Chapter Thirty-Four

KELAN SU

Des and I sat in front of Korb's desk feeling a bit like students sent to the principal's office.

"We need to talk to Crosetti," said Korb flatly. Des and I looked at each other, concerned frowns on our faces. Crosetti was a ruthless killer even if his specialty was financial crime.

"Boss, is it really necessary? He's really dangerous and he won't want to see us. How do we even know how to get to him?" I asked plaintively.

"Don't you think I have a plan?" asked Korb with a slight smile on his face. "My only question is whether we should meet him at his home or his office."

Des looked down and shook his head. I gaped at Korb.

"Both are well guarded, but his house is in Oak Park with no structures nearby. Club Victor, Crosetti's headquarters, is in Uptown, near Lawrence and Broadway, and there are several large buildings overlooking it. I think that's our best bet."

"How do we get in?" I asked.

"Why, we walk in, of course," said Korb, widening his eyes in mock surprise.

"But he's well-guarded." I looked at Des for support. He was silent, knitting his brows.

"And what if Crosetti did or contracted out the

183

murder?"

"Look, Kelan, if that is the case, he may well want to bring us under his control. What Crosetti wants most is to stay out of any inquiry regarding the Scanlon murder and the institute. I will offer him that if he will help us. I think he'll see me and hear what I have to say. The problem will be getting out after that," said Korb, looking hard at Des. Des nodded. Korb's plan seemed to be dawning on him. I was skeptical.

"Okay, here's the plan," said Korb, leaning forward over his desk.

Chapter Thirty-Five

KELAN SU

The long, varnished mahogany bar at Club Victor was packed two deep as usual for a Saturday night. The crowd was noisy and festive. The clientele was a mix of prosperous-looking, young professionals with a substantial smattering of older, overweight, puffy-faced men rasping ungrammatically at each other while leering at every unattached female—that is to say, yuppies and capos, the connecting and the connected.

I was standing in line at the reception desk with people giving their names in hopes of a table. The harried hostess was taking their names and checking her monitor for seating and point of sale info. Just then, the hubbub increased sharply starting at the far end of the bar. A tall, well-built, and nattily dressed black man was staggering drunkenly along the bar, bumping into a number of the drinkers. Several cursed him. A woman used a racist slur. One of the capos grabbed him momentarily, but the drunk shook him off and continued his erratic journey toward the exit. When he was just in front of me next to the reception desk, he lost his balance and crashed into the hostess knocking over and disconnecting her monitor. "Sorry," he slurred, righted himself, and reeled toward the door.

I helped the hostess pick up her equipment, giving her a tight-lipped, sympathetic smile. She thanked me and rebooted her machine. As she typed in the password, I etched it into my memory which, if I do say so myself, is extremely good.

As I returned to my place in the line, my phone rang. I swiped 'answer' and listened for a moment. When I hung up, I shook my head.

I looked glumly at the hostess. "I have to leave. You can take me off the list."

I stepped out of the line and left the club. People behind me in the line smiled as they moved up. The valet took my ticket and went off to fetch my SUV. When it arrived, the valet got out and held the door for me. I gave him a five-buck tip. He smiled and inclined his head in thanks, closing the door for me after I got in. I smiled at him through the window.

When I had driven three blocks, a head popped up in my rearview mirror. It wore a wide, brilliant, toothy smile. "Des, how did you squeeze yourself in on the floor back there?"

"It wasn't easy and my good suit is a mess."

"Your drunk act was great. You should have heard the comments from the crowd. Racial stereotypes are alive and well in Chicago. What a surprise!!"

"I'm used to it. Did you get the password?"

"Of course. Will that be enough for you to access the club's security system?"

"Certainly. Everything intersects. Reservations, seating, point of sale, inventory, and in case there is pilferage, security. *Voila!* Once I'm in reservations, I'm on the bus and I have the requisite transfers. See anything on the menu or being served that you liked? I can get recipes too. Not to worry. We be good."

I bit my lower lip, shook my head, and concentrated on my driving.

Chapter Thirty-Six

KELAN SU

From his previous contact with the mobster, Korb
knew Crosetti as a man of regular habits. Every Sunday
he was driven to his mother's grave at Saint Boniface
Cemetery in Uptown after an early morning mass at
Saint Giles near his home in Oak Park. After placing
fresh flowers on the grave, he and two bodyguards
walked a block and a half down the street to his office
on the second floor of Club Victor and held court for
his crew and "clients." The Club's bar and restaurant
were closed on Sunday. Korb had sent me out to verify
the morning routine.

Crosetti and two bodyguards entered at the rear
door and climbed the back stairs to the office. There
would already be a substantial security contingent at the
Club who had checked the building for stowaways and
anything that might be a threat to Crosetti. There were
two heavily armed men stationed at the front and back
doors, one in each of the two rooms on the ground floor
and two in the anteroom to his office.

Those who wished to see the mobster would go to
the rear entrance, be searched, and then wait for the
boss's summons. They would then be escorted through
the entire first floor eyed by the security men, and
mount by the front stairs to the anteroom where they
would again be frisked. Security cameras were placed

at strategic positions in the rooms and passages as well as at the exterior entrances. There were monitors in the upstairs anteroom and Crosetti's office. Bulletproof, tinted glass windows faced both the street and alley sides of the building. At 1 p.m. the crime boss ordered food from one of the local restaurants for himself and his minions.

Korb had scheduled our arrival for two-thirty p.m., following the lunch brought to the Club. He may have hoped that this would lead to post-prandial torpor, mellowing, and making careless the assembled mobsters. I had my doubts.

On a Sunday it was easy to find a parking space on the street. There was a large bank and some other closed businesses, so there was little traffic, vehicular or pedestrian. Fortunately, we did not have to walk far to the rear alley entrance of the Club. Even so, Korb was huffing and puffing by the time we reached it. He took off his homburg, pulled out a large silk handkerchief, and wiped sweat from his forehead. We surveyed the dingy surroundings. Across the alley opposite the rear of the club was a large building that seemed to be some kind of sports arena. It was closed and dark. Korb looked at me and I nodded slightly. He raised his walking stick and rapped at the heavy metal door of the Club. No response. He rapped again harder, making the door clang resoundingly. A peephole in the door slid open and two heavy-lidded eyes took us in.

"Yeah." The eyes narrowed.

"Sir, would you please tell Mr. Crosetti that Marko Korb and his associate would like to see him? We have an important and interesting proposition to put to him– one that may help him out of his predicament concerning the murder of Alan Scanlon."

The peephole slammed shut.

I noticed that a camera mounted above the door had slightly shifted position to better focus on both of us. Was that a sign of interest? I tapped Korb's shoulder and gave a slight lift of my head to indicate the device. We waited, Korb leaning heavily on his cane; me, shifting my weight from foot to foot.

Five minutes stretched to ten. I shook my head. "I guess he's not interested."

Korb frowned at me. "It's all part of the power game. I've dealt with him before. He knows what I can do. He'll see us," Korb whispered.

Then turning from the door, Korb declared in a loud voice, "Well, I can't stand here all day. Let's go."

The peephole slid open again. Different eyes appeared. "The boss'll see ya." We could hear several deadbolts disengaging. The door swung open. The eyes belonged to a hulking, bull-necked, bald man in shirt sleeves. His tie was loosened and his collar unbuttoned. He had a large caliber automatic in his shoulder holster. Two other equally large men held assault rifles at the ready.

The doorman said, "You know the drill. Empty your pockets, bend over, put your hands on that pool table, and spread your legs."

I didn't relish being frisked by these thugs. But it goes with the job and I figured they were being watched on CCTV. They were fast and efficient. No lingering at intimate places. Korb was not as easy. He was so fat that, even with feet apart, his inner thighs showed no separation, and a frisk would not reveal if something were hidden in one of the many folds of his blubber.

They supplemented their search with a metal detector. Korb grunted as he straightened up and groped for his walking stick which he had placed on the table with his pocket contents.

The doorman grabbed it first. "Whoa! You're not bringing that in."

Korb glared at the man. "Sir, if I cannot use my walking stick, you and your men will have to carry me up the stairs."

The man sullenly eyed Korb's girth. He turned to one of the security cameras and said only, "Mr. Crosetti?" I noticed that he had an earbud. Apparently, Crosetti OK'd the cane. The doorman handed it to Korb.

He led us past the two pool tables and two poker tables, prodding us ahead toward the bar. The remnants of lunch, some poker chips, and decks of cards were on the poker table. The empty barroom had a sad aura without the buzz of conversation, the tinkle of glasses, and the ripple of laughter. At the front stairs, the man motioned for us to mount. He signaled to another heavily armed thug at the top. I let Korb go first. He caned his way slowly upstairs, one hand on the banister. A security man on the second floor grimaced with impatience at our slow progress. When he reached the landing, Korb stepped to the side and leaned heavily over his cane, two hands on its crouching lion handle. He was breathing hard. When I was on the last stair, Korb emitted a loud, phlegmy cough. The guards turned toward him. I made the last step up. As the guard turned, Korb's bulk hid me and the doorman from the view of the others. I slipped the cell I had palmed while my hands were on the pool table downstairs into the security man's pocket. One should never be out of touch with the outside world.

One of the guards grabbed my arm and led me toward a desk. Another frisk? I was close enough to the man to hear a curt "Bring 'em in now" from his earbud. The office door opened and the security men pushed us toward the door. Or rather, tried to push Korb, whose sixth of a ton was the proverbial immovable object. He gave a scornful look to the putative pusher, stood up straight, and waddled in. I jerked my arm away from the thug who had grasped it and followed my boss.

Chapter Thirty-Seven

KELAN SU

Korb and I entered a paneled office. The wood was dark and heavily lacquered much like the bar downstairs. There was a dark oriental rug on the floor. At a large mahogany desk sat Crosetti. He was leaning back in a cordovan leather chair. Large, curtained windows were behind him. His wide, rugged, and florid face wore a slightly curious frown. Two henchmen standing on either side of his desk stiffened to alert.

Korb stopped in front of the desk and nodded to Crosetti. The gangster just stared. After a long moment, he rasped, "Okay. What's the proposition?"

It was Korb's turn to stare silently. He waited longer than Crosetti had before saying, "You might offer us a seat. I have walked further and climbed more stairs than I have in many years."

Crosetti sighed and turned to the burly thug on his right. Motioning with his head, he said, "The chairs over there." The underling shuffled over to the wall and picked up two padded armchairs as if they were matchsticks. He set them down in front of his boss's desk. Korb inclined his head toward the thug and lowered his massive derriere onto the chair cautiously. I took the other chair.

Korb leaned forward on his walking stick and looked hard at Crosetti. "Victor, we know that the

Shabel Institute is part of a money laundering scheme that you and your financial associates have been using for some time. We also know that there is federal interest in the arrangement and the participants. The feds would also like to link you to the Scanlon murder and they may well be able to. Furthermore, your silent partners in the scheme, the apparently legitimate donors to the institute, must be frantic that the investigation will expose their mob connections." Korb paused to be sure that this was sinking in. I was worried that the mobster wasn't buying it, but a momentary widening of Crosetti's eyes gave away his interest.

"By the way, did you know that Scanlon had a numbered account in the Cayman's with a seven-figure balance and that he was planning to leave for foreign shores?"

Crosetti smirked. "I figured he was skimmin'. A cost of doin' my kind of business. It keeps 'em loyal. I'd been happy to see him go somewhere unreachable and with no extradition."

"Did you know that Colter knew about Scanlon's game?"

"No, and I could care less."

"I don't think you committed or ordered the murder," Korb continued. "But I think your anger at the lawsuit prompted by the patent and its disastrous effect on your clever money laundering scheme was known to whoever killed Scanlon. It may have been a factor in the killer's motivation."

Korb paused. Crosetti shrugged and shook his head slowly.

Korb leaned forward. "That is why I want you to hire me to find Scanlon's murderer. The fee will be reasonable and I will identify the murderer without exposing the institute's other activities. I will need to know who at the institute was privy to the money laundering and to whom you made your anger known. Rest assured that without your agreement, I will pursue this matter but have no obligation to keep the institute's dealings out of the limelight."

Crosetti leaned forward and put his balled fists on the desk. He spat out his words directly into Korb's face. "I don't need no fuckin' help from you, you tub of lard. I'm gonna shut down the operation. The locals won't bother me and the feds are clueless. I should waste you and your assistant to stop you from prying into my affairs."

I scanned the room for anything that might allow us to escape.

Korb seemed unfazed. He leaned back, cocking his head to the right. "Balderdash!" He loved that word. He went on, "Now, Victor, there is no need for insults. I'm trying to help. You know that I am a man of my word and very good at what I do. You remember I kept your name out of the opioid case I handled when I first arrived in Chicago. The feds were looking at you on that one too. When I handed them the Russians, they lost interest in you."

"Yeah, that was then and this is now. I can handle the feds. It's you that I want out of my business," said Crosetti.

This was not looking good.

"I am deeply hurt that you see it that way," said Korb, shaking his head and giving Crosetti a sad smile. "I see that it is necessary to convince you of my resources and ability to carry out this investigation."

"And how do you expect to do that?" said the mobster with a chuckle.

There was a rap at the door of the office. Crosetti exhaled and yelled, "Yeah!" The heavy

that had ushered us into the office came in with a bewildered look on his face. He was holding the phone I had slipped into his pocket. "Mr. Crosetti, there is a call for you on this phone and I don't know how I even got this phone. But the guy says it's important."

"What are you talking about?" said Crosetti. "I don't want no calls now."

"B-but the guy said if you don't want to talk, just take a look at your monitors."

Crosetti scowled but couldn't help looking up at the monitor on the wall to the left of his desk. It was replaying the scene in the office of the last five minutes. Then the scene shifted to a gloved hand holding a cell phone. Korb said to the thug holding the planted phone, "Put it on speaker." Crosetti nodded.

A British accent with a West Indian lilt, spoke. "I have established a link and am in control of your security system and have recorded all of the recent events in your office. I strongly urge you to accede to Mr. Korb's requests and to wipe from your mind any idea of harming Mr. Korb or his associate. For a further demonstration of Mr. Korb's position, I am asking all of your men to move away from the metal door at the rear of your building and stay by the side walls."

The monitor screen now focused on Crosetti's face. "Please instruct your men to do as I say. It will prevent harm to them," said the caller.

Crosetti nodded. "Clear away from the rear door," he growled.

A ringing explosion could be heard as an armor-piercing, fifty caliber slug ripped through the peephole cover and made a hole in the floor of the downstairs poolroom. Shouts could be heard from the men in that room.

"If Mr. Korb and Ms. Su do not leave your building safely, no one else will. I have an equally skilled colleague also armed with a scoped Barrett sniper rifle covering the front door. Furthermore, if anything should happen to Mr. Korb or his associates in the future, the information I have gleaned from your security system will be turned over to federal and state law enforcement. You dig, man?" The phone beeped terminating the call.

Crosetti and his henchmen gaped at each other and at Korb. Suddenly, the room seemed stifling and smelled of the acrid odor of sweat. Des's jive closing words seemed to encapsulate the confidence in the impact of the demonstration. It was clearly very effective. I was impressed although not completely sanguine about our safety.

Korb broke the stunned silence. "Now, Victor, I hate violence. Why don't you just hire me and answer my questions? Any information you give me is confidential. I will keep my promise to find the killer and do everything in my power to disassociate the murder from your activities. Oh, you can deduct the cost of repairs to your door and floor from my fee."

Crosetti scowled and then glared at Korb and nodded.

I had been holding my breath. I let it out.

Chapter Thirty-Eight

KELAN SU

We left Club Victor through the damaged rear door. Crosetti's thugs were trying to look tough and nonchalant, but their wide-open, staring eyes following us out communicated shock at having been so easily intimidated by the fat man, the slim woman, and the unseen snipers. The detectives walked down the alley covered by Des who was perched at the window of an upper floor of the arena across the way. The armored town car was parked on the street at the end of the alleyway. I helped Korb into the front passenger seat and stowed his cane on the rear seat. Before entering on the driver's side, I looked up again at Club Victor and the conveniently situated arena. I sniffed and shook my head amazed that we were still alive.

Leaving Uptown, I headed north and west beginning a roundabout and evasive route back to our Gold Coast abode so as not to be followed or ambushed on the way, and to give Des and his colleague time to sweep and secure the house.

As I pulled the town car into the short driveway off tree-lined Buxton Place, the garage door slid open silently. From a window over the garage, Des gave us a thumbs-up.

I sighed and my shoulders relaxed as the garage door closed behind the car.

Korb noticed. "Were you worried?" he asked with a wry smile.

"Yessir!"

"Don't forget I know Crosetti. He is vicious but pragmatic. Strangely, he's also a man of his word. He'll stick to our agreement and even pay us."

I tried to hide my skepticism but it was probably evident in my worried expression.

Des met us at the door. Korb nodded to him. High praise from the boss. I clapped Des on the back. "Up, up, mesohn."

Des's teeth sparkled in his grin. "Maad, girl." He winked.

"Meet *mi esé, Gig*. He was covering the front door from the roof of the bank across the street." Des turned and indicated a broad, solid man of average height. His dark hair was gathered in a man bun and he had a moustache connecting to a goatee. He wore military boots, cargo shorts, and a sleeveless sweatshirt showing off wildly tattooed and muscled arms. He nodded but did not speak. "*Hola*," I said. "*Muchas gracias, Gig*," said Korb. Gig again nodded silently.

"Guv, I've taken two thousand dollars out of our cash reserve to pay Gig. Do you authorize the payment?"

"Certainly," said Korb. "His assistance was most valuable as to be expected from your colleagues, Desmond."

Des handed Gig an envelope, squeezed his arm, and said, "*Gracias, amigo, todavía te debo. Hasta la próxima.*"

Gig shoved the envelope into a pocket of his cargo shorts, gave Des a quick smile, and turned to go. Des followed to show him out. Korb headed to his bedroom suite, smiling to himself over a good day's work.

When Des returned, I asked, "He doesn't talk much, does he?"

Des frowned. "Don't need to, Kelan. His actions speak for him."

I felt sheepish. "Sorry. I guess you know him well."

"The bravest man I know. I watched him pull three wounded soldiers out of a firing position that was being overrun. He was hit three times in the process."

Des paused, looking into the distance. "I was one of those three guys."

I shivered not knowing what to say. The best I could do was to reach up and touch Des on the shoulder as I left the kitchen. It had been a long day.

****

As I reached my rooms on the third floor, I received a text from Korb. "A very productive day. No need for anyone to cook tonight. Let's order from The Avenue. Give Des your choices. Briefing at six p.m. Dinner at seven-thirty p.m."

The Avenue was Korb's favorite Chicago eatery and the usual go-to for delivery. Although the menu changed regularly, we three knew it well and had our favorites. I checked the menu on my phone and noted some changes. My favorites were still there. I sent Des a text message choosing the roasted asparagus on sourdough with goat's milk cheese and pickled lemons as my appetizer and then the grilled baby carrots with roasted beet muhammara, smoked trout roe, and charmoula. Korb insisted on choosing the dessert, most often a cheese plate, and the wines. My mouth watered at the thought, not that Des's creations were any less fantastic and Korb could wield a mean whisk himself.

I showered quickly and dressed in jeans and a soft tee. Didn't bother with shoes or socks, loving the feel of my bare feet on the wood floors and soft carpeting. This would be an evening at home without guests, so I reveled in comfort.

Des had on loose cargo shorts and a Lashing Dogs T-shirt, beige canvas boat shoes, and no socks. Korb was dressed informally, at least for him, in a gray pin-stripe suit, light blue dress shirt with collar buttoned but no tie, gray socks, and black tassel loafers. He eyed our casual comfort with a disdainful look but resisted commenting. We had gathered in the conference room rather than Korb's office. That too was more informal than usual for briefings. I took Korb's slightly looser approach to be a recognition of the tenseness of the successful day's work.

Korb looked from me to Des. He nodded and smiled. "Okay. We need to follow up on today's success with some hard work. Desmond, you'll be checking on a foreign account that I believe was Scanlon's. Note dates and amounts of transactions and any information indicating who the person accessing the account might be. Also, see what you can do with the Shabel Institute security system. Kelan will brief you on her meeting with a tech from the company that installed and maintained the Shabel system."

Des nodded, smiling. "Aye, Guv."

Korb continued. "I will talk to Attorney Dain. I want her to request a meeting here with our principal suspects and Ms. Merino ostensibly to discuss ending the lawsuit. Kelan, you'll deliver the messages about the meeting personally to our prime suspects. I want you to ask certain questions when you deliver the meeting notice."

Korb gave me the queries I would put to Colter, Sessions, Gould, Vrdoliak, Karlakis, and Crosetti and suggested my line of approach to assure their attendance at the meeting. It was going to be a very busy week. We discussed our assignments until the ring of the doorbell announced the arrival of our dinners.

The aromas coming from the restaurant containers took my mind off the forthcoming chores. Des had ordered the chorizo stuffed dates with bacon and a piquillo pepper-tomato sauce for his appetizer and the chicken shwarma with a vegetable mezze, hummus, olives, fermented chili sauce, and garlic toum. Korb had chosen chicken liver crostini with rhubarb mustarda and mint followed by slow-roasted pork shoulder with piri piri broth, bulgar, clams, and smoked yogurt. *Oooh*. I hoped for sharing, but didn't think Korb would part with any of his.

As I suspected, Korb ordered a cheese platter for dessert with Sequatchie Cove Walden cow's milk cheese and a crown finish Caves carpenter's wheel goat cheese. There were two bottles each of *Château Peyrassol La Croix des Templiers Rosé* and a Moroccan red, *La Ferme Rouge Terres Rouge Côtes des Romani*. I would definitely be getting a late start on my assignment tomorrow morning.

Chapter Thirty-Nine

KELAN SU

My first stop was Colter's office. It was strange entering the building in my business civvies and at daytime, so no one said, "Weren't you here cleaning up last week?" Might have been different if Marta had been there. That woman was sharp.

My appointment was for ten a.m. I glided in at nine-fifty-eight and told the security guard I was to see Colter. He checked his roster, called up to the law firm's reception desk, and motioned me through to the elevators. "Stop at the reception desk on fourteen. They'll direct you to Colter's office on fifteen." I thanked him.

When I stepped out of the elevator, the reception desk was directly opposite. I gave my name to the redhead, bespectacled receptionist sitting behind a high walnut paneled counter, almost like a judge's bench. I supposed that the effect was intended to instill the notion that one was entering the inner sanctum of the law. I was more impressed by the bank of windows behind the receptionist that looked out at Lake Michigan currently roiled by rolling breakers.

The young woman looked down at her monitor and picked up her phone. "Ms. Su is here for Mr. Colter," she reported, nodding at the response. "Ms. Su, please take the elevator on the left to fifteen. An intern will meet you there and show you to Mr. Colter's office."

I smiled. "Thank you." The woman smiled back and inclined her head. "You're entirely welcome," she said.

When the elevator door opened, a tall, gangly young man was waiting. "Ms. Su?" he asked with raised brows that made his wire-rim glasses bounce on his nose. I nodded and he introduced himself as Jeffrey Armistad.

I looked both ways down the hall, frowning to make it clear to anyone around that I was unfamiliar with the office layout. Jeffrey motioned to the left and said, "This way, please." I followed him.

He ushered me down the hall I had vacuumed four days earlier. His diffident knock on Colter's door was answered with a brusque, "Come in." Jeffrey opened the door and stood aside for me to enter.

Colter looked up from behind his teak desk and scowled. "Ms. Su," he said, nodding toward one of three brown leather chairs facing him.

"I think I'll stand, Mr. Colter. I'm just delivering a message on behalf of Attorney Dain and her client, Golda Merino."

Colter nodded.

"We would like you to attend a meeting with Ms. Dain and her client to firm up a settlement of the lawsuit."

Colter leaned forward and sneered. "I would prefer to have Attorney Dain contact me directly with an offer. My clients have always considered the lawsuit frivolous."

"Mr. Colter, we have it on good authority that your benefactors are very interested in a settlement that will end the lawsuit and would be exceedingly unhappy if you were to hinder it."

Colter exhaled loudly and sank back in his chair. It hadn't taken much to deflate him. He clearly knew that Crosetti and other heavy hitters were 'insisting' on a quick settlement. "Well, you know I must protect the interests of my clients, particularly the institute."

"We would also ask that you bring along to the meeting Ms. Gould and several documents that might aid in the settlement: the corporate articles and by-laws, any documents relating to the feraxia gene and test patent applications, Dr. Scanlon's will, key person insurance policies, and any documents relating to Dr. Scanlon's and the institute's finances. If we have to subpoena them, they would become part of the public record. I don't think you or the benefactors would like that."

Colter shook his head and then nodded, looking down at his desk. "When and where is the meeting?"

I told him. Colter nodded with a grim expression on his face.

"Thank you, sir. That's all I've come to say. No need to have anyone show me out. I know the way." I wondered if that might raise the suspicion that I had been in his office before and seen the documents he was to bring. I wouldn't mind if it did. It might convince him to cooperate fully.

****

I should have been on my way to the institute to talk to Sessions and Vrdoliak, but I noticed a familiar-looking face watching me from a non-descript silver Toyota RAV4. I got into my car, took my time getting started while scoping the Toyota's license number and calling Des to check it. I edged away from the curb slowly. Didn't want him to lose me. When I was halfway down the block, the Toyota pulled out.

I headed toward the Drive and took it going north. The RAV4 followed, keeping two cars between us. I stuck to the speed limit and exited leisurely at Hollywood, turning south on Sheridan Road.

Des buzzed me. "S'up?" I said.

"Some joy. The ride is registered to Walter Karlakis."

"Whooeeee, just who I need to get a line on. Thanks, my man."

When I got to Winona, I made a quick left turn without signaling. I wanted the shadow to think I was trying to shake him off. Midway down the 900 block, I made another abrupt turn to the right, down an alley and sped up. The tail turned and accelerated, narrowing the distance between us. I slammed on the brakes, jerking the wheel to the left. With screeching tires, the silver Toyota tried to avoid a collision. Narrowly missing my vehicle's rear left rear quarter while veering to the right, the RAV4 slammed into the dumpster on the right. I slid out the door drawing and clicking the button on my tactical baton. There was a satisfying "whhhip" as it expanded to its full twenty-two-inch length.

The man on the passenger side seemed unconscious and, in any case, his door was blocked by the wall of a building. The skinny, bearded thug I had recognized was struggling out of the driver's side. He was dazed but had drawn a gun. I jerked his door fully open and brought the baton down hard on his gun hand. He groaned and the gun dropped to the concrete. I kicked it under the car. I grabbed the injured hand, yanked him out of the car, and twisted his arm behind him, pushing him down over the hood. He screamed.

"Name?" I asked curtly. He groaned again. I saw a bulge in his back pocket and pulled out his wallet. Flipping it open, I saw the name Delbert Froman. It wasn't familiar, but his face on the license was. I dug into his bruised hand with my thumb. He groaned again. "Name?" I repeated. "And don't con me, I'll know it when I hear it."

He exhaled sharply. "Jerry Koogan."

"Riiiight. I was sure I had met you before. West Madison, one of the 'salesmen' for the industrial laundry that was extorting money from restaurants and bars in the area. I was there with the cops who busted the operation. I hear you're working for Karlakis now. Still in the laundering business, I see."

Koogan grunted. "What do you want?"

"The question is what does Karlakis want?"

"He wants his name out of this whole Shabel mess."

"And he told you to do what to achieve this result, Jerry?"

"Nothin' much, just rough you up and scare you some to convince Korb to lay off." He looked down and shook his head.

"Do I seem scared?"

He humphed and laid his head on the hood.

"Okay. You go back and tell your boss that if he wants to minimize his exposure, he'd better attend a meeting at Korb's office. I'll send him the details. By the way, Crosetti will be there. He's hired us."

I pulled him up from the hood and spun him

around to face me. "Get in your car and see if it will run. You should probably get your partner to a hospital. You too. By the way, can you drive one-handed?"

He grimaced and swore, trying to flex his right hand. I pushed him down on the car seat and he swung his legs in. I stepped away. He reached across with his left hand and shifted awkwardly to reverse. The car bucked back a few feet. He straightened the wheels, shifted to drive, and peeled out down the alley.

I shook my head watching them go. I picked up the gun that was under the car. I'd give it to Ron. He might be able to connect it to other crimes.

I was a bit insulted that Karlakis had sent a couple of dufuses to brace me. He could certainly afford better.

I telephoned Korb immediately relating my encounter with Karlakis's thugs. His response was that Karlakis was owed a personal visit to encourage him to come to our meeting.

Chapter Forty

KELAN SU

The disreputable financier was a slippery character, constantly on the move to hinder the tracking efforts of the IRS, SEC, DOJ, Interpol, and defrauded investors. Des would use his considerable technological savvy and Korb both his international law enforcement and underworld contacts to locate the peripatetic hustler and pin him down for my visit.

Meanwhile, I was to extend a personal invitation to Stanley Vrdoliak even though Crosetti would most likely require his presence. The real purpose would be to learn more about Scanlon's skimming activities and who might also be aware of them. I also hoped to encounter Dr. Sessions and get a better sense of her knowledge of Scanlon's financial diddling and who else was aware of it.

I backed out of the alley onto Winona and then north on Sheridan Road. I would go up to Howard and pick up Skokie Boulevard to the institute. Noon was approaching. The sun was beating down and I caught occasional glimpses of the sparkling water of the lake to my right. The traffic was surprisingly light. As Sheridan turned briefly west, I passed the classic tower of the former Mundelein College, now part of Loyola University.

When I got to the institute, I was glad to see

Carolyn Macready at her desk. I asked her how she was doing. She asked me about the investigation.

"We are progressing, not a little bit thanks to you."

She gave me a brilliant smile, clearly thrilled to have contributed to a murder inquiry.

"Have you heard anything about the future of the genomics lab?"

"Well, I am getting my resume together. I have a line on another position if the institute closes. I do hear that's a real possibility. In truth, I'll be happy to go. However, if Dr. Sessions becomes the director, I would stay to help her."

"I'm sorry to say that closing seems likely."

Carolyn pursed her lips and nodded.

"I'm here to see Mr. Vrdoliak if he's here. I don't have an appointment but I am sure he'll see me. Tell him it is to inform him of important developments in our investigation. It'll only take a few minutes. Also, is Dr. Sessions here?"

"Yes, Mr. Vrdoliak is here. He's been fielding almost constant calls from the board and contributors. He should be glad to have more on your progress. Dr. Sessions is due back in half an hour."

"Good. Please tell Mr. Vrdoliak that I'd like to see him, and when Dr. Sessions returns, ask her if I may fill her in on our work. Thanks."

Carolyn nodded, picked up the phone and punched an intercom button. When the CFO answered, she gave him my message. Putting down the receiver, Carolyn waved me in. "Second door on the left," she said.

When I found the door labeled Stanley M. Vrdoliak, Chief Financial Officer, I knocked. "Please, come in, Ms. Su," came a slightly muffled response. I entered. Vrdoliak smiled. He seemed pleased to see me. He was well aware that Korb and I had the support of his real boss, Crosetti.

"Please sit down. I understand that you want to brief me on the progress of your investigation."

I sat down in a padded armchair in front of his cleared, polished walnut desk. "Yes, only partly. That and I wish to convey Mr. Korb's invitation to a full briefing session at our office. Mr. Crosetti will also be there and he has probably already informed you of the meeting," I said, adding the last to emphasize the requirement that he attend.

"It's underlined on my calendar," he said with no expression. "Anything more?" Now he sounded a touch impatient.

"Well, yes. Mr. Korb and I would like to know a few things. For example, how long have you known about Dr. Scanlon's financial misdealings?"

Vrdoliak hmmphed. "To start with, he was careful. He followed old Mayor Daley's precept: A little at a time adds up. A lot at once ends in jail. However, after the feraxia discovery, he upped his take considerably. It was pretty clear he was planning a quick exit. In fact, we were happy for it. We even arranged to get him to assign the patent rights for a substantial sum to speed him on his way as well as to put an end to the lawsuit."

I was astounded by his frankness. It was clear that Crosetti had instructed him to cooperate with us.

"How much for the assignment?"

"Half a mil."

"Whew!"

"Small potatoes."

I nodded and smiled knowingly. "Who else at the

institute knew that Scanlon was planning to abscond with a substantial nest egg?"

Vrdoliak puckered his lips and looked up. He was definitely trying to make me think his answer was speculative. I doubted it.

"I discussed it with Jack Colter who is the institute's attorney as well as a board member. The Board Secretary, Tracey Gould, and the other board members were consulted on the assignment payoff. I think Elaine Sessions was involved in one of those discussions. That's all I can think of."

Or all he's willing to tell me, I thought. It sounded like a dismissal. I got up and looked down at Vrdoliak.

"One final question. Do you have all of the access criteria and codes for managing the security system, including disabling it and erasing recorded data?"

"I think you already know the answer to that. I wasn't at the institute after my work day ended at four-thirty p.m. on Friday before the murder. I was home all night with my wife and children. Check with them."

"I will." My hard look slowly morphed into a tight smile. "Thank you, Mr. Vrdoliak. I'll see you at the briefing."

He nodded solemnly.

I turned sharply and exited the office.

****

I walked down the hallway and noted that Elaine Sessions's office was two doors down toward reception. I stopped in front of her door and raised my hand to knock. She wasn't due for another twenty minutes, but I thought I would try anyway. After two sharp raps, I heard a muffled, "Yes."

When Sessions looked up and saw me, her face

twisted into a momentary grimace. She quickly regained her composure and said, "Hello, Ms. Su. Carolyn told me that you wanted to see me. Please sit down." She motioned to a chair in front of her glass and chrome desk. She closed the lid of her laptop and blanked her desktop screen.

"I was just talking to Mr. Vrdoliak and decided to try your office without bothering Ms. Macready." I gave her a slight smile. "How are things going without Dr. Scanlon?"

"Most things are on hold. I'm getting the message that the institute is probably going to shut down. I'm winding up what I can." Raising her eyebrows in an inquiring look, she asked, "And how is your investigation going?"

"Ah, yes. That is what I am here to talk with you about. Mr. Korb has scheduled a meeting with the principals in this case and he would like you to be there. It will be at our office. You've been there. We are heading toward resolution. I think your situation and prospects will improve once the shadow of Scanlon's murder is off your back."

"Maybe, but it's the kind of shadow that never totally dissipates."

I nodded. "Your presence at the meeting is essential. I will text you the details."

Sessions shook her head. "I'm not sure I care to be involved in this investigation any further."

"You don't have any real chance to avoid further participation. In the first place, you are one of the few people who have all the access criteria for the lab and the management of the security system. In the second place, you are a major beneficiary of Scanlon's will although he had indicated he wanted to change it. Did you know that?"

"When we were still together, he did mention that he would take care of me if anything happened to him. He didn't tell me anything specific."

"We have also found CCTV footage from the Bank of America branch on Oakton that has you jogging past and going toward the entrance to the park where the lab is situated at three-forty-five a.m. on the morning of the murder. Your return trip past the bank clocks in at five-ten. It puts you in the vicinity of the murder at the appropriate time."

Sessions pursed her lips and exhaled. "I jog that way every morning. That doesn't prove anything."

"That may be, but on other mornings you pass that point much later and are usually caught returning in the opposite direction within twenty-five minutes. Look, we don't think you killed Scanlon, but this information doesn't look good for you. You could have driven Scanlon's car to where it was found and resumed your run. That would account for the timing. We need to know if you were near the lab and saw anything. If you are not going to cooperate, we'll have to turn this evidence over to the cops."

"Okay, okay. I was jogging near the lab. In fact, I found a spot by the perimeter fence where I could see the side and front doors of the institute. I guess I was still infatuated and curious to find out who had replaced me with Scanlon. We used to meet at the lab in the wee hours.

"I saw Tracey Gould bolt out of the side door and drive off, leaving the door open. I then saw an arm in a black leather jacket with a patch and white, silver and green trim on it reach out and close the door quietly. The hand was gloved. I don't know whose arm it was, but I doubt it was Scanlon's. It looked like a motorcycle jacket. He wouldn't be wearing a jacket or leather gloves if he was at the lab at night. Anyway, he's not the biker type. I never entered the park or the lab that night."

"What time was it when you saw Gould?"

"I don't know. Maybe around four a.m. I didn't have a watch and didn't check my phone."

"How much longer did you stay?"

"I'd say another forty-five minutes. I didn't see anything else."

"And you never entered inside the perimeter fence or the institute building?"

"Yes. I told you that," responded Sessions with a deep frown.

I was not convinced but this wasn't the time to press. Anyway, Korb was better at it.

"Okay. Just be at the meeting and be ready to tell your story again."

Sessions' mouth opened as if to voice a protest, but she nodded instead. I turned on my heel and walked out.

Chapter Forty-One

KELAN SU

Now to tackle Karlakis. I needed Des to give me a location. Karlakis moved about with residences all over the country and all over the world. But I was hoping that he would want to stay close to what was going on at the institute. My phone gave out the "warm greeting" ringtone set up for Des.

"What've you got for me on Karlakis?"

"Okay. My canvass of local airports indicated that a Karlakis private jet landed at the Chicago Executive Airport in Wheeling two days ago. The plane is still there. It was met by a limo that picked up three passengers and took them to a house on south Kenilworth in Oak Park. The house is owned by one of Karlakis's companies. That's your best bet."

"Sounds good to me. My encounter with Karlakis's thugs earlier made me think he's in the Chicago area. I'll let you know how it goes. Thanks."

"Aye, girl, as to that I'll have your back. You won't see me. I'll be a ghost. But if you sense trouble, just say 'phantom.'"

I didn't think there'd be trouble as Karlakis should know by now that we were working with Crosetti. But Des's backup was always reassuring.

I headed south on I-94. When I got to the address Des had given me, I was facing a classic Oak Park estate, probably built at the turn of the 20th Century by one of the famous Oak Park architects other than Frank Lloyd Wright. Brown brick, mullioned windows, striped gables. There were Wright homes not far away.

I drove up to the wrought-iron gate and got out. There was an intercom next to it. I buzzed. A crackly voice said, "Yes, who is it?"

"Kelan Su from Marko Korb to see Mr. Karlakis."

"What do you want?"

"I am not prepared to discuss my purpose in coming with anyone but Mr. Karlakis. You might be familiar with what happened to the last goons who tried to ask me questions. I think Mr. Karlakis wants to see me."

There was a low grunt and then silence. I glanced down the drive and then behind me toward the street and saw no one. There was a buzz and the gate started to slide open. I hurried back to the car, wanting to get through before someone changed their mind. The tree-lined drive made an S-curve before opening up to a vast lawn at the rear of which stood the Georgian mansion. The structure lacked the large expanses of glass of Wright buildings and I doubted it would have a minimalist, open interior, but it was still magnificent. I counted three floors and three chimneys.

Two large men came out the front door and stood to either side watching me approach. One of them motioned to a parking area at the right side of the drive. I nodded and headed to it.

The other man opened my door and said curtly, "Follow me." He shut the door of the car behind me. I clicked the lock and waited for him to lead the way.

The other man was holding the front door. He fell

in behind us after closing the door. No one spoke. We were in a marble-tiled entry hall. We passed to the right of a marble staircase that was hung with portraits of Georgian era nobles and generals, none of which, I was sure, were Karlakis's kin. We crossed over huge oriental carpets that covered the floors of a dark paneled reception area and a dining room filled with heavy period furniture.

One of the men stepped up to a door at the right rear of the dining room and knocked. I heard a muffled, but curt, "Come." The man opened the door and ushered me in. "Ms. Su," he announced.

Karlakis sat behind a large oak desk in a red leather padded office chair. "Please sit down," he said. He had a slight accent that I couldn't quite place, but definitely eastern European. He looked me over appreciatively as I sat in a high-backed wing chair. It made me glad I was tall. Otherwise, I would have looked like a child in the massive piece of furniture.

Karlakis gave me a slight smile, raised an eyebrow, and nodded. "It's been reported to me that you are a hard person to get rid of. So I thought I had better see what you wanted."

I returned his nod and slight smile. "It takes better minions than you sent to make me back down. And in that, I don't hold a candle to my boss, Marko Korb."

Karlakis nodded again. "I'll remember that next time," he said, trying to sound ominous. "I understand you have a message for me."

"Yes. Mr. Korb would like you to attend a meeting in which the settlement of the lawsuit against the institute will be discussed. Mr. Korb will also reveal the murderer of Alan Scanlon. He knows that you have a considerable interest in the institute that Scanlon headed and that you would like to keep that interest out of the public eye. That is why he strongly urges you to attend this gathering."

Karlakis rubbed his forehead. "Is Korb promising to keep my connection with the institute under wraps?"

"We make no promises. But we will do our best, provided that you are not an accomplice to the murder. You know that Korb's best is damned good. He has already convinced Vincent Crosetti to come and I can add Crosetti's sincere hope that you will join him there."

The mention of Crosetti was the clincher. It caused Karlakis to draw in a deep breath. He exhaled a raspy "Okay." I gave him the details.

He must have signaled one of his henchmen from his desk because I heard the door open. Karlakis said dismissively, "Leon will show you out." I remained silent as I stood to leave. Another large man filled the doorway. As I walked toward him, he stepped to the side to allow my egress.

Chapter Forty-Two

Korb was at his desk sipping a Chateau Guiraud sauterne and munching on a slice of crusty baguette slathered with *paté de foie gras*. His eyes were half closed and his lips slightly parted as he swallowed a bite of the luxurious snack. He seized a small *cornichon* and gingerly bit into the tangy delight. He nodded approvingly.

A slight frown appeared on Korb's face as his ecstasy was interrupted by Su and Des entering the office. He took one more draft of the sauterne, emptying the flute. He acknowledged his colleagues' presence by cocking his head, indicating they should sit.

"What have you to report, Kelan?"

Su gave a thorough recount of her day. Korb listened with eyes half closed. When she got to the part about Sessions and her wee hours observation of the lab, Korb's eyes opened wide. "'A motorcycle jacket' she said?"

"Like one, but she saw nothing else," Su sounded skeptical.

Des watched the interplay of his colleagues with interest. "You think that's significant, Guv?"

Su cut in. "In truth, I think Sessions was lying about whether she entered the industrial park. I can't put my finger on exactly why I think so."

Korb nodded. "We'll take her statement with a grain of salt. Do we have video of Sessions from the bank cameras? I'll need to look at those closely. Des, will you check registrations, motorcycle clubs, and look for any reference to a motorcycle connected to anyone in the case?"

"Righto, sir."

Korb turned to Su. "Kelan, check out the Oakton Community College area for a sign of a motorcycle. Canvass houses nearby to see if anyone saw or heard a cycle around the time of the murder. If you can find any of the college library users who were there late that night, ask if they noticed a cycle."

Su frowned and gave her head a quick shake.

"You think that is a waste of time and effort," said Korb with a slight smile. He knew that as unconvinced as Kelan might be, she would follow his orders with her usual thoroughness.

"If that's what you want, boss." Su placed emphasis on the "boss" knowing that would irritate Korb. Des rolled his eyes. Korb let these reactions pass without comment.

Su nodded to Des. "Let's get to work."

****

After a long day, they reassembled in Korb's office late the next afternoon. Korb put down the book he was reading and removed his glasses. "Reports?"

Su and Des nodded. Des inclined his head toward Su, putting her on the spot.

She cleared her throat. "I spent much of last night and all morning at the Community College library and the surrounding neighborhood."

"Any joy there?" asked Korb.

"Yes and no. The library is open twenty-four-seven. I found one student who was there during the early morning hours on the day of the murder and who noticed two motorcycles parked in the lot when she left at four-thirty a.m. She knew the owner of one of the cycles. He worked the midnight to eight a.m. shift at the library. The other cycle was unknown to her. It did seem like a newer, small one. It was dark but she could make out green and white trim. She didn't think there were any other students in the library when she left. She knows nothing about makes or models. When the library worker left at eight a.m., the unrecognized motorcycle was gone. He confirmed that there was no one else in the library when my student informant left. He wasn't familiar with any other motorcyclist who frequented the library."

Korb pursed his lips and frowned. "Anything else?"

"I was able to find a nearby insomniac who heard a loud flapping engine start-up that could have been a cycle around five a.m., give or take twenty minutes. That's all I was able to get."

"Well, the timing is certainly interesting. If we can tie the motorcycle to someone in our case, we could have a breakthrough. Desmond, what have you got?"

Des had been concentrating on Su's account. His forehead rested on his steepled hands. When Korb turned to him, he lifted his head slowly. He frowned and exhaled deeply. "I am really not sure what I found."

"Let's have your best take on it," said Korb, lifting one eyebrow.

"I checked motorcycle, motorbike, and motorscooter registrations in Illinois. There were two interesting listings, but I doubt they are helpful."

"Let me be the judge of that," said Korb firmly.

"There was a motorcycle purchase and registration to Alan Scanlon last June. In early July, that cycle was transferred by deed of gift to a Michael Scanlon. At the time, Michael was fourteen years old and living with his mother, Jennifer Bridger, at an address in Waukegan. According to my investigative databases, they have since moved to St. Louis. I have that address. Jennifer Bridger was briefly Jennifer Scanlon fifteen years ago. Guv, she was married to Alan Scanlon for a year and a half."

"That is *verrrry* interesting, Desmond. We will need to talk to her and her son. But did you find any other of our suspects with a motorcycle? Have you checked motorcycle registrations outside of Illinois?"

"Not yet."

"Well, that can wait. Desmond, I want you to turn up everything you can on the Bridger woman and her son. Be quick because I want Kelan to have the information when she interviews them."

"Interview? In St. Louis?" Su's eyes widened but then narrowed as she saw the wisdom in this. "We could have another suspect."

"Another two," corrected Korb. "Make your flight arrangements for Tuesday early afternoon. That should allow Desmond enough time to brief you."

Des looked at the ceiling and cocked his head to the side. Fortunately, Korb did not see this. Su stifled a laugh.

"Willard with PlaneJockeys?" she asked.

"As usual, if he's available. He'll have to wait for you at the airport, probably St. Louis Downtown

Airport. I'd like you back by Friday. That should give you two days to locate and interrogate Bridger and her son and possibly run down any local leads. And keep me posted regularly."

"Well, Super Su will really need her running shoes."

Korb grimaced but did not respond.

Su and Des got up without further comment. Des held the door for Su and gave her a tight smile as she exited. Korb had already returned to his book.

Chapter Forty-Three

KELAN SU

I buckled into the luxuriously padded gray leather seat facing a drop-down table. We lifted off smoothly not long after I clicked in my belt. Not like a commercial flight. I perused Des's report as the plane pierced the cloud layer over Chicago. A crew member, doubling as co-pilot and steward came into the main cabin and showed me the minibar. I was already familiar with it, having used this air service several times before. I took out a diet coke and some nice brie with crackers. A little reinforcement for my lightning foray into St. Louis.

As usual, Des had put together on a moment's notice an outstanding profile on Jennifer Bridger and her son. The Bridger woman had been married to Scanlon eighteen years ago. The marriage was on the rocks from the beginning as Jennifer's wealthy father had tied up any money coming to his daughter or her son in trust funds. Not only was Scanlon cut off from the family money, he also expected his wife to stay home and cater to his every need. He was a master of psychological abuse, belittling her at every turn. She had to give up a promising career in advertising with Swain & Bridger, her father's firm. Meanwhile, the good doctor was also seeing another woman with whom he had been involved prior to meeting Bridger. This information was gleaned from the divorce papers Bridger filed seventeen and a half years ago.

Her son, Michael, was born just after the divorce became final. Scanlon refused to have anything to do with him and she didn't pursue it with him–at least as far as court records indicated. Bridger raised him by herself, having never remarried.

Bridger had resumed her PR career in Chicago and became the managing partner of her father's St. Louis firm when he retired. Most interestingly, Bridger had been in Chicago for four days, including the day before and the day of the murder. She had spoken at the National Public Relations Association annual meeting on Friday, September 7. She didn't fly out of Chicago until September 9. Des was checking with the Palmer House hotel staff on Bridger's entrances and exits from her room.

Michael, now sixteen, was an honor student at an elite private school in Massachusetts. I was surprised that his mother had kept his name as Scanlon. There was no record of Scanlon contacting her or Michael, or them contacting him until very recently.

From Michael's Facebook page and internet usage, Des had found that in the last two years Michael had been searching for his father. He seemed to have no help in this endeavor from his mother. Apparently, he had located and contacted his father in the last six months. Scanlon must have had some feelings for the boy as indicated by Michael's celebratory Facebook postings about their meetings and the gift of the motorcycle. Jennifer was not happy about these contacts.

I had checked Michael's school calendar and

found, to my relief, that classes didn't start until October. Sweet schedule for the elite preppies. I guess I can't talk with UChicago and Harvard degrees, but I was a scholarship nerd. Anyway, I'd be able to see the kid at home with his mother.

The hour-and-a-half flight was smooth and the landing was flawless. There was a rental car waiting. It was a red Mustang. Loved it, but a bit conspicuous. I hoped a stakeout or a tail wouldn't be necessary.

I headed out to Webster Groves on I-44, about a fifteen-minute ride from the airport. Driving through ritzy suburbs sporting McMansions with well-manicured lawn after well-manicured lawn was depressing. I guess I'm a snooty city slicker. The Bridger home fit the mold. It had a large expanse of front lawn surrounded by high hedges. The driveway entry had two stone pillars and a double swinging gate which, fortunately, was open.

I had checked in at Swain and Bridger and found that Jennifer was at home with her son today. This seemed almost too convenient. On the phone, Bridger had not been cordial. However, she reluctantly agreed to our meeting and to my speaking to Michael in her presence.

As I cruised up the curved driveway, I thought about the questions I needed to ask. Korb was particularly interested in the motorcycle gift. Not sure why. My intention was to grill Bridger on her stay in Chicago and whether she had contact with Scanlon.

I stopped the car in a pillared portico. The double front door had stained glass insets through which I could make out vague movement. I rang the bell, which played the *Close Encounters of the Third Kind* tones. A maid carrying a dustpan answered the door.

"Yes," she said with a slight accent. Wisps of her dark hair escaped the bandana she was using as a headband. She frowned and looked harried. I doubt she was informed that the Bridgers were expecting a visitor.

I gave her my card and said that Ms. Bridger was expecting me. She nodded and said, "Please wait here." She turned down a long hallway that led to a curved staircase. Just before the stairs, she stopped to knock on a door on the right. I heard a muffled, "What is it, Maria?" Maria stepped inside and must have handed Bridger my card. I heard "Show her in."

I entered a very stark, modern home office. Bridger sat in a high-backed, black leather chair behind a chrome and glass desk silhouetted by large windows opening out to a rear garden. There were two large computer monitors at one end of an otherwise uncluttered desk. The client chairs were Italian chrome with leather backs and seats. There was a geometric pattern rya rug in white, gray, and black on the floor. A credenza and printer stand in whitewashed oak lined the left wall.

Bridger herself mirrored the room. She was slim and angular with high cheekbones, sleek, shoulder-length black hair, and dressed in a white sleeveless pants suit with black accents. She did not rise when I entered. "Ms. Su, I presume," she said, giving me a tight smile.

I stepped up close to the desk and offered my hand. She looked at it skeptically for a moment and decided to half-rise and take it. She had a strong grip and I could see her arms were fit and muscular.

"I appreciate your willingness to see me," I said. I

sat down in one of the chrome and leather chairs and crossed my legs. I wanted to make this interview seem as casual as possible.

"'Willingness' may be too strong a word," Bridger noted. "However, I am curious about what is going on concerning the murder of my ex and my son's father and why a private detective is interested in it." She gave me a hard interrogatory stare.

I had a feeling that this was going to be a fencing match. She was much more interested in getting than giving information. Maybe if I began in a frank and open manner, it would catch on.

"My boss, Marko Korb, and I were hired by an attorney whose client was about to be charged for the murder. Although the charges were soon dropped, the client would like to remove the shadow of suspicion over her by finding the killer. The police seem to have curtailed their investigation at this time, indicating that there might be some behind-the-scenes political machinations."

"Well, I have certainly heard of Marko Korb. Our firm represents big pharma companies. Your boss has a solid reputation in those circles. But I can't say that I care greatly who killed Alan although I think my son would be disappointed if no one pays for his dad's murder. Was this woman client one of his many dalliances?"

"No. The issue revolves around a genetic patent and test developed by Dr. Scanlon at his lab that this woman hoped would be used to benefit her daughter and others with a serious hereditary disease. Your ex-husband patented the discoveries and restricted research. It's a sad case."

Bridger looked off to her right for a moment. I hoped her parental emotions were engaging. When she looked back, her face did seem to have a softer mien. "So what has brought you to me and my son?"

"Three things really. We wonder if you have any knowledge or suspicions about who might have wanted to kill Dr. Scanlon. Secondly, we are interested in the contact that your son has recently had with his father and whether he had any inkling that his father was threatened. Finally, we also want to warn you that the patents in question have some very unsavory people interested in their ownership and licensing and in deflecting attention from themselves. Your son may inherit the patents. We are in a position to protect him if we can quickly identify the killer with your help,"

Bridger frowned. Through tight lips, she asked, "Why do you think we can help?"

"May I call you Jennifer?" Bridger nodded. "Well, Jennifer, we know that you were in Chicago for four days including the day of the murder. You were speaking at an NPRA conference. Did you meet with Dr. Scanlon?"

The woman's hand went to her mouth. She remained silent.

"Jennifer, it's not unreasonable to think that you were concerned about his contact with your son. Possibly, you wished to discourage him or at least discover his intentions."

Jennifer nodded. "Yeah. I met him for lunch on Friday right after my presentation. I wanted to know if he was going to remain a figure in Michael's life. If so, I would tolerate it. But I wanted to be sure he wasn't going to disappear again. From what he told me, it seemed that he was planning to leave the country in the near future. I told him in no uncertain terms that I would not stand for any further contact between him and Michael. He whined to me about wanting to help Michael out and contribute to further his education. He told me he had scheduled a meeting with a lawyer to transfer something valuable to Michael. He was close-mouthed about the details."

Jennifer shook her head. "I didn't trust him. I told him we weren't interested in anything he had to offer and to stay out of our lives as he had always done. He just shook his head, got up and left. He even stuck me with the check. Typical! That was the last time I saw him."

I thought for a moment. "What was his demeanor? Did he seem to be anxious or frightened about anything? Did his interest in Michael seem at all related to his possible demise?" *Too many questions, too fast. Slow down, girl.*

Jennifer hesitated, her face scrunching up slightly. "You know I did think that he was anxious about something. He wasn't quite the overbearing, arrogant shit I remembered. There was a note of pleading in his wanting to help Michael. At the same time, he seemed eager to get out of the country. He gave me no clue about what or who was the cause of this anxiety."

"Jennifer, I must ask if you saw Scanlon again after your lunch meeting."

Jennifer frowned and her eyes narrowed. "I told you that lunch on Friday was the last time I saw him."

I gave her the cop stare. "Can you tell me where you were between eleven p.m. Friday, September seven and six a.m. Saturday September eight?"

She shook her head and clenched her teeth. "Look, I was alone in my hotel room that evening. I watched the Colbert late show. He had Sharon Osbourne, Kathleen Madigan, and Jay Rock. I fell asleep before the end of the show and the TV was still on when I awoke at six-forty-five a.m. I had breakfast delivered to my room for seven-thirty a.m. and left the room about nine a.m. Other than my call to room service and the waiter who delivered the breakfast, I have no other corroboration of my whereabouts in your time frame. Why would I want to kill Scanlon after all these years? Anyway, it seemed he was again making his exit from my life. Fine with me."

I realized I was holding my breath during her precise narrative. I exhaled sharply when she finished. She could have found the show details online. She also could have been to the institute in Skokie and back before six-forty-five a.m. Fortunately, I had a way to check on whether she was in her room all night. I'd get on that the moment I returned to the office. I figured that I could get no more from her.

"Jennifer, thank you, you have been very forthcoming and helpful. I would like to meet with Michael."

"I want to be here when you talk to him."

"Of course, I hope you will stay. I am interested in the motorcycle gift. You may remember things he forgets."

"Fine." Jennifer swiveled her desk chair and rose. "Let's talk in the family room." She led the way out and down the hall to a spacious, open room with a large-screen TV, a high-end stereo system, a foosball game, and a large, curved sofa as well as several comfortable chairs. The built-in shelving held games, sports trophies (presumably Michael's), and computer gaming equipment. Michael was sitting on one of the chairs with a laptop. He seemed deep in concentration over some kind of social media posting.

Jennifer went up to her son and put a hand on his shoulder. For a second he was startled, but he looked up and smiled at his mom. "Michael, this is Ms. Su. She's a private detective trying to find your father's killer. You don't have to tell her anything but she'd like to talk to you about the motorcycle your father gave you."

Michael signed out of his laptop and closed it. He turned toward Su with an interrogatory eyebrow raised. He lifted his hand in greeting and said, "Hi." He was a handsome kid with dark hair and his mom's high cheekbones. He seemed at ease in this familiar setting. "Are you really a private detective, like on TV?"

I couldn't help chuckling at his guileless curiosity. I was warming to him and hoped that he would to me. "Well, yes, I am a real private detective, but I'm afraid nothing like the ones on TV. No gun, no fast car, no tough banter."

Michael shrugged, nodded, and smiled. "How can I help? I would sure like to see my father's killer caught. I was just starting to get to know him. I had looked for him for some time."

I looked sympathetically at Jennifer who frowned and gave her head a slight shake.

"Michael, I'm very sorry for your loss. It must be hard."

He nodded. I heard Jennifer give a soft sigh.

"Tell me about your motorcycle."

Michael's expression changed to one of sheer joy.

"It's really cool. I couldn't believe it when my dad brought it. It's a Kawasaki KLX 140L. It can go both on and off-road. It rides so smooth even on a dirt track. I love the racing green color. I have a helmet and leather racing gear with trim to match."

"Was your dad a motorcycle rider?"

"No. He brought it down in a truck. He said a business friend of his who was a biker advised him on the cycle and the gear. He said that his friend had both a Kawasaki road cycle and a dirt bike and that his leather gear was the same as mine. I said I'd love to meet his friend and go riding with him sometime. Dad said he'd try to arrange it."

"Can I see your motorcycle jacket?" Both Michael and I looked at Jennifer. She nodded.

Michael fairly ran out of the room to get his jacket. When he came back, he was wearing it. He was smiling proudly. The jacket was very distinctive with black leather, green and white trim, and a Kawasaki patch on the left sleeve. "You look great. May I take a picture?" Again we both looked at Jennifer, who hesitated.

"I can just take the jacket. Although Michael sure looks great in it."

"Yes, please, just the jacket," she said. Michael pouted slightly as he took it off.

I took out my phone and snapped two photos making sure to get the left sleeve with the patch. "Thanks. I just have two more questions. Did your dad name the friend who had advised him about the bike?

Michael thought for a moment looking up and squinting. He shook his head.

"Michael, did your father seem at all worried when he brought down the motorcycle?"

"Worried, about what?" Michael looked bewildered. "Oh, he did want to be sure I would be careful when riding."

I surmised that Michael had not noticed any signs of concern beyond that fatherly concern for his son's safe cycling. "Thanks, Michael, and you, Jennifer. You've been very helpful. I'll keep you posted on any developments."

Before I turned to leave, I smiled at Michael and gave him a biker's blessing: "A long ride…a little more laughter, a little less worry, a little more kindness, a little less hurry."

Michael frowned for a moment and then he got it. He smiled broadly and sketched a goodbye wave.

Chapter Forty-Four

KELAN SU

The trip home was uneventful. Des had not been able to get the hotel security to divulge Bridger's keycard use so I took the flight time to contact a friend in security at the Palmer House in Chicago. I asked her if she would check their electronic key card data and security cameras to see when Jennifer Bridger had entered her room on the night of September 7 and whether she had left the room before the next morning. She reluctantly agreed, knowing that she owed me for the help Korb and I had given her with a jewelry theft in the hotel.

I didn't really think that Jennifer had killed Scanlon, but I wanted to confirm her story and eliminate her as a suspect. Korb would expect me to leave no stone unturned. I also couldn't believe that Michael had anything to do with the killing. It looked like Korb was right as usual. The motorcycle business would be key.

It was after 6 p.m. when I got back to our townhouse. Des was in the kitchen preparing spices for dinner–Jamaican Escovitch Fried Snapper. The fish had been flown up from Florida by Korb's favorite fish market and delivered to our door in a dry ice container. The kitchen was redolent of onions and scotch bonnet peppers.

Since I had eaten only a few snacks on the plane, I went to our industrial fridge and ferreted out some Mestemacher pumpernickel slices, smoked salmon and capers. I filched some cut up onion from Des's prep. There was also an open bottle of Edna Valley chard, one of the cheapies I like, so I poured myself a generous libation. I piled salmon, capers and onion on the dark, thin bread and ground some pepper on top. I took a healthy sip of the wine, rolled it on my tongue and swallowed, closing my eyes and inhaling the bouquet. Next, a big bite of the garnished smoked salmon. The long and hectic day started to melt away. I was glad that dinner would be soon because that would forestall the necessity to report immediately to Korb. He didn't like business to interrupt his culinary pleasures. Maybe I could wait until the next morning.

Dreamily, I watched Des's cooking artistry. No wasted motions as he sliced, diced, blended, stirred, flipped, and sauteed another wonderful concoction. The aromas multiplied and melded into a piquant rhapsody.

The atmosphere, the wine, and my impromptu hors d'oeuvre had a somnolent effect. I asked Des if there was enough time before dinner for a short nap. He chuckled. "We Tortolans are expert at being efficient at a relaxing pace. I can buy you thirty extra minutes."

"Thanks. Dinner at seven-thirty then?"

"Aye, *chakara*."

I didn't wait for the elevator. I ran upstairs to my suite, kicked my shoes off on entering, and dived onto the bed not bothering to get under the sheets or covers. I sighed and closed my eyes. Des would buzz me as soon as he was about to serve dinner. Could never be so tired that I'd miss one of his masterpieces.

****

The phone on my bed table dinged once. That was Des's signal that dinner would be served in five minutes. I slipped into comfortable moccasins and headed down. Korb was already at the table with a huge white napkin tucked between the top and second button on his cream-colored dress shirt. He was in casual mode—no tie. He gave me a sidelong glance as I slid into the chair on his left. His head was cocked to the left with a contemplative look on his face. For a moment I thought he would break precedent and ask me to report before dinner was served.

If so, I was saved by Des's prompt arrival holding two platters. With a flourish, he placed the platters on the table. He took his seat to the boss's right. Des's special white sangria was in a frosted pitcher. He poured a goblet full for each of us. He raised his glass and toasted us. "Salud." We repeated the word, clinked glasses, and drank. Then Des served up the delicacies and we ate. *Yummy*!

****

Korb leaned back and sighed contentedly. He lifted the pointed edge of his tucked napkin to his lips and daintily dabbed at them. I rose to help Des with clearing the table. Korb's eyes were closed and his fingers were tapping on the arms of his chair. He was thinking hard, probably about the next steps in the investigation. Without opening his eyes, he said, "Come back in here when you're done with the cleanup. We need to progress quickly."

I looked at Des with a raised eyebrow and gave him a half-smile. He responded with a roll of his eyes. The dinner table, even after the meal, was usually off-limits for work discussions.

We worked quickly. Des always washes pots and utensils as he cooks, and an empty dishwasher made the task even easier. As usual, there were few leftovers to pack up.

When we returned to the dining room, Korb's eyes were still closed. He slowly opened them and seemed to squint as if he didn't immediately recognize us. A sure sign of some deep thought.

Korb nodded to us. We sat down. "Your report, Kelan."

I related almost verbatim my interviews with Jennifer Bridger and her son, Michael. Korb listened intently, bowing his head at my conclusions that neither of them were likely suspects. I confirmed this with the information from my contact at the Palmer House, who verified Jennifer's statements about her whereabouts at the time of the murder.

"What did you find out about Scanlon's gift of the motorcycle to Michael?"

"Definitely a Kawasaki, and there were also the leathers. The jacket was black leather with green trim and a Kawasaki patch. I have a picture of it. Michael said that his father got his information of what cycle to buy from a friend who had Kawasaki bikes. He didn't know who the friend was."

A throat-clearing "Ahem" from Des, indicated that he had something to add. "I've searched our investigative databases for all of the suspects. Vrdoliak, Colter, Karlakis and Crosetti all have summer and/or winter vacation residences. No joy in finding motorcycles registered to any of them. However, Colter's summer residence is in Algoma, Wisconsin, and my searches indicate that he is or has been a member of a motorcycle club, The Algoma Roadrunners. Checking out their website, I saw pix with a lot of Kawasaki riders."

"Excellent, Desmond. I am interested in Colter. Do we have any pictures of him?" said Korb, his head bobbing up and down.

"The only recent photos I've found are head shots. I have his general info."

"Go on."

"Okay. He's forty-five. He's been practicing law for nineteen years since his admission to the Illinois Bar. The last twelve years with his present firm of which he is a founding partner. His expertise is in corporate and commercial law. He was born and raised in the Chicago suburbs. He graduated with a bachelor's degree in Business Administration from the University of Wisconsin in 1994. He received his law degree from the University of Illinois Champaign-Urbana in 1997. He and Scanlon go all the way back to UW where they were in the same fraternity. They also roomed together for a year at Illinois where Scanlon was getting his Ph.D. Interesting, but probably not relevant. I did see a non-headshot UW yearbook photo of him. He was on an athletic scholarship and was a power forward on the UW basketball team."

Korb leaned forward with his hands slapping down on the table. "What was that? Power forward? Basketball?"

Des shook his head and looked bewildered. "*Yessss*. That's a big man front line position in basketball." Something clicked for me but I couldn't focus on it.

"Hmmm. I see. Let's look more closely at Mr. Colter. Kelan, you'll need to go to Algoma and talk to the motorcycle club people."

"Right, sir." Another trip, but at least it should be scenic.

Des was still frowning and shaking his head slightly. "What more can I do?"

"Find anything more you can on Colter and his work with the Shabel Institute. But you can split the time with work on some of our other pending cases. I want to be well-prepared for a confrontation. Meanwhile, I will talk to Cook County State's Attorney McGovern and a certain County Commissioner who shall remain nameless for the nonce."

Chapter Forty-Five

KELAN SU

The flight to Austin-Straubel International Airport in Green Bay was rough but short–only fifty-five minutes. There had been a storm brewing over Lake Michigan. The sun never broke through the cloud cover, nor was the small PlaneJockeys jet able to rise above it. The lightning and driving rain made me nervous, but the flight crew seemed unconcerned as they bantered about a fishing trip to the Upper Peninsula of Michigan.

Just as we arrived at the private plane arrival area, the clouds parted and rays of sunshine reflected blindingly off the terminal windows. The storm had brought with it a drop in temperature and the wind was still strong. I donned my leather jacket and zipped it up to my neck. I slung the strap of my bag over my shoulder and stuck both hands in the jacket pockets as I descended the portable stairway to the tarmac.

There was a black Audi Q3 SUV waiting for me— part of our arrangement with the air service. I tossed my bag in the rear seat and got behind the wheel. I took a moment to familiarize myself with the controls and glanced at the GPS screen. The route to On the Lake B&B was already programmed in, ETA eleven-fifty-seven a.m. Forty-seven minutes, assuming I could find my way out of the airport.

Fortunately, private plane arrivals were well taken care of. The airport exit was nearby and clearly marked and there was no traffic to speak of. The exit was directly opposite the ramp to I-43 North, the first part of my itinerary.

The B & B lived up to its name. A 100-foot lawn sloped down from the back of the building to three docks. Two of the docks had fifty-foot pleasure boats tied up and the third had a collection of kayaks and jet skis probably for the use of guests. The lawn was dotted with Adirondack chairs and a few wrought-iron tables.

My room looked out toward the lake. It was lovely. The walls were a sunny yellow. There was a handmade quilt on the queen size bed. Too bad I wouldn't be spending much time in it.

I stowed my overnight bag in the closet and went back out to the foyer. The friendly young man who had checked me in was still at the front desk. He smiled at me charmingly.

"Is everything all right? Can I get you something?"

"Oh. The room is beautiful. But I do have a question."

"Yes."

"I'd really like to tour this area by motorcycle. I ride with a women's cycle club back home and several of our members have had great things to say about cycling here. They say there's a road club here that rents cycles. How would I get there?"

"Right. The Algoma Roadrunners. They are well known. I'll give you their address and phone number."

That confirmed my information. "Thanks. I really appreciate it."

****

The address the front desk man had given me was just out of town, but not far from my B & B. The headquarters was in a two-story frame building. There was a large parking area in front jammed with cycles, most for display. On entering the club, I saw that half of the first floor was furnished like a pub. Dark wood, tiled floor. There was a bar along the back wall with high stools and there were five square tables with chairs. There were ten or so folks dressed in leathers drinking and talking about cycling.

The rest of the first floor to the right of the pub area had trophy and cycling paraphernalia cases, and some things for sale. There were vintage Indian and Harley cycles on display. Behind a wooden counter was a Goth young woman whose heavily mascaraed eyes followed me as I approached.

"Hi. I was told by someone at On the Lake B & B that I could rent a cycle here and get some suggestions for touring the area."

"Yeah, we can do that. In fact, there's a group of women members going for a coastline ride in half an hour. That suit ya?"

"Yes. It sounds interesting. What have you got to rent?"

"Depends on your riding experience."

"I haven't been riding recently, but I've done some big hogs."

"How about a Kawasaki 350? The riding group are no speedsters or daredevils and won't be going off the road too much. They're interested in the spectacular scenery from the coastal high road." Her bored expression belied the description of the landscape.

"Great. And do you have a helmet?"

"Sure and we got protective leggings and a jacket you can rent. The whole shebang for the day including gas and insurance will cost ya two hundred dollars."

"I'll take the protective gear too. Here's my credit card."

She pointed with a black-nailed finger to a card reader on the counter. "Just put it in the reader. The insurance sign-off and liability waiver will come up there so you can authorize them. After that, I'll bring around your cycle and introduce you to your cyclemates. They're gathering outside now."

"Sounds good." I checked the boxes and signed the e-docs. "See you out front."

"Oh. I'm Tricia, by the way." She smiled crookedly.

"And I'm Kelan," I said, returning her smile.

The young woman waved her black ringed hand and the chains on her skull bracelet tinkled.

I went outside and saw six women standing near their cycles and exchanging greetings. The women wore leathers, some very stylish, but all well-used. They ranged in age, as far as I could tell, from the mid-twenties to the mid-fifties. They seemed to know each other well and there were several hugs.

The weather was perfect for a ride–not much wind, sunny, temp about 65. I only hoped I wasn't too rusty and that the group would allow me to keep up. I hadn't ridden since my law school days. I also hoped to get a chance to talk to them about Colter. I wasn't sure how to approach this.

Tricia rounded the corner of the building wheeling a red 350–a beauty. It looked brand new. The chrome glittered in the sun. The helmet sat on the seat. She handed me the protective gear. The chaps in a brown faux leather buckled around the waist, calves, thighs, and ankles. Tricia helped me with them. The jacket was trimmed in red matching the cycle. What I could see reflected in the chrome of the cycles made me look good.

By now the other women were looking me over. Tricia turned to them and introduced us all. She told them I was an experienced rider who was interested in seeing the sites along the coast. The women looked at each other questioningly and after several nods smiled their acceptance. Now it was up to me to live up to Tricia's build-up.

One of the older women said, "*Andiamo.*" We all mounted our bikes and kicked them into life. The muffled roars brought back some great times I had had cycling. Thankfully, the group set off at a leisurely pace.

The lake shore was indeed beautiful. The coast road went along a cliff above the dunes lining the shore. After an hour, the group stopped at a scenic roundabout. Suze, a lean, thirty-something blonde who worked for the local chamber of commerce, gave me a rundown of the sights. A lighthouse was visible in the distance. Suze recounted its history and the wrecks and rescues connected to it. Lois, who had given the signal to start off, passed around some energy bars.

Time to get to why I came here. "Thanks. This is really great. A colleague, Jack Colter, told me that this area was breathtaking, and the club was a great group. Do you guys know Jack?"

There was some looking around and shuffling of feet. Then Suze said, "Yeah, Jack, the Green Glider. He was usually the front door of the pack. He was very active but recently he sold his cycles to the club. They have a special deal where you can rent your bike back when you want to. The club takes care of maintenance, insurance, and rents the cycle when the original owner isn't using it. We haven't seen Jack around lately."

Darlene a dark, intense, young woman piped in. "I wonder if Mr. Colter has given up biking. Don't know what happened to turn him off. He was a regular weekend warrior. But he hasn't been on any group rides for two weeks."

"Do any of you know if Jack might have rented his cycle for a trip recently?"

This was a step too far. The women looked around at one another and turned to me with a distinctly wary look. There was a palpable silence.

Lois broke the silence. "Time to cruise. We'll head back by the old logging road. A different type of scenery and a more challenging ride."

I had all I was going to get from this group. We mounted and continued our ride. In two more hours, we were back at club headquarters. It was a spectacular ride. The dense woods we went through had helped make Algoma a lumber center. From the tops of hills on the road, we could also see rolling green dairy farms. The hills and hairpin turns made for a thrilling ride. I was glad my muscle memory was staunch, but when I dismounted at the end of the ride, my thigh muscles and buttocks complained mightily.

I thanked the women and we said our goodbyes. They were noticeably cool. Some talking quietly and looking back at me as they left. I went in to give my gear to Tricia. There were three guys having a beer at the bar, but Tricia wasn't there. I left the gear on the counter. One of the women from my ride came in and whispered something to one of the men at the bar.

As I turned toward the door, the three men swiveled their bar stools toward me and got up. They moved together to block my path to the door. I saw clenched fists and narrow-eyed looks. There was the bulge of a weapon under the untucked shirt of the shortest of the group. I nodded and returned their squints. "What's on your minds, gentlemen? And I use the last two terms loosely." The woman from the riding pack who had just come in must have reported my questions.

"You a cop?" sneered the short one.

"Nope."

"We don't like folks comin' here asking questions about our members." This was from a meaty, red-faced guy wearing a Harley hat and a plaid flannel shirt. The sleeves were rolled up revealing biker tats on both massive forearms.

"Got something to hide?"

"We ain't no outlaw club, but we still protect our own. Who you workin' for?"

They moved closer. The third man, the silent one, brought his hand from behind his back holding a heavy wrench.

"So, fellas, I am working for a mother with a very sick child whom your friend Jack Colter robbed of a medical discovery that might have led to a cure for the disease the little girl has and might have saved her life and that of other children with the same condition. In addition, Colter may be a murderer. So I will continue asking questions of your members and employees. It's me or the cops. Take your best shot, gentlemen. You will find you have bitten off more than you can chew."

I stepped closer to the big guy. I'd feint at him and hit the guy with the wrench first. I didn't think the little guy would use a gun in here.

There was a look of bewilderment on the big man's face. He stepped back and stuck out his arm to hold back the other two.

"We don't have any personal connection to Colter outside of the club. In fact, he hasn't been around much and never wanted to hang with us after a ride. You say he hurt a sick kid?"

Interesting that he didn't seem concerned about the murder. "That's right."

"And you're not a cop?"

I nodded.

"What do you want to know?"

"Whether Colter checked out a cycle on September six or seven of this year?"

The big man glanced at the other two. He pursed his lips and nodded. The others shrugged. "Tricia," he yelled.

The Goth girl stuck her head out of the doorway behind the counter. "Yeah, Chuck?" She raised her eyebrows.

"Answer any questions you can about Jack Colter for this lady. Let's go, guys." Chuck turned toward the door. The other two hesitated for a moment and then followed him out.

"Hi, Trish," I greeted her with a big smile. "I was looking for you earlier. Thanks again for arranging my ride. I just have a couple of questions."

Tricia sighed. "Well, if Baker says it's okay,

shoot."

"Did Jack Colter sign out a cycle on September six or seven?"

"Let me check the records," Tricia said, tapping on a keyboard on the counter.

"Yes, he did on the morning of September seven."

"Do you record the mileage when a rental cycle is out?"

"Let's see. He returned it on September nine. There was two hundred and fifteen more miles on it."

That wasn't enough mileage for a round trip from Algoma to Skokie. It was enough for one way.

"Could Colter have transported the machine by a truck?"

"Didn't see a truck. He rode the bike to and from the club."

"Thanks, Tricia. Take care of yourself." I turned to go. I'd drive by Colter's place before I left here and see if there was a truck or trailer. Des could also check DMV registrations.

"Hey. I heard what you said earlier. Hope you can help that lady and her kid."

"Thanks. Me too."

Chapter Forty-Six

Korb's eyes closed and his fingers tapped a staccato beat on the arms of his chair. He was processing Su's report through his high-power intellect. Su's hands were fidgeting behind her back as she reported to her boss about the Wisconsin trip. His eyes snapped open. "I think we need to concentrate on Colter."

"Yes!"

"As I said before."

"Des said that Colter owns a pickup truck."

"So do a myriad of others," said Korb with a slight smile.

"And I found his truck at the parking garage near his office." Su was drawing the story out to keep Korb on tenterhooks. It didn't work.

"And you found oil stains?" Korb smirked.

Su rolled her eyes.

"Have you sent the evidence to the forensic lab at U of I Chicago Circle to see if it is motorcycle oil?"

"Of course, boss."

"How long before we get results?"

It was Su's chance to smirk. "I put some pressure on Sam Goralick to speed up the process. Two days."

"Okay. Meanwhile, I need to talk to McGovern and County Commissioner Cordoba."

****

Korb had spoken many times with the commissioner and had provided information to her about an associate who was taking bribes. That information had saved Rena Cordoba's early political career. He might be able to do the same again. Over the years, he had more than a few encounters with States Attorney Kevin McGovern–some positive, but most negative.

Korb thought he had the entrée he needed to get Golda Merino off the hook and to turn in a killer without implicating his recent client, Crosetti, exposing the institute's illicit activities, or outing a key federal informant.

He picked up his desk phone and dialed a private number. A woman, probably a maid, picked up the phone after three rings. With a slight accent, she said, "Señorrrra Corrrrdoba's residence."

"Is the Señora in?"

"Who is this?"

"Tell the Señora that Marko Korb is calling."

"Yais, Señor Korb, I will tell her." The maid dropped the standard pretense of checking whether the lady of the house was in. She must have recognized Korb's name and that he was someone the commissioner would surely want to talk to.

A deep, resonant voice came on the phone. "Marko, how are you?"

"Rena, I'm well, thank you. And you?"

"Very well."

The ritual pleasantries out of the way, a flatter and matter-of-fact tone entered the Commissioner's voice. "What can I do for you, Marko?"

"Rena, I think it is more what I can do for you?"

"And that is?" The temperature of her voice had dropped a few degrees.

"As you know, Dr. Alan Scanlon, the Director of the Shabel Institute, was murdered."

"That's old news, Marko."

"At the moment, it is little known that you have been a donor to the Shabel Institute."

Cordoba grunted. "'Little known' is not unknown, particularly regarding a murder investigation or politics."

"Right you are. But it is also key to keep it off the record and out of the public eye. Wasn't that your reason for pressuring McGovern to drop the charges against Golda Merino?"

"Granted. But that was only a temporary respite." Cordoba sighed heavily. Her voice took on a hoarser tone. "What are you getting at, Marko?"

"I can turn in a confessed murderer for Scanlon's killing. No trial."

The commissioner was no stranger to political deals. "I like the sound of that, but what'll it cost me?"

"I'll turn the killer over to McGovern, but I don't want him to just go public claiming credit for the arrest. I need him to make a clear statement that Golda Merino had no connection with the murder.

"Okay, if you can pull it off as you say."

"I am assuming that you will see that McGovern does not mention any of the benefactors of the institute."

"You think!" Cordoba hmmphed. "Well, Marko, it was good talking to you. I'll have to invite you over to taste some excellent 2009 *Figeac St-Émilion* I cellared."

Korb closed his eyes and licked his lips, of course, unseen by the commissioner. "You know I don't like to leave my home, but your offer is sorely tempting. Possibly, you would consider dining here and bringing some of that nectar with you?"

"It might be arranged, Marko," said Cordoba with a smile that Korb didn't see.

****

Korb grimaced and rubbed his chin. Slowly his face composed itself into a sly smile. He punched in another number. After two rings, a recorded, nasal, female voice answered with "Office of the Cook County States Attorney. If you know your party's extension, please enter it now. If not, please listen to the following options."

Korb quickly entered States Attorney McGovern's personal extension which he had received during one of those few positive interactions with the man. After two rings, a gruff voice answered, "McGovern."

"Kevin, how nice to speak with you again," Korb's voice fairly dripped with sarcasm.

"Korb, ya sonofabitch. I can't believe you got this number. Whaddaya want?"

"Kevin, Kevin, Kevin." The repetition and tone conveyed oceans of disdain. "You gave me this number when I helped you out of a very sticky situation and I am calling because I may be able to do so again. I can be a good friend."

"I'm not interested. With friends like you, who needs enemies?"

"Before you reject my assistance so rashly, you should listen to what I'm offering."

A low grunt came over the line. Korb looked up to

the ceiling and waited.

"Let's hear it," McGovern finally responded without enthusiasm.

"A wise decision. When I heard the plea offer you made to Cheryl Dain and then your dropping the charges when her client didn't take it, I knew you were taking political heat."

"Yeah. So what else is new?"

"I can provide the ice or maybe the icing on the cake."

"Hardy, har. Eighty-six the cute metaphors and cut to the chase."

Korb knew he now had the States Attorney's undivided attention. "I can give you Scanlon's murderer with a confession obviating the need for a trial and embarrassing revelations about the institute's funding.'"

There was a skeptical, but not dismissive hmmph from McGovern. "And how do you propose to do that?"

"That I can't tell you at this time, nor can I tell you who the perp is."

"You're wasting my time then. As I thought. Goodbye." But he didn't hang up.

Korb knew he still had a hold on the man. "Don't be hasty. I can turn the killer over next week. Thursday to be exact. Directly to you if you wish or to an assistant or the Skokie cops."

"Of course, this isn't a freebie."

"Kevin, you're such a cynic. I guess that goes with the territory. Don't worry. I'm not asking much. All I want is a letter from you to Golda Merino apologizing for the filing of murder charges and stating that she was never a suspect in the case only a person of interest as a possible witness. That's close to the truth. We will not make it public. She may use it if questions are asked or any further charges arise."

McGovern hesitated momentarily. "No letter until the killer and the confession are in my hands."

"As expected. Come to my office on Thursday with the letter and a cop to make the arrest. You'll get what you want. There will be no resistance to the arrest."

"Korb, whenever I deal with you I feel like a victim." He hung up abruptly.

The detective clicked off thinking, *Whenever I deal with you, Mr. States Attorney, I feel dirty.*

Chapter Forty-Seven

The stage was set. Between Su's "friendly persuasion," Cheryl's overtures for settling the civil suit, and the worried curiosity of potential suspects, the parade of interested parties was complete. As they arrived, Su and Des showed them, one by one, into the large, sun-lit dining room on the second floor which also doubled as a conference room. Each was seated around the highly polished, oval oak conference/dining table according to Korb's plan. The first to arrive were Golda and Cheryl. They had left Golda's husband, Sam, and her daughter in Korb's office. Su seated Cheryl at the point of the oval facing the door next to a supersized chair that was for Korb. Golda was seated to her right. As she sat down, Golda looked around the empty room and glanced uneasily at Cheryl, who gave her a quick nod, a reassuring smile, and squeezed her hand. Golda, who had been holding her breath, exhaled sharply. Her tight expression relaxed a bit, but not as far as a smile.

Su exited to usher in another arrival. The door opened to disclose a dour Stanley Vrdoliak, the institute's CFO. Just like a CPA, crooked or not, to arrive right on the dot. Des reached through to hold the door and guide Vrdoliak to his seat on the left side of the table with his back to the sunlit windows. He nodded to the women as he sat down. He placed his attaché case on the floor next to him. He looked around the mostly empty room impatiently and then placed his forearms on the table and stared stonily at the Peter Uka print of a woman in a green dress on the wall opposite.

When the door next opened, Jack Colter, the institute's lawyer, entered with Su, followed by Tracey Gould with Des. Three heads turned to watch the new guests. Vrdoliak nodded to Colter, ignoring Gould. Cheryl acknowledged both. Golda's eyes were closed. Not a word was spoken. The tense silence in the room was only broken by breathing, fidgeting, and the door opening and closing. Su seated Colter mid-table facing the windows. Des put Gould to Colter's right.

Crosetti's entrance was accompanied by wide-eyed stares from the earlier arrivals. It was also considerably noisier. Des had blocked Crosetti's henchman from entering the conference room. "Sorry, dude. Only the boss." The man was as tall as Des and wider. He stepped close and initiated a chest bump expecting the lighter man to stagger back. Des did not budge. He gripped the larger man's shoulder. The thug tried to shake it off, but Des's grip only tightened.

Bringing his face right up to the larger man, Des's eyes narrowed. "I said '*just* Crosetti.'" The man stared. Crosetti turned back. He shook his head. "It's okay, Robi. Wait outside for me." The large man pursed his lips, nodded, and stepped back as Des's grip loosened. He shot a look of pure hatred at Des, who only shook his head sadly.

Crosetti looked around the conference room from the doorway. He turned back to Des. "Where's Korb?"

"He'll be here when everyone is seated."

"Wants to make the grand entrance, huh?"

Des raised an eyebrow and cocked his head to the left. He showed Crosetti to the seat directly facing Colter. The gangster placed both hands on the table looking hard at Colter as he sat. The lawyer blanched and nodded almost imperceptibly. Crosetti did not acknowledge the nod.

Elaine Sessions was the next to arrive. She was stylishly dressed as usual with a tailored black blazer, black straight-leg pants, an ivory cotton knit top, and a gray and blue patterned scarf. However, her face was drawn and haggard. The scientist's confident stride into the room faltered as she surveyed the occupants. She frowned and sat down hesitantly in the seat between Crosetti and Golda indicated by Su.

Su went down in the elevator to the first floor. She glanced at the monitor showing the front entrance. Walter Karlakis, the shady financier, was walking up the path with a suit carrying a briefcase, most likely his lawyer. They moved hesitantly as they were in deep conversation. Karlakis vigorously shook his head and made as if to turn around and depart. The lawyer grabbed his arm and said something that halted the financier. Karlakis first shook his head again, but then with a grimace nodded and turned back toward the entrance.

Su wished she had heard what they were saying. She opened the door before they reached it so as to forestall another change of mind on Karlakis's part. When the two men saw the door open, they hesitated a moment, frowning. Then smirky smiles appeared on their faces as they stepped up to the open door.

"Welcome to our humble abode," she said with a half-smile, closing the door behind them.

Karlakis flashed her a tight-lipped look of hatred and grunted. He started toward her menacingly, but the lawyer restrained him uttering an exasperated "Walter!" Karlakis dropped his head and dejectedly followed Su to the elevator.

Before they reached the conference room, Su told Karlakis's lawyer that he should stay outside but could watch the proceedings on the CCTV monitor. The lawyer protested but Karlakis shrugged it off and told his attorney to stay put.

As Su and Karlakis entered the conference room, Su noticed a lot of fidgeting and grumbling. Korb was still absent. The cast of characters was getting restless. She sat Karlakis down to the left of the empty chair next to Colter. She took the seat at the cusp of the oval with her back to the French doors.

Outside the doors in the hallway, Des took up a post facing the elevator. The door slid open noiselessly and Korb waddled out. He nodded to Des who turned and opened the French doors. Korb stopped momentarily after stepping into the room. He surveyed the seated occupants, all of whom looked up at him expectantly. Korb stepped past Su, looking down at her and nodded. He proceeded to the oversized chair on Cheryl's left at the far end of the table.

"Cheryl, are you ready?" the detective asked.

Golda's lawyer smiled and inclined her head.

Before taking his seat, Korb again surveyed the assembly. "You have been invited here to discuss the settlement of the lawsuit brought by Ms. Merino on behalf of her feraxia support group. Attorney Cheryl Dain, for the plaintiffs, will lead the discussion." Korb held up his hand indicating Cheryl and then sat down.

Cheryl rose slowly. She leaned forward and placed both hands on the table. She looked first at Colter, then at Karlakis, next at Crosetti, then Sessions and Gould, and finally back at Colter. "I thank you all for coming. I am sure we are agreed that this matter must be put to rest as expeditiously as possible." The interested parties gave Cheryl tight-lipped nods.

Cheryl continued. "I understand that Dr. Scanlon had assigned the patents of the gene and the test for the gene to the institute. To the end of a quick settlement, the plaintiffs suggest that the patents now be assigned to the feraxia support group for the consideration of one dollar. I also understand that there was a key man insurance policy on Dr. Scanlon's life in the amount of one million five hundred thousand dollars payable to the institute. The plaintiffs contributed family data, tissue samples, and money to the institute for the work on feraxia. In addition, they have incurred attorney's fees and other expenses in pursuing this lawsuit. We propose that the institute make a payment of two hundred thousand dollars to the feraxia support group."

Cheryl looked at Colter. He seemed to be absorbing the terms and showed no immediate signs of rejection. But he had a good poker face. Cheryl frowned and addressed him directly. "Mr. Colter," she said with a half-smile, "isn't it time for you to ask what the plaintiffs are offering?"

Colter gave the attorney a tight smile. "No. I would prefer that you state your offer."

The heads of the other participants swiveled from Cheryl to Colter and back to Cheryl as if following a tennis rally. It was clear that their interest in this settlement was substantial.

Cheryl let out a long breath. She looked at Golda, whose eyelids drooped as she nodded slowly.

"Of course, we will withdraw the lawsuit, release all claims against the institute, and execute an NDA with regard to the financial settlement, patent assignments, and research restrictions imposed by Dr. Scanlon.

Colter nodded and looked around at the institute benefactors. Karlakis inclined his head slightly. Vrdoliak, the institute's CFO, looked at Crosetti and raised his eyebrows. Seeing no visible sign of opposition, he gave Colter a slight shrug. The lawyer took this as assent. When Colter's questioning gaze moved to Crosetti, it was caught by a hard, squinty stare. A look of panic crossed Colter's face. Colter's expression eased when Crosetti broke his stare and gestured his approval with a short wave of his hand.

Colter blinked and nodded. With eyes half closed and a long exhale, the lawyer gave Cheryl a conciliatory look. "Looks like you win, Ms. Dain," he said. "My office will draw up the agreement."

Cheryl gave Colter a half smile. "No need. I have the agreement right here."

"You were pretty confident," conceded Colter.

"I just assumed that you and your clients could see the justice of our terms as well as the protection of their interests."

Colter raised his eyebrows and shrugged. Cheryl handed out copies of the agreement.

Chapter Forty-Eight

There was a pregnant silence only broken by the crinkle of paper as each of those around the table perused the agreement. Karlakis and Crosetti gave only cursory looks at the document. Karlakis made to rise and depart.

Korb halted him and drew the attention of the rest of the group by leaning forward, slapping both hands on the table, and half-rising from his chair. "I suggest you all remain seated," growled Korb. Karlakis frowned but resumed his seat.

Korb also settled back in his chair and continued in a more even tone. "There is yet one more matter to deal with. As you know, the non-disclosure agreement cannot shield information requested in a criminal investigation. We know that the interest of all concerned is to limit the exposure of institute activities to such an investigation. It is also in the interest of Ms. Merino to have a definitive resolution of Dr. Scanlon's murder. She has been the continuing victim of suspicion and speculation."

Korb looked around the room. There were concerned frowns on all of the faces. Colter shook his head. "I don't see a need to discuss anything further. I understand that the charges against Ms. Merino will be dismissed with prejudice once this agreement is finalized." He started to gather up his papers and put them in his briefcase.

Crosetti cleared his throat. He gave Colter a look that froze him in his seat. The crime boss then turned to Korb. "Yeah. We need to hear you out. What do you have in mind to close out this matter to everyone's satisfaction?"

"I intend to reveal the identity of the murderer and present that person with good reasons to make a confession," said Korb.

Crosetti harrumphed but nodded his assent. Colter shook his head and whined uncertainly, "I really don't see a need to..." Crosetti cut him off. "We're doing this." That settled the matter.

Korb nodded and sat back. He closed his eyes and lowered his head. His fingers tapped out a rat-tat-tat rhythm on the arms of his chair. When the detective raised his head again, he surveyed each of those connected with the institute with an appraising stare. There were uneasy shiftings of position by those around the table—except for Crosetti who was stock still gazing straight ahead.

A low growl came from Korb. All eyes turned to him as he began. "It is often said that ascertaining the perpetrator of a crime depends on motive, means, and opportunity. Everyone around this table except for Attorney Dain, my associate Ms. Su, and myself had a motive for getting rid of Alan Scanlon." There was general head shaking and grumbling from the seated company.

"There is no point in denial. Messrs. Karlakis, Vrdoliak, Crosetti, and Colter, you were very much concerned that Dr. Scanlon's patenting and restricting research on the feraxia gene, along with Ms. Merino's and the support group's lawsuit, would put an end to certain very profitable, but best concealed, activities of the institute. It seems that the good doctor was not about to give up his rights at least without substantial remuneration. He was also quite vain about his scientific reputation and wanted to parlay his discovery into a prestigious and, might I say, genuine scientific appointment. He was planning to go abroad to find such a position."

There was grumbling and head shaking from those Korb had just mentioned but no immediate protestations of innocence.

Korb continued, "This cuts two ways regarding motive. While killing Scanlon clears the way for ending the lawsuit before the institute's finances were exposed, it starts a criminal investigation that would open up the institute's operations."

"And that brings us to Dr. Sessions and Ms. Gould." Korb glanced from one to the other. Sessions glowered back. Gould put her head down. "You each were infatuated with Dr. Scanlon. It is a mystery to me how sensible and intelligent women could have been ensnared by such a transparent womanizer. But when he threw you over both romantically and professionally, Dr. Sessions, he definitely gave you a strong motive for vengeance. He did make you a substantial beneficiary of his will. A will, I might add, he was preparing to change. In addition, you might also accede to the institute's scientific directorship if he were eliminated."

Sessions only looked down at her hands tightly clasped on the table. Korb decided to let her stew and turned his attention to Tracey Gould.

"Now, Ms. Gould, you were willing to risk your

job and the funding of your children's education to have an affair with Dr. Scanlon totally on his terms and at his convenience. Then he intimated that he was leaving the country definitely without you. Men have been murdered for less." Gould, eyes wide, shook her head in a vigorous denial.

With a rumbling exhale, Korb turned to his right and looked at Golda. She looked down at her hands folded on the table. He gave her a crooked, apologetic smile. "Of course, I can't forget Ms. Merino. Her motive is also obvious. Dr. Scanlon took money and personal medical information from her and from the group she headed and when that resulted in a breakthrough, he patented the discovery and restricted its availability to researchers. This was not only a betrayal but also dashed hope of a cure for her daughter, Teri."

Cheryl covered Golda's hands and gave them a squeeze. Golda turned to her with a sad smile.

"Can you move this along, Korb? Some of us have better things to do than watch you grandstand," said Colter, shaking his head and grimacing. There were a few "hmms" which the lawyer could have taken as agreement.

Crosetti rasped sharply, "Let Korb make good on his promise in his own way." That put the kibosh to any mutiny among the assemblage.

With a crooked half-smile, Korb readdressed the seated parties. "Next, we have the question of means. In one sense, anyone of you had the means as Scanlon's own weapon, presumably already in the lab, was used for the murder. However, the use of that weapon and the apparent opportunistic nature of the crime does seem to exclude some of you. It is hard to imagine that Mr. Crosetti, Mr. Karlakis, or Mr. Vrdoliak doing their own, shall we say, hands-on criminal violence. Nor would they react rashly in such a situation. Their experience and organizational positions would militate against such a conclusion. Scanlon was a problem, but one to be handled by professional minions."

There were nods from Su and Dain and eyerolls from Karlakis, Vrdoliak, and Crosetti. The others were silent, looking glum.

Korb again glanced around the room, stopping at each face. He cleared his throat. "However, the opportunistic nature of the murder and some indication of desperation does not exclude Dr. Sessions, Ms. Merino, Ms. Gould or Mr. Colter."

Korb sat down heavily. Both he and his heavily padded chair sighed deeply. He nodded to Su, who rose and opened the door behind her. When the double doors into the room again opened, Des was leading in a dark-haired, tattooed, young woman dressed in jeans, boots, and a black hooded Nirvana sweatshirt. The woman looked around nervously and glanced back at Des, who smiled reassuringly and sat her down on Colter's left. "I'll be right outside the door and Su will be at the table," he said.

Colter looked up as the young woman sat down. Des cocked his head toward the attorney, "Donna, this is Attorney Jack Colter." Looking at Donna, Desmond said, "Mr. Colter, this is Donna Walsh, the security guard on duty at the kiosk on the morning of the murder." Colter looked surprised and quickly turned his head away, muttering a hoarse hello. Donna looked at Des and shrugged her shoulders. Karlakis on Walsh's left glanced toward her and leaned away with an inquisitive half grimace.

Des moved to the door behind Su. Instead of going out, he stood in front of the exit, feet spread, hands clasped before him. His impressive physique and impassive stare made it clear that no one was leaving without his permission. Korb looked at him and smiled approvingly.

Korb turned toward Donna Walsh. "Ms. Walsh, thank you for coming all this way to help us." Walsh raised her eyebrows and shrugged. Korb said, "Ms. Walsh was the security guard at the science park kiosk at the time of the murder. She has graciously flown in from Florida to provide assistance in this inquiry." There was consternation all around.

Chapter Forty-Nine

"The time has come to talk of many things: of opportunities and vehicles and alarms–of trajectories and killings," Korb announced, smiling smugly and paraphrasing Lewis Carroll's Walrus to whom he bore a resemblance. There were collective "phews" and much eye-rolling and head shaking, not the least of which came from Su. She thought, *Korb's a genius, but never as clever as he thinks he is. Wit is not his forte.*

Oblivious to the reactions, Korb continued. "Opportunity is the key to this case. It is that aspect which has compelled me to eschew Messrs. Karlakis and Crosetti. There is nothing connecting them to the crime scene at the relevant time. For the same reason, I have excluded Ms. Merino. Her arrival at the scene was at least two hours later than the latest estimate of time of death. Her entry was not recorded at the kiosk due to a mixup as the security officers changed. However, her exit in her own car was recorded at seven-thirty a.m. This meant she could not have driven Scanlon's car from the science park." Golda closed her eyes and exhaled slowly. The unnamed suspects squirmed in their seats.

"Let us begin with Ms. Gould." Gould's head jerked up with an open-mouthed look of surprise on her face. "She acknowledges that she was at the lab and had a tryst with Scanlon. She says he was alive when she left and her car, although she had given an assumed name, was recorded as leaving the science park at four a.m. It would have been very difficult for her to return on foot and then drive Scanlon's car out of the park. If, in fact, that is what the murderer did."

Korb paused and looked at Walsh. "Ms. Walsh, do you recognize Ms. Gould?"

Walsh looked at Gould. Her brows wrinkled as she squinted at the woman. She had to look past Colter to see Gould. Colter turned his head away and leaned back.

"Yes. She came by the kiosk several times in the evening and generally left in the wee hours."

"And did you see her on the night before and day of the murder?" asked Korb

"Well, she used a different name and drove a car I had never seen before."

"But did you recognize her?" Korb insisted.

"Yes. I did. I missed her coming in as I was checking out something on my monitor, but I definitely saw her leave at four a.m. on the morning of the murder."

Korb pressed on. "Could she have also been the person you saw driving Scanlon's car later that morning?"

Walsh twisted a strand of her black hair. "I don't think so. This woman is very short. The person I saw in Scanlon's car must have been tall. A man, I think. But it could have been a tall woman."

"Thank you," said Korb. "You may leave now. If you wish, Ms. Su can take you back to your residence. You may wait in my office next door."

Donna Walsh stood, nodded to Korb, and left the

room. On her way past Su, she said, "No need to drive me. I have my wheels." Su nodded and patted her arm. "Don't forget you'll need to make a formal statement for the prosecutor, Mr. McGovern, who is right outside." Korb watched Walsh leave.

Tracey Gould had relaxed back into chair, evincing relief that she had been excluded by Walsh's statement. But Korb was not about to let her off the hook easily.

"However, Ms. Gould, you could have murdered Dr. Scanlon if someone else had driven his car away— someone who had reason to protect you–possibly someone who did not want to see the mother of his children go to jail."

Gould blanched and sobbed. Colter groaned.

"Yes. We checked on your supposed niece and nephew's birth certificates. They are your children, not your sister's, are they not?" asked Korb, staring hard at Gould.

The woman nodded between sniffles.

"And, Mr. Colter, you are not just an altruistic friend paying for the children's care and education, are you? You are their father."

The lawyer just shook his head dejectedly.

There were looks of surprise which were bolstered when Korb seemed to drop questioning Gould and Colter.

Korb turned to the bewildered researcher. "That brings us to Dr. Sessions. She could be described as a tall woman who might have driven Scanlon's car from the Science Park."

There was muttering around the table. *Why was Korb so circumspect? When was he going to identify the killer?*

Korb went on, seeming oblivious to the reactions. "Dr. Sessions, you were at the industrial park in the early morning hours of September eight. You said you did not enter the park itself, but observed from outside the fence. You lied. We have found a security camera video that shows you passing a local bank going toward the institute at three-forty-five a.m. and your return trip at five-ten a.m. The interesting thing is that on the return trip, there is an obvious grass stain and scrape on your shorts and leg that were not there at three-forty-five. There is also a torn-up portion of grass on the berm directly between your supposed vantage point at the fence and the side door of the lab. You were inside the park that morning."

Sessions's eyes widened and she gaped at Korb.

Korb pressed on. "Dr. Sessions, no need to look so shocked. You could have killed Dr. Scanlon and driven the car to the community college, left it there and resumed your run, passing the bank's video camera at five-ten a.m."

The scientist moaned, "No, no, no!"

"Calm down Dr. Sessions. I am not making an accusation–yet."

Korb looked hard around the room and his gaze settled momentarily on Jack Colter. Then he turned toward Stanley Vrdoliak. "Mr. Vrdoliak, only you and Dr. Scanlon had access to all of the necessary codes and passwords for turning off the security system and editing the security data."

Vrdoliak frowned and squinted at Korb. "I told your investigator, Ms. Su, that I was with my family all that Saturday night and Sunday morning. She talked to my wife."

"Yes. Your wife verified your account. But close family is not the most credible source of an alibi."

"Well, that's the best you're gonna get and it puts me in the clear," grumbled the CFO.

"Fortunately for you, you also have an insomniac neighbor who was letting his dog out into the backyard at five a.m. Saturday morning. The dog was yapping and he saw you close your bedroom window. That verification is a bit more trustworthy. It would make it impossible for you to be leaving the industrial park in Scanlon's car."

"Thank you for your trust in me," sneered Vrdoliak. Korb bestowed a beatific smile on the executive.

Turning to the attorney, Korb said, "That brings us to you, Mr. Colter."

Colter blanched. "Are you accusing me of killing my friend and client, Dr. Scanlon?" he blustered.

"Now, now, Mr. Colter, I am not accusing you of anything. I am just laying out the facts of the case relating to the opportunity to commit the murder," said Korb calmly.

"Well, I, for one, will not stand for any more of this rigamarole," rasped Colter, turning red and rising from his chair.

Korb also rose and slapped his hands down on the table with a loud crack. "Sit down, Mr. Colter, we are not through here."

Colter remained standing. He looked at Crosetti. Crosetti, tight-lipped, jerked his head in a downward motion that clearly meant for Colter to sit. The attorney collapsed back into his chair. His shoulders slumped and his chin sank to his chest.

Korb sat back in his chair, breathing hard from the effort to stand and pound the table. He looked briefly at Crosetti and then turned back to Colter. "Mr. Colter, I understand that you are a motorcycle driver."

Colter shook his head in confusion.

"Am I correct, Mr. Colter?" Korb's voice rose in volume.

"Yes, but what has that to do with anything? I keep my bike in Wisconsin with a cycling club."

"The Algoma Roadrunners, I believe," said Korb. "A Kawasaki 350 that you signed over to them. They maintain it and loan it to you when you want to use it. Is that correct?"

"Yes," said Colter, shrugging.

"You checked it out on September seven and returned it on September nine."

"Is that a question?" Colter growled.

"No, it's a fact verified by the clerk at the motorcycle club. Where did you ride the motorcycle, Mr. Colter?"

"I'm sure I tooled around the Algoma area. Might have gone as far as Green Bay."

"The weather was good those days. About how many miles do you think you rode?"

"Don't know. Maybe a hundred twenty."

"According to your club, you logged two hundred fifteen miles. That's just a bit more than the mileage to Skokie."

"Maybe one way. But I made a round trip, bringing the cycle back to the club." Colter smiled smugly.

Korb nodded. "You also have a pickup truck in which my operative found oil stains in the bed along with bungees and ties for transporting a motorcycle.

Colter emitted a "Pfff. So, I do often transport my bike in the truck but not that weekend."

"As you know, Scanlon's car was found parked near the Community College. A woman who was studying at the college library has said she saw a motorcycle with the characteristic green and white trim of a Kawasaki parked in the library lot at four-thirty Saturday morning."

Colter shook his head. "I have no connection with any of this. Your insinuations are pure speculation."

"Right you are, Mr. Colter. But let's see if we can provide some more context," said Korb, sucking in air noisily through pursed lips. "Do you have a Kawasaki emblazoned leather motorcycle jacket?"

"No. I do not," said Colter with staccato emphasis on each word.

"Ah. But you did own such a jacket according to Alan Scanlon's son for whom you bought a similar jacket on his father's behalf. Michael was told it was just like yours."

"So what! This is getting more far-fetched and ridiculous." Colter shook his head and grimaced with disgust.

Korb first looked at Colter with narrowed eyes and then turned to Elaine Sessions. "Dr. Sessions, will you tell us what you saw in the early morning hours of September eight at the side door of the institute."

Sessions seemed startled to have the attention returned to her. She looked at Korb wide-eyed. Her mouth opened and then closed. Korb nodded encouragingly. "Go ahead," he said. "What did you see at the side door?"

Sessions frowned and then nodded. "Oh, yes. I saw

Tracey Gould exit through that door and head to her car, which was parked at the side out of sight of the road."

"Yes. And what else did you see?"

"Well, it seemed that Ms. Gould was in a hurry and left the door partly opened. I saw an arm reach out from inside the lab and a leather gloved hand grabbed the door handle, closing the door. The sleeve of the arm was from a leather jacket that had a green and white emblem which I later discovered was the Kawasaki logo." Sessions leaned back in her seat.

"Thank you, Doctor." Korb turned back to Colter. "Mr. Colter, were you at the lab in the early morning hours of September eight?"

"N-no. I was not," said Colter. It did not sound like a confident denial.

Korb took a photograph out of a folder that was on the table in front of him and passed it to Gould on his left. "Please look it over and then pass this to Mr. Colter."

The woman looked at it and frowned and then looked at Colter to whom she slid the picture. "Mr. Colter, please look carefully at this picture. It is a copy of one found in your office. The police are now prepared to search your office as well as check your cellphone photos and presumably find the original. Can you tell me what is in that picture?"

"This is absurd. That picture could have been taken any time. How did you get it?" Colter glared at Korb.

Korb only smiled. "Ms. Gould, can you tell me what is in that picture?"

Tracey Gould exhaled sharply. She reached over in front of Colter and picked up the picture. "It's Alan and

I embracing in the corridor of the lab leading from his office."

"And is there any way you can tell when that picture was taken?"

"It must have been on the morning of the murder. It was the first and only time I wore that top. I had just bought it. I thought it was sexy and Alan would like it." Gould dropped her clasped hands into her lap, leaned back, and closed her eyes. Korb nodded to her.

Colter's lips were drawn into a tight line. He stared straight ahead.

"Mr. Colter, how tall are you?" asked Korb, taking another tack.

Colter's eyes flicked momentarily toward Korb but returned to his grim stare. He did not answer.

"I'm sure we have all noticed that Mr. Colter is quite tall. Even taller than my associate, Mr. St. Clair. I understand that in his college days, Mr. Colter was something called a 'power forward' on the University of Wisconsin basketball team. An old roster lists his height at six foot seven inches." Korb let this sink in and noticed the questioning looks of the people around the table.

He continued, "The medical examiner's report indicates that the trajectory of the bullet that killed Dr. Scanlon was downward from its point-blank entry at the right temple. Dr. Scanlon had been sitting on a high lab stool when he was shot. It would take a shot from a very tall person standing next to the victim to create that path. There is—"

Korb was interrupted by Colter's shout. "I've had enough of this. You don't have enough evidence to convict me of anything. No jury would find me guilty based on this claptrap."

Korb gave Colter a pitying look. "Oh, Mr. Colter, I don't have to convince a jury of your guilt. Actually, I only have to convince one person that you murdered Scanlon. Am I right, Mr. Crosetti?" said Korb, acknowledging the crime boss.

Crosetti nodded and looked hard at Colter. The attorney blanched.

"And are you convinced, Mr. Crosetti?" asked Korb.

"Yeah. I am," agreed the mobster.

"What would you suggest Mr. Colter do?" asked Korb pleasantly.

Crosetti knitted his brows, nodding and giving the attorney a menacing look. "I would strongly suggest that, if Mr. Colter knows what's good for him, he oughta turn himself in, confess to the murder, and plead guilty."

A sob escaped Colter. His hands on the table were shaking.

Korb spoke calmly and persuasively. "Now, Mr. Colter, if you were to confess to killing Dr. Scanlon, it would be very important for you to let the authorities know that you did not intend to harm the doctor when you arranged to meet him. You didn't bring a weapon. As I see it, you wanted to convince him to free up the patent for research and to find out what he and Tracey Gould might be up to romantically as she is the mother of your children. You were also concerned about how her relationship with Scanlon would affect your access to the operations of the institute. It was he who became hostile and first reached for the weapon at his side. You, being stronger and more agile, were able to grab it and wrest it away from Scanlon's grip. In the process, it went off. Isn't that the case?"

Colter put his head in his hands.

Korb continued. "It is also imperative that in your confession you make no mention of the institute's financial dealings or connection to certain people in this room. There are important people with an interest in the institute who have quite a bit of political influence. If you follow these instructions, I am sure they will see that you can enter a plea of reckless homicide and receive a minimum sentence. The State's Attorney Mr. McGovern is waiting outside to take you into custody. Have I made myself clear?"

Crosetti interjected in a loud growl. "Do I hafta tell ya the grave consequences of going to trial or talking about the financial backing of the institute?"

Colter was in tears. He looked down at the table, then up at Crosetti and croaked, "I understand."

Korb signaled to Su, who rose and came around to Colter. She tapped him on the shoulder and helped him to rise with her hand on his elbow. Des had come around to take his other arm. They led the sobbing attorney out.

Korb leaned back in his chair and closed his eyes for a moment. The people left around the table, except for Crosetti, were dumbfounded. They gaped and goggled. When the door opened again and Su strode in, there was a collective exhale and questioning looks. Su handed Korb a piece of paper. He read it, nodded, and handed it to Cheryl Dain. "I hope this is satisfactory. It's States Attorney McGovern's press release concerning the arrest and confession of Jack Colter. It absolves Ms. Merino of any involvement in the crime."

Cheryl leaned forward to kiss Korb on the cheek. He almost fell out of his chair trying to avoid the contact. The attorney smiled at him, shaking her head. She looked up at Su who was trying hard to stifle a laugh. Cheryl then held out her hand to Korb. After a brief hesitation, he deigned to shake it.

When her lawyer showed the press release to Golda Merino, the woman sobbed and hugged her. Over Cheryl's shoulder, Golda looked at Korb and mouthed, "Thank you."

The others at the conference table looked at one another uneasily. Crosetti was the first to rise and leave the room. The rest of the assemblage got up to go, avoiding each other's eyes.

Golda turned again to Korb. "Mr. Korb, I don't know how to thank you. I will manage to pay your fee. Please send me the bill."

Korb smiled. "Good lady, it was a *mitzvah* to help you and your family. Besides, I have another client who will be paying my substantial bill. It will be no problem for him."

Su gaped at Korb, having never heard him use a Hebrew or Yiddish term before nor ever heard him indicate that any work he did was done for any reason but pride or recompense. Hiding her shock, Su commented, "It sure was a lucky coincidence that Tracey Gould was wearing a brand new top in that picture."

Korb smiled cryptically. "Ah, Kelan, you know I don't believe in luck or coincidences."

A word about the author…

Lawrence E. Rothstein is a retired lawyer and university professor, who specialized in constitutional law, privacy law, and labor law. He was born and raised in Chicago and since 1974 has resided with his wife and family in beautiful southern Rhode Island. He has lived and traveled widely in Europe. An avid reader of detective fiction, Rothstein has always wanted to write detective novels. Venetian Bind is his first novel of a prospective series involving the corpulent detective, Marko Korb, and his Chinese-American, right-hand woman Kelan Su. Ripped Genes is the second book of the Tri-Star Investigation series.

www.Rothsteinsmysteries.com

Thank you for purchasing
this publication of The Wild Rose Press, Inc.

For questions or more information
contact us at
info@thewildrosepress.com.

The Wild Rose Press, Inc.
www.thewildrosepress.com